Final Call

Book Two of the Call series

Emma Hart

Sometimes you will never know the value of a moment until it becomes a memory.

Dr. Suess

Chapter One

You know life has taken a shit turn when your underwear doesn't match.

And the quality of that underwear is a guide to measure the shitness on.

Me? I'm pretty sure I have a hole on the waistband of these boy shorts, so, yeah. My life is at Epically Fucked with a heavy dose of Heartbreak Hell on the life quality guide.

But what can you do?

Tuck your change from the cashier into the pocket of your sweatpants and grab your ice cream—that's what.

I get into my car, my ice cream snug on the passenger's seat, and pull away from the store. Tonight is my final night of the allotted seven-day mourning period after the breakdown of a relationship, so basically, it's my last chance to be a miserable bitch in public. Okay, so I added a couple of days onto the mourning period, but whatever. I plan to milk it for everything it's worth—ice cream, wine, and my best friend.

It doesn't matter that I never wanted the relationship in the first place. It doesn't matter that it was only a handful of days that the relationship had felt truly real to me—like it was something I could hold on to and something I could really change my life for. What matters is that it *was* real and it happened.

It doesn't matter that a small part of me wishes it hadn't. That I was stronger.

I press the button on the keys to open the garage and drive in. The door shuts behind me with a whir, and I rest my head on the steering wheel. I wish I didn't still feel it—that keen sting of betrayal reminding me of what he kept from me.

Since I stepped foot on the plane—*his* plane—I've wondered if I have been overreacting. More so since I touched back down in Seattle. Should I have stayed the night? Talked to him? Listened to the full story? The same one he couldn't get out because of my angry hysteria?

The part that loves him says yes. It says that he deserved that— to tell me what happened. To tell me why he didn't say anything.

The part that is still ruled by common sense says that I was absolutely right to walk away from the secretive bastard.

I dump the ice cream in the freezer, barely glancing at my aunt's state-of-the-art kitchen, and find her in the front room.

"More ice cream?" She looks at me over the top of her book. I peer at the title. It's a romance. *Figures.*

"Yep. I'll just kill myself in the gym tomorrow to make up for a few days of bumming around."

She shakes her head, her dark hair swishing over her shoulders. "Honestly, Dayton. I don't understand all this nonsense. You knew the risks when you took the job."

"When I was forced to take the job."

"Oh, come on, honey. You know as well as I do that Mon can push and push, but she won't make you take a job you're truly not comfortable with. You knew exactly what you were getting into."

I raise an eyebrow at her placid expression. "So it's my fault he hid his wife from me?"

Aunt Leigh opens her mouth, pauses, then closes it with another shake of her head.

"Exactly. Did I know I could fall in love again? Yes. I knew that. Did I think he would hurt me this way? Keep something so important from me? No. Never in a million years did I think the man I knew would keep secrets like that."

Her dark eyes regard me, never changing, and she rests the book in her lap. "Well, maybe the man you knew isn't the man he is today."

I swallow and look out the window. Isn't she right? Every day I was finding a little something about Aaron that had changed despite all the things that were so familiar to me. Every day I realized that he was different from the person I fell in love with the first time around.

"Yeah." My gaze finds my aunt's again. "I think that was the problem. Maybe I was in love with a memory."

❦

"I can't believe he's married."

"Mm."

"I mean, he has a *wife*."

"Yep."

"Married. A fucking wife." Liv shakes her head.

I slam my spoon on the coffee table. "Say it again. Go on. I don't think it quite cut deep enough the first ten times."

Her eyes soften when they find mine, and I jab my spoon into the ice cream tub.

"I'm sorry, babe. I just can't believe it."

"Yeah, well, take a number and join the line." I look flatly at the laden spoon and drop it into the tub. Nothing like the reminder of your broken heart to sour the taste of your comfort food.

"I can't believe Monique didn't tell you." Liv runs her thumb over her lips. "You'd think she would because of your past."

"Monique has her own reasons for doing things," Aunt Leigh butts in, entering the room. "And my niece is the only person to ever question them."

I fix my aunt with a hard stare. She's definitely not one for comfort. Nope. I told her what happened, and she asked me when I was going back to work.

Welcome to the glamorous world of an escort.

"That's because her reasons are bullshit. Client confidentiality?" I laugh bitterly. "She can shove that."

"Dayton."

"No. I have every right—*every…fucking…right*—to be pissed off with her, Aunt Leigh. She deliberately withheld an important bit of information from me. For what? Money? That money means shit when it's at the expense of me."

She sighs and picks up her book, tucking it under her arm. "Why don't you try talking to her instead of ignoring her?"

"How do you know I'm ignoring her?"

"She called me an hour ago. Despite your current emotional upheaval, she's still your agent and you still have a job to do."

See? Apparently balding men's need for sex is more vital than me soothing my broken heart. Oh, sorry. *Emotional upheaval.* Like my fucking cat just died or something.

I stare after my aunt with the expression equivalent of a 'fuck you' and jam the spoon in my mouth. What do you know? I got my appetite back.

Liv pours two glasses of wine and hands me one when my aunt has left the room again. "So what are you going to do?"

"I'm going home tomorrow. Then I'm going to have a hot bath and call Monique, I guess."

"Really?"

"No. I'll probably have a hot bath and curl up in front of some trashy TV show. There's plenty of them to choose from." I lick the spoon clean. "Then I'm going to call Monique and go back to work."

My best friend raises her eyebrows with a shake of her head.

"What?"

"How can you do that? Leave the guy you're in love with and think about sleeping with other guys?"

"I'm kidding myself that maybe there'll be a hot hunk of a guy waiting for me this weekend and he'll fuck all the heartbreak out of me."

Liv stares at me blankly.

"Kidding. I'm kidding. Geez."

"I wondered there for a minute." She taps a long fingernail against her mouth. "Do you have to go back to work? You have savings, right?"

"I'm not retiring at twenty-four because of a fucking guy, Liv. I'm going to have one hell of a good cry tonight, let it all out. Then, tomorrow, I'll get my shit together. If I sit at home every day, I'll spend my life wondering if I made the right decision or not."

"You did. Make the right decision."

"Thank you. So I have to get on with it. I can't spend forever on the past."

"You're missing one huge point though."

"How am I? It's over. He'll go back to New York and his cushy little rich-guy life, finalize his divorce, take over the company, and find a second wife that isn't me."

I think it before she says it.

"No. No, Liv. Don't even."

"Or he'll come looking for you. He knows where you live, remember?"

Fuck. Fuck. *Fuuuuuuuck.* "He won't," I say through shaking hands. "I told him never to contact me again. He wouldn't."

Her lips twitch. "He paid three times your rate just to keep you in his life. You think he's gonna let you walk away now?"

"Shut up."

"Get back to it, Day. You can try and live your life like you never happened, but you're gonna be fighting him the whole way for it."

"You're a really shitty best friend, you know that, right?"

"Just keeping it real." She grins and grabs her jacket. "Besides, you'd kick my ass if he does exactly that and I *didn't* warn you."

True that. Oh, how well she knows me.

I hug her before she goes. "Thanks for coming over tonight."

"It's my job. By the way, you need that bath."

"Bitch." I shut the door behind her. She isn't exactly wrong.

Heartbreak does funky things to you.

Her words in mind, I jump under the shower before climbing into bed and snuggling under the covers. I cocoon myself between the thick sheets, my legs still wet from my lazy towel drying, and my mind runs rampant.

It's the same thing it's done every night since I left. This time though, it's not going over every word of our conversation. It replays the final night in Paris like I'm watching it in HD and slow motion, but there are no words. No sounds. Only feelings and emotions and the truth of them.

Without reminding myself of the words that shattered the possibility of a future we'd never set in stone, I see more. Everything. I see the raw pain in his eyes when he realizes I'm going. I see the shake of his hands that lingers all night and only intensifies when he finds me packing my suitcase. I see the brutal agony and guilt swamping him, and I see the defeat that beats against his usually determined and assured stance.

And I hear through the silence. I hear the begging through the desperate way his mouth forms his words. I hear the anguish every time his lips say my name. I hear his realization that his secret did the very thing he was trying to avoid—that it was all for nothing.

But mostly, I feel. I feel the shattering pain all over again, this time combined with his. I feel his desperation to keep me there and my need to go. I feel him reach for me at the same time I step away, and I feel the heaviness that settles when I walk through the door. Away from him. Again.

I feel the crushing of my hopes, the helplessness of my heart, the rapidly increasing flow of my tears. And I realize that I'm not remembering anymore. The tears cascading down my cheeks are real, so very real, and so is the hollow ache in my chest. The twisting of my stomach with bitterness is the same as it was then, and the hopeless feeling penetrating my bones hasn't eased a bit.

I miss him. Despite the pain, I miss him as much as I hate him, and I hate him as much as I love him. I miss his body next to mine at night. His breath on my neck. His arms around me. His legs and feet tangled in mine. I miss the gentle way he'd whisper my name to wake me up and the look he had reserved just for me and the notes I never knew he was leaving. Everything. Every. Fucking. Thing.

I shouldn't. I shouldn't miss him at all. But I do.

I miss him the way I love him.

Entirely.

Chapter Two

Home smells like home. That scent that always lingers no matter what, the same one that comforts you.

I leave my suitcases strewn in the hallway and collapse onto my bed upstairs. It's soft and familiar. More comforting than the warm, fruity smell of home. I reach into the drawer of the nightstand and pull out some matches. Lighting one, I lower the flame to the wick of my bright pink Yankee candle, letting the strong Dragon Fruit scent assault my senses almost immediately.

Goddamn, I love these candles.

I close my eyes for a long moment. Now I need to get changed. As much as I don't want to, these sweatpants aren't going to cut it much longer. They're two days old, after all.

I strip and throw all my clothes into the laundry hamper. My drawers are half empty, but I find a pair of pajama pants and a tank.

This house feels huge after a month of living in what were essentially apartments. And kind of lonely too. Like someone should be walking around the corner and knocking into me or sitting on the sofa, in the kitchen, or in the bathroom. And only pulling one mug from the cupboard and placing it under the coffee machine feels alien. So does not hearing creaking floorboards just before it's stolen from me.

I swallow and put the mug down. *Seven days, Dayton. One week. Time to get your shit together.*

I survived it once. I can do it again—if only because I've done it before. Because I know I can. Because I have to.

Because I'm stronger than to let love be the death of me.

My cheeks sting as my palms connect with them sharply. It's cheek slapping or head knocking, and the closest thing I have to hit myself with is a saucepan. I'll pass that one up, thanks.

A loud ding-dong echoes through the door followed by the sound of it opening. Monique. Not even Liv walks in. I turn around and brace myself for the first conversation with her in days.

She stops in the doorway, her waist accentuated by her tailored blazer, and runs her eyes over me. "You look like fucking shit."

"Nice to see you, too, Monique. So kind of you to drop by without calling."

"Leigh called. You think I was gonna let you run away before I could talk to you?"

"A chance would have been nice." I smile tightly and perch on a stool at the breakfast bar. "What do you want?"

"Any coffee left in there?" She nods to the machine and pours one before I can answer. Typical Monique. Why wait for an answer when you can just find out yourself?

I roll my eyes as she sits down and sips casually at her coffee. Fuck her and her games.

"What do you want, Monique? You're not my favorite person right now if you hadn't guessed."

She sighs heavily and sets the mug down. "I came to apologize."

"Does Darren need a new car again?"

"Not this time." She smirks, but it drops quickly. "I should have told you before you left."

"So why didn't you?" I hold up a finger at the opening of her mouth. "And fuck your 'client confidentiality' bullshit. I'm not interested in that. The truth, Mon."

Her tongue wets her lips, and she stares at me.

"Do I need to find a new agent? One who won't keep important information from me?"

She laughs. "Well played, Dayton. We both know you won't find another agent, but well played all the same. All right. You wanna know?"

"No, I'm asking for shits and giggles."

"He paid extra if I didn't tell you. That's why the money was wired through me and not into your account."

I get up and cross my kitchen. I grip the counter, facing away from her, and close my eyes. He wanted to keep it from me that badly that he paid her off? What the fuck is that?

He must have really thought I'd never find out.

"How much?"

"You know I can't tell you that."

"How much?"

She sighs again. "Five grand."

"Shit!" Five fucking grand for her not to tell me? I don't believe it. I don't believe him. I don't believe *her!* "Why did you take it?" I turn, and she blinks harshly. Monique never loses her composure or acknowledges our emotions, so I know she can really see how pissed off I am.

"Money," is all she says.

"And that's more important than my wellbeing?"

"You fuck guys for a living, Dayton. I make sure they're legit. That's looking after your wellbeing."

"And for big jobs, important clients, you're supposed to make sure there are no fucking skeletons hiding in fancy-ass, designer-clothing-lined closets."

"Everyone has skeletons, Dayton. Even you and I."

"This is a skeleton I should have known about. I can't forgive you for not telling me. Not yet." I point to the door. "You know the way out."

"You're the only person I take this shit from, y'know?" She stands.

"Good. I would hope you don't give the other girls the shit you give me."

"Touché." My agent inclines her head in my direction and makes for the door.

"Monique?"

She pauses at her name and looks over her shoulder.

"Call me when you have a job for me. But I'm not fucking anyone yet. Escorting only."

"You're coming back to work?"

My lips curve to one side. "Someone has to pay for your crap."

"Just answer the fucking phone this time, all right?"

She leaves, and I lean back against the counter again.

Five grand to keep a secret.

I shouldn't be surprised. He paid enough to keep me. It's just a fucking shame it wasn't quite enough to keep me there.

Money can keep something, but it can't guarantee it. You'd think he'd know that. He has enough to throw around.

* * *

I need some control back in my life.

That's my problem. Since Aaron came back into my life, it's spiraled so crazily out of control that I can barely put my panties on the right way. Now, with the last few weeks all said and done, I can untangle them and get back to my life.

The way it should be. Focused. Controlled. Planned.

I ignore the niggling empty feeling in the pit of my stomach as I roll my stockings up my legs, the lace tops hiding just beneath the hem of my dress. Six knocks drift up the stairs to me in Liv's signature knock. Tap tap. Tap tap. Tap tap. The sound is followed by her opening the door and yelling up at me.

It's not my preferred method of control, admittedly, but when your best friend insists that a night out will cure your blues, you go along with it. Well, you do if your best friend is like mine.

It's easier to do what she wants and save myself the headache.

Liv stops in the doorway and runs her blue-green eyes over my body. I pause, my fingers still looped under the lace on my thigh, and raise my eyebrows at her.

"That dress is too long."

"Excuse me?"

She rolls her eyes like I'm a petulant toddler. "The dress. It's too long."

"There's nothing wrong with my dress." I smooth it over my legs. "Less is more, you know."

"More material won't get you laid, you know."

I stand and grab my lipstick. "I'm not trying to get laid, Liv. I'm trying to get over him."

"And getting under someone is the best way to get over someone else."

"Did your mind get swapped with a teen boy at some stage of your life?"

She smacks her pink lips together and grins. "No. While you were fucking for work, I was fucking for *fun*. I learned more than a few things after I broke up with Ross."

Ah, the boyfriend she only kept around for his finesse in the bedroom.

"I'm sure I'm aware of all the things you've learned." My tone is dry, and I drop the lipstick into my makeup bag. "Look, I just want to relax tonight. No guys, no getting laid, nothing."

"Fine. But you're missing out."

"I'm sure." I grab my bag and follow her out to the waiting cab. Liv directs him to the wine bar where she works, our usual first stop, and settles back in the seat.

Night is falling as we head into the center of the city, and the bright lights from the skyline drown it out. A golden tone climbs into the inky blue, both colors fighting in the sky for their space. They collide in a gorgeous pinky-purple band that stretches out before me, providing an illuminating backdrop for the buildings that reach high up.

I wriggle my toes inside my shoes. I want to go home, change into some pajamas, and eat ice cream. Even if my ass is feeling the numerous tubs over the last week or so.

No, I tell myself. I'm not doing that anymore—being a whiny teenage girl over something she couldn't help. Something she couldn't stop. I'm going to be the strong, independent woman I am.

After all, a man can't make me, so there's no reason to let him break me either.

Mental pep talk done, I follow Liv into the bar and to our usual table by the window. It provides the perfect spot for people-watching, something I've found myself doing a lot since we went to Italy, and it gives Liv the perfect view of the door just in case a hot guy should walk through.

Our friendship is kind of skewed, I'm realizing.

One bottle of wine appears on the table in front of us. "A bottle? Big spender tonight?" I tease her, grabbing it and pouring two glasses.

"Ha! As if." She grins and nods her head behind me. "Nope. The two guys in the suits bought it for us."

Of course. Only my best friend could walk in somewhere and get the first drinks bought for us.

I glance at her chest. The girls are definitely out to play tonight. "I wonder why."

Her smile widens. "Hey, if they get us free drinks, are you going to complain?"

I want to remind her that I can buy my own drinks, but even that reminds me of Aaron. *Fucking hell.* Is there anything that won't?

"I have a job this weekend."

"Hmm? Where to?"

Liv chews on the inside of her lip and hides behind her wine glass. "I didn't want to tell you before, but I took your advice. I went to the Stone agency."

"Why wouldn't you tell me? Regardless of the asshole level of the guy in charge, they're still an incredible agency. Are you signed with them?"

"Not yet. This weekend is a kind of trial, too. If the pictures come back okay, they'll be drawing up a contract next week."

"I'm happy for you." I grab her hand across the table. "Really, I am."

Apparently even now my best friend will remind me of him. Maybe I should move to Australia.

"I thought it would be kind of awkward."

I force a laugh. "No. What happened with us happened. One of those things."

She arches a perfectly shaped eyebrow. "Right. We can go with that."

"I was planning on doing so." I sigh into my glass. "Can we stop talking about him now, please? I'm done moping over him."

Liv stands and grabs my hand. "Let's finish this then find somewhere we can go dance. And with any luck, there'll be some hot guys to look at."

She has a one-track mind.

"My feet hurt," I whine, sitting on a stool. I pull my shoe off and rub the ball of my foot with my thumb. Two hours of nearly solid dancing has just about killed me.

"Wine?"

"The drink or the action?" I mumble. "If I can, both."

Liv laughs and leans over the bar. She gives her eyelashes a quick flutter, squeezes her boobs together, and grabs the attention of the bar guy right away. I'd roll my eyes if I weren't so used to it.

Two glasses of wine appear in front of us. I pull out the money, but a hand rests on my forearm. "Let me get those for you," a deep voice says into my ear.

I turn to face the guy offering with a polite smile. "Thank you, but no thank you. I owe her a round." I'm done having drinks bought for me.

"Really, let me get it for you."

"That's very kind of you, but no, thank you." My voice firms toward the end. I don't give a crap if he's good-looking and has that rugged thing going on that melts panties. My panties aren't melting, and I'm buying my own drink.

He opens his mouth to speak, but he's interrupted by another voice. One that sends shivers down my spine and stops my heart.

"You heard the lady. She can buy her own drink"

Liv's eyes widen, and my throat goes dry. No. He's not supposed to be here. America or Seattle. No. No.

"And who are you?"

"I'm the owner."

Liv's eyes are as wide as saucers, but I'm not even surprised. Am I surprised he's here? Yes. That he owns the place? No. I know nothing about his business. Not really.

More words are exchanged behind me, words I can't make out through the spinning inside my body. Every part of me is on edge, and my stomach is clenched with apprehension. I can't breathe.

I grab Liv's arm and shake my head. I can't stay here—not with him. She understands, grabbing my hand and leading me toward the door. I step out into the night air and take a deep breath, leaning against the wall, but the eyes I look into aren't the blue-green ones of my best friend.

They're the electric-blue ones of the man who owns me so entirely.

"What the fuck are you doing here?"

"I own this place with my uncle. He saw you were here and called me."

"Not that it has anything to do with you." I straighten. "Where's Liv?"

Aaron grabs my arm to stop me going back inside and spins me into him. I look up at him coldly, ignoring the way a fire sparks at his fingers wrapped around my bicep and threads through my veins until my body is alive and humming.

"I wanted to see if you were okay. That's all. Then that guy—"

"I can take care of myself." I snatch my arm back. "I'm more than capable of it, thank you. I certainly don't need saving from someone who has no right to do so."

"Is that what you think?"

I step back. "That's what I know. You gave up every right to have anything to do with me eleven days ago."

"Twelve."

"What?"

Aaron swallows, and I see a flicker of regret in his eyes. "Twelve days. But who's counting?"

"Not me, evidently." I turn away, but his next words make me stop with my hand on the door handle.

"It's over. Naomi finally signed the papers two days ago."

A lump builds in my throat, one that threatens tears as strongly as it threatens vomit, and I struggle to swallow it back down.

"Congratulations," I croak. "Now perhaps you can find someone and have a real relationship with them."

"I already found her."

"Then it's a shame you fucked it up, isn't it?"

He curls his fingers around the handle above mine, his chest against my back. I'm still on fire, still reeling from his touch, and now his breath across my skin is cracking the façade I'm struggling to keep in place.

"It took me seven years to find you again, and if you think I'm giving up now, you're so very, very wrong."

"I don't doubt that for a second, but it doesn't mean you'll get anywhere."

"This isn't over, Dayton. We aren't over."

"Oh, it is. We're very over. Trust me."

I tug on the door and he releases it. I can feel his eyes on me as I find Liv at the bar, and when I turn, he's inside, staring at me. Determination clouds his eyes, and I know I'm in for a fight.

"What the hell?" Liv hisses in my ear. "What's he doing here?"

"He owns this place." I grab her hand. "And we're leaving."

I can't stay around him any longer. Just when he's stopped consuming my every thought, here he is, standing in front of me like a dream come to life. Like my own personal heaven and hell mixed together in one gorgeous, heartbreaking package.

Because that's what he is—everything that's good and bad spun together into something intoxicatingly addictive, something you can't help but want. Aaron Stone is and always has been my drug. He's the one thing that can make me lose my head and send my body into overdrive. He's the one thing I'm completely powerless against.

I can't fight the effects he has on my body or stop the pounding of my heart whenever I hear his voice. I can't change the way I feel when he looks at me or the way I jolt whenever he touches me, but I can't live with it.

I also can't live without it.

But I've made it this far. Twelve days without him seems like a lifetime, but it's not really. It's a small slice of nothing when he's everything.

Chapter Three

"And what did you tell him?"

I stab my fork into my pasta with a little too much vigor. "I told him it was over. Done. Fini."

"I assume he didn't take that very well."

I drop my fork without taking a bite and look at my aunt, a heavy sigh falling from my lips. "You assume correctly. Naturally, my words went right over his head."

"So what are you going to do?"

"I'm going to go to work and pretend he didn't show up and ruin my night out."

Aunt Leigh nods approvingly. "Make sure you use plenty of concealer. You could carry your fucking groceries in the bags under your eyes."

"You know something? Sometimes I wonder how I'm not the most insecure person on the planet."

"Insecure people are that way because they have people wrapping their asses up in bubble wrap all the time. Honey, if you'd rather me tell you that you look gorgeous and ready to go to work, I will, but next time I do, you'll be wondering if I'm lying or not."

I can't argue that point.

"No? I didn't think so. What time is your client?"

"Seven."

She checks her watch. "It's almost six. You go shower and I'll clear this away. Your dishwasher works, correct?"

I hold up my hands, showing her my perfectly manicured nails. "Of course it does. Monique would shit a kitten if I turned up with—god forbid—soap on my fingers."

A smile twitches the corner of my aunt's mouth. "Just one kitten? She'd shit the litter."

I giggle into my hand as I head upstairs. This much is true. Monique is Ms. Perfection herself.

I shower quickly, the hot stream of water beating away some of the tension knotting my shoulders, and wrap myself in a fluffy towel. I almost feel like I can breathe easily after that—if it weren't for the new fear of Aaron popping up everywhere I go.

I tug a black dress from the closet and some red heels to go with it. Red isn't a color I want to be wearing right now, but Mr. Alexander Carlisle was very specific on how he wants me to dress. And the client always gets what they want.

As long as they've paid for it, that is.

I blow dry my long hair in record time and twist it into a sleek updo before stepping into my outfit for the evening. Some of the control I know so well seeps back into me as I roll the tan stockings up my legs and pull the dress down to cover the tops. I feel even more in control of my life as I slide my feet into the red heels and apply my makeup.

That same old rush floods my body. The knowledge of what I have to do—how I have to act, how I'm expected to behave, how I'm expected to speak.

Tonight, at Mr. Carlisle's request, I'm Kelly York, a woman from a small town just outside Portland. I'm about to graduate from law school, and we met when I interviewed for an open position at his law firm. Of course, he couldn't hire me because he's a respectable man who doesn't mix business with pleasure, and he decided I was better for the pleasure.

And the irony is that he's hiring an escort.

Very respectable, Mr. Carlisle.

It's hard not to judge. It's my job not to, but sometimes I can't help it. Thankfully I rarely take away my brain-to-mouth filter, so my judgments stay firmly inside my own mind.

"Better," Aunt Leigh declares, running her eyes over me. "Who's your client?"

"You know I can't tell you that."

"Fine. I might just stop by the Southfall later for a drink or two."

I purse my lips at her. Goddamn woman. "All right, but if Monique finds out…"

"I worked for her for twenty years. You don't need to tell me to keep it quiet. I'm just nosy."

I tell her everything, and she nods the whole way through, reminding me to use my upper-class mannerisms she spent hours teaching me when I decided to do this job. Like I need reminding—but I get it.

This is her crazy way of looking out for me.

Our relationship is dysfunctional, like so many of the others in my life, but it works. Like the others do. Well, mostly.

I climb into the cab—five minutes early, much to my annoyance—and lean back in the seat. I take a deep breath when a thought flashes through my mind.

Shit. Alexander Carlisle is one of the top lawyers in Seattle. This is a high-profile event.

What if Aaron's on the guest list?

"This better be good, Dayton."

"Do you know who's on the list tonight?"

"Funnily enough, that's not something I charge for," Monique replies dryly.

"Fuck off, Mon. Can you find out?"

"Why?"

"In case Aaron is there. He's in Seattle. I saw him last night."

My agent sighs. "I'll try to find out."

"Quickly!" I hang up as the cab pulls up outside the hotel. There's a sinking feeling in the pit of my stomach as I remember the last time I was here—and the events that unfolded after that chance meeting.

My instinct tells me to get the cabbie to drive me home, but I hand him his fare and get out instead. Where the fuck was that instinct six weeks ago?

The same girl is even behind the counter—Rachel, was it? — and recognition flashes in her eyes. "Can I help you, madam?"

"Yes. I'm looking for Mr. Carlisle. It's Kelly York."

She nods and picks up the phone. It's like déjà vu as she requests someone to take me to the private booths in the bar where he's waiting. As the young guy takes me there, I almost expect to see Aaron when the curtain is opened.

But I don't. It's a thirty-something good-looking guy, and he oozes confidence.

"Ms. Lopez," he greets me in a hushed voice and kisses my hand. "Alexander Carlisle."

"It's a pleasure to meet you, Mr. Carlisle."

He motions for me to have a seat. "Please, call me Alexander. Can I get you a drink?"

"A white wine would be wonderful. Thank you."

He orders, and when the waiter disappears, he slides a brown envelope across the table to me. "The fee agreed with your agent."

"Thank you." I slip it into the lining of my purse. My drink is delivered, and I wait until we're alone until I speak again. "Is there anything specific I should know for tonight? I know the general information about our 'meeting' and your company from what my agent passed on, but I'd like to make sure we're on the same page before we go out."

"Of course. I believe all the necessary information was already given. The only thing would be that, after three months, my parents are under the impression we're very much in love." He quirks an eyebrow over a dark eye "Fortunately they live in Nevada now, so it will be easy to convince them."

I swallow some unwelcome bile. Of course we'd be crazy in love. Why the fuck wouldn't we be?

"Of course." I smile. "When would you like to go out?"

"We can join the party now if you'd like to."

"Perfect." The sooner we get there, the sooner I can leave. Three hours of my time is all he booked, and I'd like that over as soon as possible.

I link my arm through his in the elevator. Why hasn't Monique called yet? She knows not to fuck about with this stuff. I need to know.

We stop outside a function room thankfully different than the one Aaron had his party, and Alexander smiles at me before opening the door. The room is full, but I spot two familiar heads by the bar.

Fuck.

I step back and take my client with me. "I'm afraid I have a problem, Mr. Carlisle."

"Alexander, please. What's the problem?"

What fucking isn't these days? "My ex-boyfriend's parents are at your party. I'm sure you understand that it's not convenient for me. We broke up only recently."

"Ah, of course."

I take the envelope from my purse and discreetly tuck it inside his jacket. "I'm so sorry. I'll call my agent on the way down, and she'll send someone else to accompany you. She'll be here within half an hour. If anyone asks, there's heavy traffic, which is delaying her. Reception will call up for you."

"It's a shame, Ms. Lopez. I was looking forward to an evening with you."

"And I you. I'm sorry for the inconvenience." I smile and step back into the elevator. My cell buzzes.

"He's not, but his parents are."

"Yeah, thanks for the heads-up on that. Luckily I noticed before we went in. You'll have to send someone else."

Monique sighs. "Lori can do it. She'll have to learn her shit quickly. What's your story?"

I tell her exactly what I just told Alexander.

"Good. I'll call her now and get her ass down there. And Dayton?"

"Mm?"

"Good call."

"Thank you." I smile and hang up. Then I hail a cab and climb in.

What are the chances of that? Thank god for small miracles.

Not that there's anything wrong with the guy, but I'm not in the mood to be the loved-up girl of some mogul lawyer who represents half the city. He's probably from the firm that deals with all the Stone stuff.

Of course, now I have nothing to do for the rest of the evening.

Or I can keep a certain businessman off my property.

I throw a few bills at the cab driver and slam the door behind me as I get out, my eyes tracing the silhouette of Aaron Stone sitting on my bench.

"If this happens again, Mr. Stone, I may have to look into taking legal action. Two nights in a row? I hardly imagine your sitting outside my house is a coincidence."

He looks up, his eyes piercing in the evening darkness. "Back to work, Miss Black?"

"I have a job. As much as I'd love to sit around and feel sorry for myself, I'm afraid I have far more important things to do." I stroll past him and put my key in the door.

He closes his hand around mine. "Things, or people?"

"I fail to see what business it is of yours."

"It's very much my business, as you're well aware."

"Perhaps in your opinion. But if it will make you feel better, it's things, not people." I turn around. "I'm not back to work fully. Yet."

"Yet?"

"I have to earn money somehow, and my big spenders aren't pretty little rich boys who need a date for the night. So yes, yet."

"Never," he growls, leaning into me. "You aren't fucking another guy, Dayton."

"That's not your decision, Aaron. You had your chance to decide that, and you blew it. Now if you'd like to remove yourself from my property, I'd appreciate it."

His lips touch mine in a scorching, forceful kiss that knocks me backward. I gasp at the sudden touch, and he slides his tongue between my lips. His hands cup my face, holding me against him, and my back is flush against the door. He tastes of the woody whisky he adores, of power and determination and finality.

"Tell me one thing," he says, his lips brushing across mine with his words. "Has anyone else kissed these lips?" His thumb comes between us and flicks my bottom lip.

Who the fuck does he think he is asking that question? I'm ready to push him away, to shove him on his ass, but instead, what happens is a whisper of, "Fuck you."

"Answer the fucking question, Dayton."

My chest heaves at the thickness of his voice. I can hear the emotion beneath the demand. "No. They haven't," I answer.

His lips crash against mine once more, this time rougher, harsher. I can feel nothing but his palms rough against my cheeks and his lips soft against my own. His tongue sweeping through my mouth and owning it completely. The ball of need building in my lower stomach and sending aches down through my pussy.

He kisses me deeply, completely dominating my mouth, possessing me until I'm consumed by him, and for a long moment, I forget why this shouldn't be happening.

Until he pulls back, his nose resting alongside mine, and I remember again.

I take a deep breath, meeting his eyes as the reality of what just happened settles into a heavy ball in my chest. "You have five seconds to get your ass out of here before I go crazy at you."

He smirks, igniting a new kind of fury inside me. "Remember that the next time you think what you do is none of my business." My cheeks feel cold when he drops his hands, and he walks backward, his eyes fixated on me. "Good evening, Dayton."

He climbs into a waiting black car. I watch, frozen to the spot, as it pulls away. My hand trembles as I turn the key and scramble inside my house. I slam the door shut and lock it—like a few bolts and a chain can keep him away from me.

I need the barrier. I need a ten-foot-high wall.

I lean against the door, my heart thumping and my chest heaving, and slide down to the floor. I can feel the ghost of his lips on mine. I can taste him on my tongue, rich and woody, and the warmth of his body is still threading through mine.

My anger dissipates before I have time to process it. It's replaced by that hollow, empty hole I thought I'd filled, and tears fill my eyes. I look up at the ceiling as the tears spill over and drip down my cheeks.

Fuck.

I run my fingers through my wet hair, my eyes closed. The water beats down on my face in a futile attempt to wash any traces of Aaron Stone from me. If it were that easy, I would have done it a long time ago, but he's seared into my skin. He's burned in, like I'm branded by him.

My lips still feel swollen from his forceful kiss, and there's a light red rash on my chin from the stubble that covers his jaw.

I feel like I've spiraled back to where I was when I left Paris. Like I'm back in the dark pit of heartbreak and longing and disbelief. I still want him. I crave his touch whenever I'm alone, and I crave the sound of his voice through the silence.

I want him to fight so I can say no. So I can beat him back and so he can feel even an ounce of the pain I feel whenever his name is mentioned. Whenever I think it. Whenever he turns up in front of me like a little fucking surprise and drives me to insanity.

It doesn't matter that it's been more than twenty-four hours since I found him outside my house. It doesn't matter that I should be working right now but I can't because of him.

What matters is that I can still feel him all over me.

I can still feel his breath and his fingers wrapping around mine and everything. I can feel everything.

I step out of the shower and dry off, throwing on some sweatpants and an old tank before heading downstairs. The doorbell goes off as I open the fridge, and I leave it open as I answer the door.

"Hello?"

"Miss Black?" A young girl peers at me over a bunch of flowers.

"Uh…" I look at the extravagant bouquet and back to her. "That's me."

"Delivery for you."

"Who from?"

She shoves the bouquet at me and shrugs. "Doesn't say. Have a good day!"

I frown and back into the house, kicking the door shut. I don't need to ask who they're from. I know.

I set them down on the island in my kitchen and carefully look through the lilies and roses and blossoms and god knows what fucking else until I find a card.

Tu me manques, Dayton.

"You are missing from me," I whisper, rubbing my thumb over the scrawled words, and close my eyes.

He said them a thousand times to me when we were in Paris—the first time. Whenever we weren't together, he'd text me or get the concierge to pass a message on, and it was always the same. I didn't know what it meant until I finally plucked up the courage to ask him.

"The French don't say 'I miss you,'" he whispered. *"They say, 'You are missing from me.' And that's true. Whenever we're apart, I feel half complete. That's why I tell you, 'Tu me manques.'"*

That was the moment I fell entirely in love with him. Whatever part of me was holding back, that was the moment I really, truly lost my heart to him.

I felt the same. Whenever we weren't together, I was convinced I was missing a part of myself. Whenever we were together, I felt whole.

Exactly the way I feel now.

I grab my cell, snap a photo, and send it to Liv. My cell rings almost immediately, and I balance it between my ear and shoulder as I pour some juice.

"Holy shit!" she exclaims. "Is that from Aaron?"

"Yep. Just got delivered."

"He can break my heart any day. They're fucking gorgeous."

"Yes, heartbreak is a real hoot," I reply dryly.

"Shit. Sorry. Didn't think."

Obviously, Liv.

"What are you going to do?"

"With the flowers? Fill my sink with water and put them in it until I find a vase large enough for them."

Her sigh is heavy and a little pained. "Not about the flowers, asshole. About the guy."

"Pretty sure everything I'm considering would be considered illegal."

"We're thinking different illegals here, aren't we?"

"Probably." No doubt she's thinking of sexy things. I'm thinking of not-so-sexy things—unless you're into dead bodies. "But what the fuck, Liv? Flowers? Who sends flowers?"

"Guys who haven't forgotten how to romance a girl."

"I'd rather be romanced in the bedroom, if I'm honest." I nudge the fridge door closed and stare at the flowers. "They are pretty though."

"Pretty? They're freakin' gorgeous! Seriously, are you letting him grovel?"

"There's nothing to grovel for."

"Okay. Not having this conversation. Call me when your head is screwed on properly. I love you. Goodbye."

My jaw drops and I stare at the phone.

The bitch just hung up on me.

Chapter Four

"Ms. Lopez, you'll be dining in one of the private rooms upstairs. Please follow me." The host leads me up a short flight of stairs and toward a white door with gentle gold embellishments. "Someone will be along for your order shortly. Your drink is waiting for you."

"Thank you." I wait until he disappears before opening the door. The room is empty—which means my client is late. Fantastic. Just what I need.

I pour a glass of wine from the bottle on the table and set my purse by my feet.

"Dayton."

I freeze. "Please tell me this is a bad coincidence and not something you organized."

Aaron says nothing as he takes the seat opposite me. "We need to talk."

"We've spoken plenty over the last few days, don't you think?"

"Not nearly enough." He fixes me with a hard stare. "Sit down, Dayton. You're not going anywhere."

"Really?"

"The door is locked from the outside." His lips quirk. "And on my orders, it won't be unlocked until one hour from now."

"Let me guess. Your uncle owns this restaurant, and that's why you're playing caveman."

"I could walk into any restaurant in Seattle and have a private room booked quicker than it takes you to blink." He looks up at me, and I feel the truth in his words. "Now, you can stand while we talk or you can sit. I really don't mind, but we're most definitely talking. You're not leaving this room until I'm finished."

"I think I've made it perfectly clear I don't want to talk to you."

"And I've made it perfectly clear you're going to, and we both know who is going to get their way. You'd be much more comfortable sitting down, I'd imagine."

I sit back down and take a deep breath. "This is underhanded, you realize that?"

He shrugs one shoulder, leaning back casually on his chair. "I'm not above playing dirty to get you back. I'm not above anything to get you."

I take a long sip from my glass. "What are you doing in Seattle?"

"That's the middle of the story."

"Fine. Why don't you start from the beginning? I'm always good for a fairytale."

He chuckles lowly, and I feel it down my spine. *Fuck you, body. Fuck you.*

"When you left, after…" He pauses.

"After I discovered you'd been lying to me for weeks."

"Ah, it wasn't really lying."

"It was a lie of omission, and that's still a lie." I hold his gaze for a few beats. "But we're not discussing your idiocy, so please continue."

"When you left, I confronted Naomi, and eventually she admitted she organized the party deliberately. She was trying to make my life difficult for me, and she's succeeded." He runs his finger around the rim of his glass. "I spent the next few days in Paris doing business and headed back to New York. A divorce agreement was already drawn up—my final offer—and if she didn't sign it, we'd go to court and she'd get a hell of a lot less. She agreed. Dad flew her into the city and we signed the papers."

"Congratulations," I repeat my halfhearted sentiment from the other night.

"And then I fired her."

"Excuse me?"

Aaron smirks and loosens his tie. "Our lawyer, Mr. Carlisle Sr., pulled out the documents and I took over the company. Then I fired her. She no longer has a place at Stone Advertising or modeling."

"Making your mark quickly, aren't you? Starting off as ruthless as you intend to carry on?"

He rests his elbows on the table and leans forward. "She fucked with you, Dayton. I don't take kindly to people fucking with the most important person in my life."

"Are you firing yourself then? Because you fucked with me pretty damn good too."

His eyes darken. "I don't need to. My punishment is my own personal pain in knowing I hurt you. Not to mention the way your eyes haunt me. I can't close my eyes without seeing your face as you found out about her."

"Good." I grab my glass tightly. "I hope it hurts like a bitch."

"Worse," he says honestly. "Being without you is like my soul has been shredded in the most brutal way. There isn't a second where I'm not thinking of you and the way you feel in my arms or the way you taste when your lips are against mine. Being without you is the worst kind of torture, and I brought it on entirely by myself."

I swallow. *I know,* I want to say. *I know because I feel that and more.*

"So why are you here? In Seattle? Other than to harass me, of course."

"I control the Seattle branch now. The person in charge here before me was all too happy to relocate to New York."

"Happy to relocate? I'm sure he was."

"I may or may not have convinced him a false happiness was better than no job."

I shake my head. "You're a bastard in and out of the boardroom."

His lips quirk to the side. "I prefer powerful or influential, personally."

"I'll stick with bastard, thanks." I meet his eyes. "You should have stayed in New York, Aaron. It would have been better for us both. You should have stayed just like you did the first time around."

"And the first time around, I made a colossal mistake. I fucked up. I should have come running after you and never let you out of my sight, but I was too weak to do that. I didn't realize you were the best thing I would ever have in my life. Now I know differently. Now I know that nothing or nobody will ever compare to you, and I'm not giving you up again."

"It's not a choice, Aaron."

"I'm not giving you up. Hear that, listen to it, understand it, and accept it." His eyes are focused, his voice edged with a rawness that hits me hard. "No matter what you convince yourself, Dayton, you're mine. Your heart and your body belong to me. You know it as well as I do."

"I'm not convincing myself of anything. Only what I know to be true."

He stands now, leaning closer to me—so close I can feel his breath across my lips as his eyes search mine. "Then start convincing yourself of how entirely you belong to me and the fact it isn't changing anytime soon."

The cab pulls up outside Monique's house, and I slam the door behind me. Anger is circulating crazily in my body, so much so I can barely think. Yet again, she knew. She knew he was there and she made me go.

I see red as I storm up to her house and shove her door open.

"Monique! Monique! Get your ass here now!"

Her husband, Ross, appears in the living room. "Dayton? Are you okay?"

"Where the hell is she, Ross?"

"She's upstairs. Hang on." He eyes me curiously as he passes me, and I take a deep breath. My fists are clenched at my sides, and footsteps on the stairs alert me to her presence.

"Dayton. What a surprise."

"Surprise? I'll give you a fucking surprise, Monique!" I follow her into the kitchen. "What the fuck? Are you trying to drive me insane?"

"You'll have to explain yourself." She pours herself a cup of coffee. "I'm not following."

"Of course you're not following the fact you just sent me to lunch with my ex-fucking-boyfriend boyfriend who broke my heart for a second time just two weeks ago!"

"Ah."

"Ah. Ah. Fucking ah! What the fuck, Mon? You knew! You knew he was there and you sent me anyway!"

"I know."

"Why? Why the hell did you let me go?"

She turns, her coffee clasped to her chest. Her ice-blue eyes are warmer than I've ever seen them. "You told me you wouldn't fall in love."

I desperately rake my fingers through my hair and spin on the spot. "I loved him, Mon. Do you get that? Once upon a time, I loved that man so fucking desperately that my life wasn't worth living without him. I loved him so damn fiercely that he was the center of my universe, but I moved on. I stepped into this world after my parents died, into this world where love isn't allowed. I forgot what it felt like, what love and adoration were, what it was to be addicted to the touch of another person. Until I saw him again. Until he took me on a fucking worldwide trip *you* allowed to happen, one you shouldn't have allowed. And now... Now I know a secret everyone knew but me, and I've had my heart shredded into a million inscrutable, unfixable pieces because of it. Because of him. And you let me go. You let me go!"

She looks at me hesitantly, regret filling her eyes the way tears are filling mine. I wrap my arms around myself.

"I am so in love with him that it hurts every time I breathe. Every time my heart beats, I feel the pain of not having him by my side, and you let me go. Why, Mon? Why the hell did you let me go?"

Her heels click along the tiled floor as she approaches me and wraps me in her arms in the first comforting contact I've ever had from her. I bury my face in her shoulder and cry, the hot tears soaking her shirt. She sighs as I sob so hard that it really does feel like my heart is being torn from my chest.

"Because," my agent says in a soft voice, "despite my job and the way I act around you girls, I believe in true love. I believe in the power and the magic of true love, and I will always send you down that path if you're lucky enough to ever cross it."

"This isn't love," I whisper. "This is pure pain."

"There's no love without pain. When it hurts as much as you do now, that's when you know its love." She smooths her hand over my hair. "Dayton, honey, when it feels like your whole world has been tipped upside down and shaken so hard that nothing makes sense except for the steady pounding of your broken heart, that's when you know it's true love."

Liv's apartment is quiet when I let myself in. This is the only place I can bear to be right now. It's the only place he hasn't been.

I know she won't be back until tomorrow since her shoot was today, but her tabby cat, Angus, immediately rubs himself against my legs.

"Hey, buddy." I bend down and scratch his back, much to his delight. "Let me in, will ya?" I lock the door behind me and dump my purse on the table. "Hey, Angus, do you know if your mommy has any wine in this place?"

He jumps onto one of the barstools and purrs loudly. I sigh. Of course he wouldn't know. His food tray is nearly empty, so I grab a can of food from the cupboard and dump it into the bowl before I turn to her fridge.

There's a bottle in there. *Bingo.*

I pour a glass, kick off my shoes, and curl up on her sofa. After I find some trashy TV show and Angus curls up on my lap, my eyes close briefly.

I'm exhausted. Completely, utterly, mentally, physically, and emotionally exhausted. I think the only thing that could revive me now is a year on a remote island with no contact with people, a stack of books, and a supply of wine.

And possibly my vibrator, because, y'know. A year is a long time to go without an orgasm.

I smile at my own thoughts and shake my head. *Jesus.*

A heavy sigh leaves me. I wish I could go back a couple of months, back to when everything was simple. When I knew exactly what to expect from my days and where my life was going. This crazy limbo I'm hanging precariously in is almost too much to deal with.

I could end it all now. I could give in and give Aaron what he wants. Me.

I just don't know if I can. I love him, but I don't know if I respect him anymore, and I sure as hell don't trust him. How can I? How do you trust someone who kept something so critical to their life from you?

That doesn't stop my heart or my body crying out for him though. It doesn't stop the heavy thumps in my chest when he's around. I still want to sink into his arms and never leave the comfort of them.

I almost want him to convince me he's worth it all. He took so much from me so readily, but he never really gave me any of himself in return. He so easily told me to give everything up for him when he couldn't even give up a skeleton rotting in his closet. And now... Now he's fighting.

Now that he's sorted his shit, he's back and he's fighting. I wonder if he knows what he's fighting for. I wonder if *I* know what he's fighting for.

I don't. I don't have a clue what he's doing.

All he says is that I belong to him. I do. I'm not naïve enough to believe I don't... But it's not enough. Maybe if he said them, the words I want to hear, it might change things.

Telling me that he never stopped loving me isn't enough. If he stands in front of me, looks me in the eye, and tells me that he loves me, then it could change everything. I'd know what he's fighting for, I'd know why he's fighting, and perhaps I'd be willing to fight for the same thing.

Perhaps.

Chapter Five

"Um, hi?"

I stop my absent dipping of my finger in the sugar pot and look at Liv. "Hi."

"Not that I don't love you being here, but why the fuck *are* you here?" She drops her bags and kicks the door shut.

"I'm hiding."

"Right."

"Angus has been keeping me company. He's not one for conversation, is he?" I cast a glance at the cat. He hops off the stool, his tail in the air, and stalks off. "Kind of moody, too."

"He's a cat," she replies flatly. "Why are you hiding?"

"Don't ask." I lick my finger free of sugar.

"I wish you wouldn't do that." Liv wrinkles her face. "It's disgusting. I'm going to have to replace my sugar now."

I shrug and dip my finger back in. "I'll carry on then."

"It's Aaron, isn't it?"

I roll my eyes. "It's always Aaron. He's a pain in my fucking ass. A relentless pain—like that annoying muscle ache you get after working out too hard."

"Why don't you just tell him to fuck off?"

"I did."

"And?"

"He told me I belonged to him. Do I look like I have a collar with a nametag on to you?"

Liv's eyebrows arch. "Okay, Dayton. I think you've had enough sugar." She takes the pot from me, slams the lid on, and puts it on top of a cupboard I can't reach. "And enough alone time with my cat. How long have you been here?"

"Two days. I told the guy who lives opposite you that he didn't have to feed Angus. He seemed kinda happy about it." I would be, too, if I'm honest. This cat is a menace. "Anyway, I thought you were coming back yesterday?"

"I was, but I decided to stop by and see my parents. I wasn't expecting your mopey ass to be here, was I?"

I shrug. "Whatever. I thought Monique might have called me with a job, but she hasn't."

Three days with nothing is unusual—even without the sex side of the job. In a city like Seattle, there's always someone who needs a lunch or dinner date or even someone to accompany them to an art gallery opening or some shit.

Three days of complete silence is unheard of.

"Really? Nothing?"

I shake my head and take the cup of coffee she offers. "I've checked my cell about a thousand times. No calls or messages. I don't know what's going on."

"Have you tried calling *her?*"

"No. I spoke to Aunt Leigh this morning and she said it was probably just a quiet week with everyone preparing for the new art gallery opening this weekend."

"Aren't you going?"

"Yeah. I'm supposed to be escorting someone. I haven't heard anything about it though, which is odd since it's in a few days."

Liv waves my phone in front of my face. "Again with the calling."

"All right, all right. I'll call her when I get home. I think Angus hates me now anyway."

My best friend glances over my shoulder at the cat, who's eying me evilly. "Angus hates everyone if he has to spend longer than two hours with them. He's a temperamental little bastard."

"Like his momma," I mutter and finish my coffee.

She smacks my leg. "Get out of my apartment."

I grin and grab my stuff. "I'll call you later when I've spoken to Monique."

"You better."

I leave her apartment and climb into my car. It's fairly early in the morning still, so there isn't much traffic, and it doesn't take long to get across the city to my house.

I ignore the message alert on my phone and head straight for the shower. Once I'm dressed and looking and feeling somewhat human, I lie back on my bed and call my agent.

"No," she answers. "Nothing today."

"Jesus. Mon, that's three days now. There has to be something."

"You have no jobs booked, Dayton."

"Why? Clients don't just drop off the edge of the Earth—even with my reduced list. What's going on?"

A long silence follows. I wet my lips with my tongue, my stomach clenching into a ball of fear. Like I know what she's going to say.

"You're booked," she says softly. "Permanently. I can't book you any jobs."

I sit up and look at myself in the mirror. Eyes wide, lips parted, cheeks flushed. "If you say his name, I'm going to go ten shades of batshit crazy."

"I'm sorry. He's paying for you indefinitely."

I close my eyes and rest my hand across my forehead. "Aaron's booked me? Permanently?" I clarify although my gut knows it.

"Yes."

"Jesus fucking Christ!" He really wasn't kidding when he said that I'd never fuck another guy. "He has more money than sense. Shit! What's he playing at?"

"You know what. This is up to you now, Day. I can't do anything. I had no choice but to accept his offer. It was that or he could close this business now."

"He threatened you?"

"He's that desperate. I can't be mad at him. If it were Ross, I'd do everything I could to get him back."

"I can't fucking believe him. Unreal. I gotta go." I hang up and throw the phone down.

I stand in the middle of my room, my breathing coming hard and fast, and look around aimlessly. Who the fuck does he think he is? To buy me and threaten my agent?

Without another thought, I pull some boots on. Standing here in my room isn't going to get this straightened out, so I'm going to give him what he wants. I'm going to go to him, but I'm not going to roll over submissively.

I'm going to kick his sharply suited ass until his balls turn blue.

My car beeps as I unlock it from the key fob, and I tear out of my driveway angrily. I hope Aaron isn't busy, because he has an unscheduled meeting with me.

My heels click against the floor as I cross to reception. A gorgeous blond woman smiles up at me.

"Can I help you?"

"Yes, you can. What floor is Mr. Stone's office on?"

"Floor forty-seven, madam, but I'm afraid you're not allowed there unless you have an appointment. He's in a meeting."

"It's okay. I'm his girlfriend. He's expecting me." I smile convincingly and head toward the elevator. Yeah, his girlfriend who doesn't know where his office is. Super convincing, Dayton.

Still. Meeting or no meeting, this shit gets sorted today.

I take deep breaths as the elevator takes me to the top floor. It's all glass doors and walls up here, and it takes me seconds to find the boardroom Aaron's having a meeting in.

I push the main doors open and walk right past his receptionist, who does her best to stop me. I ignore her calls of "Miss, miss! You can't go in there!" and shove the door open.

Six men in tailored suits sit around the table. Aaron is at the head of it, and he slowly comes to a stand when he sees me. Silence descends on the room as everyone turns to look at me, eyebrows rising and lips pursing as eyes settle disapprovingly on me.

"Dayton?"

"Who the fucking hell do you think you are, Aaron Stone?" I point my finger at him. "How dare you!"

He smiles apologetically at the shocked faces between us. "Excuse us, gentleman. It appears I've done something to anger my girlfriend."

"Anger? This is beyond damn anger! You'll be lucky to be breathing when I'm done with you, you presumptuous bastard!"

Aaron takes my shoulders and pushes me from the room. He leads me across the floor, past his bewildered receptionist, and unlocks the door to what is presumably his office. I don't pay any attention to the room around me as we step inside and he releases me.

"I'll be back in five minutes."

The door shuts behind me, and my mouth drops open when I hear the click of a lock. I grab the handle and shake it. That asshole! Where the hell does he get off locking me in his office—*again*?

I pace angrily, my fists clenched at my sides. Thankfully his office doesn't have glass walls. I'd probably bear a great resemblance to a caged animal to anyone walking by. A rabid bear or hungry tiger are my guesses.

I stop and perch on his desk, leaning my head back with a deep sigh. Pacing is doing nothing but hurting my feet. Stupid fucking boots. I pull the evil heeled boots off and look around his office.

The windows to my side are floor to ceiling, giving an uninterrupted view of Elliott Bay and the fat, green-and-white ferries running back and forth between the city and Bainbridge Island on the opposite shore. It's a soothing sight, and a little of my anger trickles out of my body.

The desk I'm perching on is thick glass, perfectly cleaned, and covered in neat stacks of paper and files. I lift some of the files, drag my fingertip across the glass, leaving a long smear across it, and smile. Immature, yes, but now I feel slightly better.

Aside from a leather corner sofa at the far end of the room and two leather chairs in front of me, the rest of the office is empty. Nothing on the walls, nothing telling where the two doors behind me lead to…

The lock clicks once again, and Aaron strolls in surrounded by an aura of calmness. Like I didn't just storm into a meeting and scream at him.

I fold my arms across my chest and watch him as he shrugs off his jacket and hangs it on a hook behind the door. He brings a strong hand to his neck and loosens his tie, his nimble fingers deftly undoing the top button of his shirt.

A flutter hits my lower stomach. I may be vibrating with anger at him, but he really does look hot as hell right now. He's tall and commanding, and when he finally turns to me, I can see his own annoyance in his eyes along with a glare of pure power.

His gaze flicks to my feet before roaming leisurely up my body and finding mine once more. "Making yourself at home, Dayton?"

"Why not? For all I know, I could have been here for a while. You should really get a coffee machine in here if you're going to lock women in your office."

"Not women. Just you."

"I'm flattered. Really."

He tilts his head slightly to one side, and his lips curve into that smirk that's so dangerously alluring. "Care to explain why you interrupted my meeting?"

I mirror his movements. "Care to explain why you called my agent and threatened her with closing her business if she didn't let you buy me indefinitely?"

"I told you, Dayton. No one but me gets to touch you."

"And I told you, Aaron. You lost that right when you fucked me over and broke my heart." I stand. "Threatening Monique was absolutely unnecessary and marks you as a downright bastard in my books. How dare you do that to her when she kept your secret from me?"

"I wouldn't have shut her down. I was calling her bluff." He walks around his desk, and I stand, following him with my eyes. "I may not understand her chosen…profession…but I respect her."

"At least you respect someone."

His eyes flash at my words. "I have never disrespected you."

"No, of course not." I laugh bitterly. "You only lied to me about your wife. Remember that? Oh, yeah." I tick that off on my fingers, and a bit of the righteous attitude leaves his eyes. "And you continue to push me, and then you freaking *buy* me, yet again, when I've made it quite clear I have no desire to have anything to do with you now. You continue to force me into situations I'm not comfortable with.

Where's the fucking respect in that, huh, Aaron? Because it's lost on me."

He fiddles with the cuff link at his wrist, his eyes steadily holding mine as he does so. The intensity in his stare makes me tremble a little, and the silence lingering heavily between us is uncomfortable. Turn-around-and-run-like-hell uncomfortable.

He places his hands flat on his desk, leaning toward 'me. "You're right. Lying about Naomi to you wasn't respecting you at all."

"Thank you."

"But I refuse to agree with the second part of your statement. If you were uncomfortable around me, sweetheart, you wouldn't be here right now."

"I'm here to kick your ass, not fuck you."

"You're here because, regardless of my paying for you, there's nowhere else in this world you're supposed to be."

I know he's right, but the tug in my heart that wants me to move closer is still clouded by my anger.

"You might own my heart, Aaron Stone, but that doesn't give you the right to abuse it. It doesn't mean you get to decide what I do, who I see, who I sleep with, where I work. I'm not your employee or someone who even gives a crap if you get your own damn way or not. It doesn't mean you get to throw your money around until I see things your way and give in to you the way everybody else does!"

"Then please enlighten me as to what it does mean."

"It means if you're sorry, you man the hell up and stop hiding behind your money. It means you *show* me you're sorry, because right now, all I see is a man unwilling to admit his mistakes." I put my own hands on the table and lean into him. Our breaths mingle as his eyes flick to my lips, and mine to his, before our gazes crash into each other's. "And for a man so confident and powerful, it's not a good look for you."

"Insults now?"

"No, the truth. Isn't it a bitch?"

He runs his thumb along my jaw, sending an electric current across my skin, and cups it softly. "Do you want to know what is a bitch? It's seeing you here, touching you, and knowing there's a part of you that doesn't want it. It's looking into your eyes and seeing contempt mixed with a slither of hatred because of what I did to you. It's knowing you only belong to me by default. That's the real fucking bitch here—that I lost you." He leans forward so his nose brushes mine. "Is that the kind of showing you want, Dayton? Do you want me to strip myself naked emotionally for you?"

"Yes." The word escapes my lips. "I want you to throw words and honesty at me, not underhanded contracts with my agent. I want realness, not sneaky payments in an attempt to get me to bend to your will. But you can't do that unless I kick and scream, can you?"

I step back and his hand drops limply. Aaron closes his eyes, pinching the bridge of his nose, and straightens. He turns his back to me to face the Bay.

"Why did you do it?" I lift my chin although he can't see me, like standing taller will give me the strength I need to continue this conversation. "Why did you really keep her a secret from me?"

"You know why. I didn't want to hurt you."

"Bullshit. Bull-fucking-shit!"

"I didn't want you to think any less of me for marrying a woman I didn't care for!" His words are sharp, and he turns just as suddenly as he shouted. "Happy?"

I step backward and shake my head. "Why would I have thought less of you?"

"Because I wasn't man enough to find you although I've been in this city a hundred times since we first met, but I could promise my life to a woman I didn't care about or love. What does that say about me, Dayton?"

The same thing it says about my not having another relationship since you.

"It says you were afraid of being hurt again, so you took the only option you had that meant that wouldn't happen."

He runs his fingers through his hair, and when I look into his eyes, I see the same pain I know is in mine reflected in them. "What am I supposed to do? I talk so easily about you belonging to me, but we both ignore the fact I belong to you. You own me. You always have and you always will. That's the very bottom of it, the defining line. You own me so fucking completely that I have to buy you because, dammit, Day, if I can't have you, no one else is going to either."

Aaron crosses the room, his long stride swallowing it up in a second, and frames my face with his hands. His thumbs run under my eyes and rub away the tears I didn't realize were falling, and he takes a deep, ragged breath.

"Jesus, woman. I can't let you go again. Do you understand that? I have to know, one way or another, that you belong to me."

"Buying me isn't the way to do that," I whisper. "I'm not a fucking toy, Aaron. If you want me, you have to prove that to me. You have to fight for me until you're blue in the face and struggling to breathe, because that's the only way I'm ever going to believe you. Your money, your power, your status—they all mean nothing to me. Nothing."

"I will spend every day of the rest of my life proving to you I want you if only you'll let me."

"It shouldn't matter if I let you. If you want me that badly, you'll do it anyway."

He rests his forehead against mine. "I want to show you something."

Chapter Six

Aaron takes my hand and leads me to one of the doors off his office. I chew the inside of my lip as he pulls out a key and unlocks it—just to lock it again once we're through it.

"Won't you be missed?"

He shakes his head. "I got Dottie to clear my schedule for the rest of the day, and as for that meeting, it's rescheduled for tomorrow morning."

"Dottie?" I can't help the curving of my lips. Seriously. Dottie?

"My assistant."

"I know who she is. She yelled at me a few times."

"And obviously, you ignored her."

"Obviously." I look around. "Oh, an apartment adjoined to your office. How very cliché of you."

"Sometimes leaving the office after working late isn't appealing."

"Oh, so it's purely for a work sleepover? Not a fuck pad then?"

"I can honestly say I've never fucked anyone here." His eyes flick to me. "But it can be arranged."

I roll my eyes and snatch my hand from his. "So what do you need to show me?"

He waves a hand over his shoulder and walks into the main room. I follow him, playing with the hem of my shirt. I'm suddenly feeling uncertain. Do I really want to see whatever this is?

Wait. I'm supposed to be mad at him.

Fucking hell.

Aaron pulls a box from a walk-in cupboard and carries it over to me. He motions to the sofa, and I sit as he pulls out something wrapped in brown paper. He hands it to me, and I rest it on my lap. It's light but large.

"What is it?"

"Open it. I haven't seen it yet."

I frown but flip it over and slide my finger beneath the tape holding the paper down. I do it on all four sides and pull the paper away

My breath catches when I flip it back over. "This is…"

Us, sitting on the beach in Australia, our foreheads together, both of us smiling. His arms are around my waist and mine are around his neck. I run my finger across the canvas, my throat tightening as I do so.

"Us," he finishes, sitting next to me.

The tug inside my chest grows and spirals into an all-consuming ache I feel deep into my bones. I can see it now—the love we never knew existed circling us. The love, so pure and real, clouded by reality and lies.

I can't take my eyes from it, the picture of us. We look perfect. Like we were meant to be there. Like its right—*right,* right. Wouldn't-have-it-any-other-way kind of right. It cuts and it hits and it twists inside me. An evil reminder of what we had. What we have. What's buried beneath the same reality that sliced it apart.

"How did you get it?" I ask softly.

"I called Joel while we were in Italy and asked to see the pictures that weren't chosen. Then I bought them from him and had these done. They were waiting for me in New York when I got back last week."

I swallow the lump forming in my throat. "What were you going to do with them?"

He smiles. "What one usually does with pictures."

"Shut up." I nudge his arm.

"I was going to hang them in my apartment when you moved in. I know, I know," he adds at my raised eyebrows. "Presumptuous bastard."

I can't help the twitch at the corner of my mouth that pulls my lips into a small smile. "Very much so."

Aaron takes the canvas from me. "Then you left, and I couldn't have them at home, so I brought them here."

"And you're going to keep them here until you get your way and I move in, right?"

"That was plan B, yes." He puts it on the table in front of us and leans back.

I pull my legs up and hug them to my chest as I turn, resting my head against the back of the sofa. My eyes find him and I trace his profile, my eyes lingering far too long on his lips and strong jaw. The urge to reach out and rub my thumb across the stubble shadowing it overcomes me, and I tighten my grip on my legs to stop myself doing it.

Even angry at him, I want him. Badly. I want to fold myself into his arms and let the ache in my chest go away, even if it's just for a minute. I want to feel his heart beating against my cheek and the steady rise and fall of his chest as he breathes me in, savoring me.

"You know, I don't think you've apologized for not telling me," I whisper, breaking the tense silence between us.

"That's because every time I try, I can't find the right words. There's nothing I can say that will show you how sorry I am."

"'I'm sorry' is a good start."

He turns to me with a raised eyebrow. "That wouldn't cut it."

"It might dent it a little."

A small laugh leaves him and he slides across the leather seat to me. He closes his hands around my wrists and pulls my arms from my legs. My skin hums, goose bumps coating it, when he lifts my legs and rests them over his.

Slowly, he brings a hand to my face and pushes my hair from my eyes. "Believe me, Day. If I thought 'I'm sorry' would even nudge it, I'd have said it a thousand times. Nothing I could say could show you how much I regret it."

He softly touches his lips to mine. His hand curves around my neck and pulls me closer to him, and his rich, masculine scent envelopes me. I respond to his kiss on instinct, curling my fingers into his collar.

This is slow and tender, filling me with warmth. Tingles spread through my body, reaching every part of me, and they heighten when Aaron wraps his arm around my body and pulls me closer.

This is his apology. And I feel it.

Every bit of his regret, his remorse, his guilt—it's all perfectly clear in the gentle brushes of his lips. It's louder and more meaningful than any words, but the ache is there still. It's still prevalent in my chest. It's still consuming.

This won't make it better. This won't make it go away.

"I have no idea what I'm doing with you half the time," he whispers, his eyes still closed. "You are the one thing that's unexpected, the one thing I truly have no power to control. I'm totally winging this, you know that? Like right now, I'm sitting here, completely lost, all the while hoping you'll walk out that door with me."

"One kiss won't change it. It won't heal my heart, Aaron."

He opens his eyes, and the brightness of them holds my gaze on his. "I can't change anything if you refuse to be around me." He fingers ghost along my neck and collarbone and come to rest above my heart. It beats faster at his touch, and his lips twitch. "I broke your heart, and now you have to let me fix it."

"What if you can't?"

"You have to let me try. Please, baby. Let me try and right my wrongs the easy way."

The easy way. I smile. That's his polite way of saying, "Let me, or I'll be forced to make you."

God, he's so frustrating and endearing mixed into one annoyingly sexy package.

"I don't have a choice, do I?"

He smirks. "Not at all."

"Fine. You win this time. I'll allow you to try." I put my finger over his lips to stop him from speaking. "But if you fuck up, even once, that's it. I mean it. Everyone deserves a second chance, but you're not getting a third. And I haven't forgiven you yet. Understand that."

He kisses my hand before taking it away from his mouth. "That's fair. I suppose."

"You suppose?"

A boyish grin appears on his face. "Yes, I suppose. Now go and put your shoes on. We're leaving."

He gets up, and I lean on the back of the sofa. "What if I want to stay?"

"Then we're going to break up before we make up, and that's quite the feat." He quirks an eyebrow. "Come on."

I mirror his expectant expression when he opens the door and waits by it. "You're incredibly bossy for someone who's supposed to be making things up to me."

I cross the room with a sigh, and he grabs my arm.

"Dayton." He lowers his mouth to my ear. "I said I'd right my wrongs. Not that I'd stop being a domineering, presumptuous bastard. Now get your pretty little ass into my office and get your shoes on before I carry you out of here without them."

My mouth goes dry. Oh, this is going to be no fun at all. And judging by the way my pussy is clenching because of his last sentence, he's going to get his way sooner rather than later.

I fake a heavy sigh and walk through the door. His hand connects with my ass sharply and I jump and squeal loudly.

Rubbing my hand over my stinging butt cheek, I turn and glare at him. "Not looking good for you already, Mr. Stone."

His eyes darken. "Call me that again and the only thing looking good will be you lying back on my desk completely naked."

I put my boots on, fighting my smile, and he unlocks the door. I stop in the doorway and glance up at him. "Is that a promise, Mr. Stone?"

"Dayton," he growls, and I laugh, walking into the reception area. He grasps me round the waist and steers me into the elevator, waving to his receptionist, who looks on, still bewildered. Poor woman.

When the elevator doors close, I lean up and whisper in his ear, "I can play dirty, too."

"And if I wasn't trying to behave, I'd have this elevator stopped and you against the wall so I could fuck you senseless."

My breath catches when he pulls me to his body.

"I play more than dirty, sweetheart. I play downright filthy." He presses a chaste kiss to my lips. "And if you keep playing dirty, I'm not promising I'll be able to behave for very long."

"Behaving is overrated," I mutter.

"You would know," he responds with more than a little amusement and leads me out of the elevator.

Through the glass walls of the reception, I see a black car pull up. The door is opened as soon as we step foot outside, and Aaron motions for me to get in.

"Efficient." I slide in, and he folds himself in after me.

"I'm the boss." He flashes me a grin like that explains everything.

Actually, it does.

"Where are we going?" I shift in my seat, and Aaron looks at me.

"To my apartment."

☙ ❧

This place is a bachelor pad. For real.

From the wood-paneled walls and U-shaped sofa in the living room, complete with wall-mounted TV, to the home bar with an empty whisky glass on. The colors are all neutral with the exception of the sofa, which is a dusky orange color. A half-full bookcase curves around the back of the sofa, and my eyes flick to it more than once.

Since I realized I really don't know much about Aaron, I've been filled with a burning desire to know more about him as the man he is. Something which has only intensified since I walked through his door five minutes ago.

"This is my office." He pushes a door open and ushers me into the room.

A desk runs wall to wall beneath the window that overlooks the Seattle skyline, and a cream sofa is pushed against the wall opposite another television. Piles of paperwork and folders are stacked on the desk, and a shining chrome laptop sits closed in front of the chair. A large mirror covers the wall behind me, and I look at Aaron.

"Why do you have a mirror in your office?"

He shrugs. "The interior designer put it in, so I went with it."

We leave the room, and he takes my hand.

"How long have you had this place?"

"About a year or so. The main office is in New York, as you know, but I was constantly flying between here and there. It made sense to buy somewhere instead of staying in a hotel each time." His eyes find mine when we stop. "I'm very glad of that decision now."

"Oh yes. Imagine having to take me back to your hotel to seduce me." I roll my eyes, and he laughs quietly.

"I seem to remember you saying you don't get seduced."

"You ought to remember it, Mr. Stone."

His eyes darken, and he pushes open another door. "And my bedroom."

Ah. There are more wood-paneled walls in here, and they're broken by dark brown quilting on the wall above the king-sized bed. A TV is built into the wall in front of the bed, and a side door is open, revealing a large walk-in closet.

I pull my hand from Aaron's and walk to it, sticking my head through the door. Rows of perfectly pressed shirts are hanging alongside a range of tailored jackets, and a rack of ties is attached to the wall. Various pairs of shoes are lined beneath the shirts and jackets, and there's floor-to-ceiling shelving that holds all his pants and every day t-shirts.

"Someone's inquisitive today." Aaron stands behind me, his hand resting on the doorframe above mine.

"You can tell a lot about someone by their closet."

"Is that so? What does mine tell you?"

"It tells me your suit-to-everyday ratio is way off, which means you either work too much or you simply have no idea about fashion."

His chest vibrates against my back as he laughs. "Anything else?"

"Yes. It tells me you don't have the closet space for even half of my wardrobe."

"Warming to the idea of a move, are you?"

"No. Believe me, no." I spin and look up at him. "Just gathering another reason against it for when it inevitably comes up again in conversation."

His lips tease into a small smile. "We'll see."

I duck under his arm and walk out of the bedroom. "Your apartment is really boring, isn't it?"

"Nice of you to notice."

His tone is dry, and I grin at him. "No, really. It is. It's also very manly. So, yes. Boring is the perfect word. I hope you didn't pay the designer much."

"A fortune."

"You were ripped off." I open every door in the hallway, my eyes skimming over the huge claw-footed tub and double shower unit in the main bathroom, until I reach a cupboard. It's full of fluffy towels and sheets, and I rummage through them a bit.

"What are you doing?"

"Looking for skeletons." I glance at him over my shoulder. "Just in case there are a few more hanging around I should know about."

I almost feel guilty at the sadness that fills his eyes. Almost.

"What? Did you think I wasn't mad at you anymore? I am. I'm still fuming. A string of promises and soft words followed by a cozy home tour isn't going to change that."

He shuts the door and takes a deep breath. "There are no more, Dayton. Naomi was my one and only, very ugly skeleton. If there's anything you want to know, you can ask. I'm an open book now."

I chew the inside of my lip and search his eyes. The pained shadow hits me hard. Jesus. I'm a real bitch sometimes. "I'm sorry. That was uncalled for."

"No, no, it wasn't." He brushes his thumb across my cheek. "I deserve everything you can throw at me and more. I know you don't trust me. I can see it in your eyes."

I sigh. "I do trust you, Aaron. As a person, I do. But I just don't know if I trust you with my heart again."

"I'll prove you can." He softly touches his lips to mine. "I don't deserve this second chance, but I'm going to make every second of it worthwhile. For the both of us."

"Deserve it or not, you were going to take it," I mutter. "Easy way or the hard way. I know when to pick my battles."

"Oh yes. Because I wholeheartedly believe you aren't going to fight me every step of the way."

I follow him into the kitchen and nod when he pulls a bottle of wine from the fridge. "I will never stop fighting you. It's way too fun."

He places the glass in front of me. "I know."

"Crap. I drove to your office. My car is still in the parking lot."

He shrugs a shoulder. "I'll drive it back tomorrow."

I curl my fingers around the stem and watch him as he pulls a clean glass and pours two fingers of amber liquid.

"Aaron?"

"Dayton?"

"I'm still mad at you. Really, really mad."

He smirks. "I know."

My thumb hovers over the screen of my cell. The green call button taunts me, challenging me. If I press it, I'll be making a huge decision. Something that could potentially change my life.

I take a deep breath, throwing caution to the wind, and press the button.

It rings.

And it rings.

And it rings.

Monique's voicemail cuts in, her sharp voice telling me to leave a message and she'll get back to me. The beep is harsh and seems louder than usual, as if it's giving me an extra half second to make my choice.

"Monique." I pause. "Cancel Aaron's payments. I'm still off the books, but I don't want him to pay for it. You understand."

I hang up and drop my phone on the bed. I stare at it for a long time, and my hands tremble as I wring them in front of my body.

I either just made a really smart move or a really stupid one.

Time to start finding out.

Chapter Seven

I always know when he's looking at me. My skin hums when he walks into a room, but his gaze makes it burn. It's always hot and heavy, laden with raw want and desire.

It's amazing how something so small and simple can hold so much weight. How it can take your breath away in a split second. His eyes have always had this effect on me—this mesmerizing feeling that stills my whole world until he looks away again.

I bite the inside of my lip as I pull some underwear on. He's filling the doorway of the spare bedroom, his arms resting on either side of it and his legs crossed at the ankles. I'm trying to ignore the way his dark jeans are hanging low on his hips, his belt forgotten, the band of his boxer briefs peeking above the waistband of the denim.

Trying to ignore the way that 'v' curves over his hips and dips teasingly below them.

I'm not doing a very good job.

I pull a tank over my head and tie the string on my shorts before turning. His lips are curved into a smirk, and his eyes are sparkling.

"Those shorts are practically underwear," he says, a hint of huskiness coming through his voice.

"Tell that to Victoria's Secret." I tap his arm and he drops it, allowing me to step by him.

"Believe me, sweetheart. I have no plans to tell Victoria's Secret a damn thing."

I glance over my shoulder, and his gaze is fixed firmly on my butt. I roll my eyes and pull the fridge open. "I didn't think you would." My eyes skirt across the shelves. "Why is your fridge half empty? And why is none of the food in it actually edible?"

I shut the door again and turn. He leans forward on the bar, bent at the waist. The muscles in his arms flex, and I blink harshly to pull my own gaze from his body. Jesus. The man awakens some kind of crazy primal attraction inside me that means I'm addicted to staring at his body.

"Because," he says with amusement, "I don't eat much at home. If I'm not out for dinner, I'm ordering something at the office. Keeping edible food at home seems pointless when it'll merely rot."

"And I suppose you never factored in the fact I might want to eat."

He raises an eyebrow.

"Well, for someone so presumptuous and certain of everything, I would have thought he'd have prepared for my basic needs."

"I was more focused on your other basic needs." His eyes flick to my hips and back up again.

"They're not basic needs. They're extracurricular needs."

"This is where men and women differ, Dayton. To me, exploring your body and making you come in my arms is absolutely a basic need."

"For you." I turn and swallow, grabbing an empty glass from the cupboard. "Food is a basic need for me."

"So I'll order in."

His cell rings on his words.

"Hello? Mom… No, no, I didn't forget. I just, uh, I have company… Yes, Dayton's here… Yes, I know."

I spin back, and his face is creased into a pained expression. I can hear the buzz of his mom's voice on the other end of the line, and by the way Aaron's bringing his shoulder to his ear in an extended wince, I'd guess she's giving him a few choice words.

"Mom… Okay, hang on." He covers the mouthpiece and mouths, "Fuck," with his eyes closed. After a quiet sigh, he opens his eyes again and looks at me. "Dayton, my mother would like to know if you'd care to join us for dinner tonight."

"I don't want to intrude." I bring my glass to my lips in an attempt to hide my teasing smile.

Aaron catches it anyway. "You could never intrude. In fact, I think Mom would love it if you'd join us."

"In that case, I'd be happy to."

He brings the phone back to his ear. "Add another reservation. I'll see you in an hour."

I watch as he places the cell facedown and rubs a hand down his face.

"Fuck. I forgot they were here this weekend."

"Gosh, Aaron, I can feel your delight from here."

He looks at me flatly. "Tonight will be close to hell for me. In fact, it's probably better you're there. Then they'll be a little politer."

I follow him into his bedroom, leaving the glass on the bar. "Why wouldn't they be?"

Almost as soon as the words leave my mouth, I realize. Our situation is awkward to say the least.

"Mom made it clear from day one that she didn't like Naomi—and she wouldn't try to either. You, however, have always been somewhat of a golden girl in her eyes. So naturally, when she learned of the events in Paris, I transported to the top of her shit list."

I cover my mouth with my hand. Shit list. Hearing such a juvenile term from him amuses me so much. It's so out of line with his usual composed speech.

"That's because your mom obviously has good taste." I drop onto the bed tummy-first and prop my chin on my hands. Aaron emerges from his closet, minus his jeans, and my mouth goes dry.

Holy shit, the man cuts a fine figure in those boxers. I can't decide if I prefer the underwear look over the suit.

"That's a matter of opinion."

Wait. What was the question?

"Hey!" I shake off my haze. *Clearly, I need sex. Fast.* "What are you saying?"

A grin spreads across his face as he pulls his pants on and buttons them. He walks to the bed and bends down in front of me. "I'm saying you're a very refined, exquisite taste, Dayton. That's all."

"I'm trying to decide if I should be offended by the 'refined' part of that."

He runs a thumb across my cheek. "No. My taste is very refined and I happen to like you very, very much."

My breath catches when his lips hover in front of mine. "Me, or my taste?"

"Both," he murmurs, his lips brushing mine with his words. "Your taste more so when it's on my tongue."

I hum low in my throat when his mouth lingers on mine. He smiles and straightens, and he threads a belt through the loops on his pants.

"I don't have anything to wear to dinner."

"So we'll stop by your place." He shrugs. "As long as you put some decent clothes on first."

"I take offense to that. Shorts and a tank are proper clothes."

He pauses, his fingers halfway through buttoning his shirt. "Dayton Lauren Black." His voice lowers, heat flaring in his eyes. "If

I can see the curve of your gorgeous little bare ass beneath the hem of your shorts, they're unsuitable for anyone's eyes but my own. Get changed. Now."

I smile sweetly and stand. "Is that a request or a demand?"

"It's a fucking requirement."

I laugh my way to the spare room and pull some jeans on instead. The shorts lie discarded on the floor when I meet him in the main room, my house keys in my hand.

His shirt is open at his throat, the buttons undone just low enough to give a tiny glimpse of a smattering of dark hair on his chest. His jacket perfectly stretches across his shoulders, and he's left it open, meaning I can see how his shirt fits his body and his trim waist. Shit, I'm staring so hard I can almost see each individual pack of muscle hiding beneath the white cotton covering his stomach.

Aaron clears his throat, and I look up. *Dammit, Dayton. Mad. Be mad.*

"Let's go," I mutter, tugging on the strap of my tank.

He laughs quietly behind me and secures an arm around my waist once we're in the elevator. "Like what you see?" he says into my ear.

"More than I probably should, but not as much as you think."

His fingers flex. "A simple 'yes' would suffice."

"Why build you up just to have your parents tear you down tonight?" I raise an eyebrow, my lips twitching.

"Because you're supposed to soothe me, baby." He leads us through the lobby to a waiting car. These things come from fucking nowhere.

I snort, getting in. "Right. I'm going to soothe you when you deserve everything your mom will throw at you. No, I'm going to be sitting there grinning my fucking head off and agreeing with everything she says, *baby*."

He sighs heavily. "I suspected as much." His eyes cut to mine. "You're going to kill me tonight, aren't you?"

"It can be arranged. I spent enough time thinking of all the ways I could when I arrived back here, so I'm certainly not short on ideas."

"Of course she assumes it in the physical sense," he murmurs, reaching over and tucking a lock of hair behind my ear. I fight my smile, and he turns my face to his. "I meant kill me with your beauty."

"Of course I am. I plan on making tonight as hard for you as it possibly can be." I glance at his pants so there's no mistaking my meaning. His jaw tightens.

"And to think, I've only just gotten rid of the erection your shorts gave me."

"Those shorts are magical. Ask the cop who waived my speeding ticket when I was wearing them two years ago."

His eyes harden. "You've worn those in public?"

I smile sweetly. "I thought I had a flat. It was convenient timing, I must admit."

Aaron pulls my face to his and nips my bottom lip. "I'm confiscating those shorts."

"Don't you dare!"

"The second we arrive back at my apartment, I'm picking them up from the floor and hiding them. I can promise you that, woman. No one else is going to see you the way I do." He opens the door and slides me across the seat and out of the car.

I narrow my eyes at him and walk up the path to my house. I leave the door open behind me, and he follows me in.

"Wait here, you shorts thief." I point to the sofa. "I'll be back in a minute."

I leave him downstairs and walk into my second bedroom—my lingerie room. I haven't been in here for three weeks, instead living in sports bras and my 'period' panties—a.k.a. normal sized panties. It smells a little musty, but the lavender undertones of my scented pots on the shelving above the rails soon break through and fill me with their rich, relaxing scent.

I breathe in deeply, pausing in the door, and exhale softly. My eyes scour the rails I installed, past the basques, corsets, and baby dolls to the rail that holds my every day, matching underwear. I pull a brand-new red set from the hanger and stroll into my bedroom, ready to tackle my closet.

I finger the black Prada dress Aaron reserved and made me get. Bitterness fills me and a little bile rises in my throat at the memory of that day. Of standing in front of a woman who knew more about him than I did, a woman who put me down because I don't fit into her ideal the way Naomi does.

Fuck her. I love my extra three pounds. Okay, it's more like six now, but let's not be picky.

I tap my butt and pull it out anyway. The scoop neck and knee-length pencil skirt in a clinging material is perfect for tonight. I know the way it'll cling to me will drive Aaron insane, and the way his eyes will light up when he realizes I'm wearing something of his is almost worth having let him buy it.

I lay it on the bed while I change my underwear and roll some stockings up my legs. With a rub of my temples, I push the Italian memory aside, slink into the tight material, and look in the mirror.

It hugs my body perfectly, and I can imagine the look on his face when he sees it. It'll be somewhere between pleasure and anguish, delight and torture.

Exactly what I'm going for.

I apply my makeup and paint red onto my lips. The shade matches the heeled pumps peeking at me from my shoe rack in the closet, and I slide my feet into them easily. My toes wriggle to get my feet comfortable, and I stand.

Aaron's standing at the door to my lingerie room, and I bite the inside of my lip. Shit. *Should have closed the door...*

"Like what you see?" I ask, repeating his words from earlier.

"Do you have stock in the lingerie business?" he looks at me.

"No, but I probably should." I look in my room proudly.

"You've worn all of this?"

"Not all of it. Some still have the tags. Sometimes it didn't fit the description of the client's needs. A lot I bought because I liked it."

He's silent for a long moment. His eyes flick across the room, and when I think he's about to walk away, he steps inside. "If I know anything about you, I'll bet you have it all organized. Old and new separate. Correct?"

"Uh, yes." Control freak, I am.

He runs his hand across the hangers until he reaches a midway point. After flicking a couple of sets back and forth, he grabs the worn things and lifts the hangers from the rails. They clatter to the floor, and he does the same to the baby dolls and other outfits.

My mouth drops open. "What the hell are you doing?"

He ignores me, dropping four corsets to the ground. "Clearing out your lingerie closet. Or rather, room."

"I can see that. My next question is why the fuck you're doing it."

He stops in the middle of the room and his chest heaves before he raises his head to look at me. His gaze burns into me, and I don't move when he approaches me and stands right in front of me.

"Because"—he cups my chin and tilts my head back—"I refuse to fuck you in something you've fucked another guy in."

"It didn't bother you before."

He grabs my hips and flattens my body against his. I turn my head when he pulls it into his chest. His breath crawls over my neck when he lowers his mouth to my ear.

"That was before, sweetheart. This is now. This is different. This is a new start and another chance for both of us. That means we put shit in the past and leave it there, and for you, that starts with getting this stuff out of your house."

"I'm not throwing out my underwear," I say through clenched teeth.

"It's nonnegotiable, Dayton. Your old underwear will sit collecting dust." His fingers dig into my lower back. "I'll replace it all, but you will get rid of it. You won't be needing it again anyway."

"You're failing on the making-it-up-to-me thing."

"There are a thousand ways I can make it up to you, Dayton, but none of them begins with lingerie you worked in. Get fucking rid of it."

I take a deep breath. *Fucking man.* "And the new stuff?"

He kisses my jaw. "The new stuff I will enjoy removing from your body very, very much. Most of it, anyway. Some of it I like so much I might just have to fuck you in it."

The mother of all aches starts in my clit. Goddamn him.

"We're going to be late," I manage, pulling back from him.

He smirks knowingly. "I don't think you'd need much convincing to be even later."

I stop at the bottom of the stairs and slide the shoulder of my dress down, revealing a red strap. "Don't go there, Mr. Stone. If we start, we won't be stopping. Now get your ass in your car."

"She's bossy." He places his hands on my waist and guides me from the house, only stopping so I can lock the door.

"She's taking tips from this demanding, possessive guy she knows."

Aaron eases me into the car, keeping me close as he can. "You demanding is kind of sexy." His finger trails down my side and thigh. "And so is this dress."

He wraps his arm around me, and I rest my head on his shoulder with a small smile. When it's so easy and natural between us, like it is right now, it's hard to stay mad. It's hard to remember all the bullshit from a month ago and remind myself why this might not be the best idea.

When the beat of my heart matches his, it's hard to consider a life without him.

As it is, I already don't know how I lived for seven years without looking in his eyes and kissing him and touching him. I don't know how I lived without the electrifying spark born of his skin against mine or the trembling bliss of his body covering mine.

I know it's not healthy. To be so distracted by someone, to be so attracted to them and so... obsessed... It's not good and nothing good can come of it. I proved that to myself when I walked away. The pain that tore through my body at the reality of leaving him behind in Paris once again was too much to bear. The more time I spend around him, the worse that pain will be if it happens again.

I don't want it to. As much as I convinced myself that I didn't want anything to happen between us again, especially after he showed up in my home city, I don't want a life that doesn't have him in it in some way.

I don't want a day where I wake up to find that he's no longer there.

That's why I'm giving him this godforsaken stupid second chance he doesn't deserve. That's why I'm giving him what he wants, because really, I want it, too. I want us. I want us the way I thought I knew us. I want to find out what us really is. Who we really are together, who we are alone, and where that will take us.

I want to know that, in the end, the pain will be worth it. I want to know if the fights and the doubts and the hurtful words thrown carelessly in the heat of the moment are worth it. If they're worth the feeling of wholeness, of the complete and utter clarity he brings to my life. If they're worth giving up my control forever and handing it to the man who already controls my heart so completely.

I need to know if everything is worth the love he's yet to admit to.

And I need to know those words. I need to hear those three tiny words fall from his lips, because they're the verification I need for this relationship. Three tiny words that will lay to rest every single doubt I have about our situation.

I've never needed love, not from a man. I've never needed to feel loved for my life to have any sort of meaning. I looked at those women and believed they were weak because they needed someone to lean on, but perhaps I was wrong.

There's nothing weak about love, and needing to hear Aaron tell me that he loves me doesn't make me weak either.

Chapter Eight

"Dayton!" Aaron's mom stands and opens her arms to me when we enter the restaurant. I step into her warm embrace, then his father's, and take a seat opposite them at the table.

We're seated in the back of Glassini, an upscale restaurant that neighbors the Southfall hotel. The curved shape of our booth means we're practically invisible to prying eyes, and the lighting is just bright enough to make out the shade of red velvet on the chairs but low enough to be cozy and romantic.

"It's wonderful to see you again." Carly smiles across the table. "I'm glad for the chance." She flicks her eyes to Aaron.

He tenses next to me. "Mom."

She smiles and raises a wine glass to her lips. His dad steps in, offering us both a glass of wine, and pours them.

There's a heavy awkwardness between Aaron and his mom. It's palpable, and I know he said that she didn't like Naomi, but I can feel it. Her name hasn't even been mentioned and I can feel the hatred for his ex-wife glittering in her eyes. And I can see the anger that she came between us—and that Aaron let it happen.

We order our food, and as we wait, Aaron engages in a conversation about the company with his dad. Turns out, Brandon isn't as comfortable being retired as he thought he would be, and as I listen in, the conversation is more a comforting session for the older man.

Carly rolls her eyes in a move that makes me smother a laugh. "Men," she sighs. "I can't take those two anywhere without them discussing work. Someone needs to inform them that the world doesn't revolve around it."

"Have you tried?"

"Several times. They're too stubborn to listen to me. I'd hoped Aaron would skip his father's need-to-be-in-control gene, but it took to him and it stuck."

I nod my head. *If only she really knew.* "You don't need to tell me that. He honestly drives me crazy with it sometimes."

"Darling, Aaron delights in driving women crazy. Mostly myself."

Our food is placed in front of us, and we eat in near silence. The only words exchanged are from Aaron and Brandon, who are still discussing work.

"Oh, for goodness' sake, you two," Carly snaps. "You're at a family dinner, not a work one. Dayton and I do not want to hear about it. I for one hear enough about it at home."

I bite my bottom lip to hide my smile.

"Of course, honey," Brandon soothes her, patting her hand. "What would you rather we discuss? Clothes? Shoes? The latest installment of The Bachelor, perhaps?"

"My guilty pleasure." Carly winks at me.

"I've never seen it," I admit. "I don't watch much television."

"Oh my. We'll have to rectify that. I can't say I'm much for the women on the show—they're all rather catty—but the bachelor is always worth it."

"That was a rhetorical question, Mom." There's a hint of a groan to Aaron's voice.

"Really?" I ignore him. "Maybe I'll have to start watching."

"Dayton."

"You really should. It's rather addictive though. Goodness knows Brandon has come home to me shouting at the television more than once. Those girls are vile sometimes. It's hard to believe they're real at all, but I've had the displeasure of meeting one or two over the last thirty years of my life."

"Mom!"

Carly turns to her son. "Yes?"

"Are we done with the trashy TV talk?" Aaron grinds out. "You're making it a little personal now."

His mom delicately chews a piece of pasta, her eyes on him, and the tension rockets up. She doesn't say a word. She merely pins him in place with her stare until he backs down and looks away.

I look between them. Ha! He might be CEO of the family company, but his mom can still give him a look that makes his tail go between his legs.

Oddly, I love it. He obviously respects her enough not to challenge her too much. And that warms something inside me.

The rest of our meal is finished in silence. Brandon looks at Aaron when the plates are cleared by our server.

"Let's go and get a drink at the bar, son. Perhaps then we can discuss business in peace." Brandon throws Carly an affectionate smile. "And replace the empty bottle of wine on the table."

They leave us alone for two minutes. Aaron brings an opened bottle of Pinot over and places it between us, his hand on my upper back. He pauses before leaving and drops his lips to my forehead. I close my eyes at the brief touch, aware of his mom watching us but not really caring as his gentle kiss warms my skin.

I pour our glasses without a word and bring mine to my lips. I'm not prepared to be left alone with his mom. If I'd known this would happen, I wouldn't have come. Not because I don't like her—I do, very much—but because I'm not sure if I'm ready for the conversation we're about to have.

"She was a bitch. If you'll excuse my language." Carly smiles slightly.

"Naomi?"

She nods. "She was one of those people I took an instant dislike to. You know when you meet someone and something about them rubs you the wrong way? This was akin to a cat rubbing against a scratching post vehemently."

"Funnily enough, I felt the same way when I met her," I reply dryly.

"I imagine you would. She's a very unlikable person." She runs her finger around the top of her glass. "I couldn't imagine why Aaron was entering into a relationship with her. The last person he saw seriously was you. The two of you are so incredibly different, and it surprised me. Naomi was and is everything I'd never wished for him. She was vindictive and selfish and very one-minded. She took so much but never gave anything. All she ever truly was was something pretty on his arm for dinners and functions."

"Why did he marry her?"

"Who knows, honey? Guilt? I know that Brandon's assistant at the time convinced him it was for the best. He would be stronger for taking over the company later if he was married and had a good woman beside him. Not to say I don't agree with that statement, but a good woman isn't enough. He needed the right woman, and unfortunately Naomi was neither."

She's silent for a moment before she continues. "I told him to tell you. When he told me you were going with him on the trip, I told him you had to know. You weren't just anyone. You've never just been anyone. Not to him."

I swallow and look down. "What did he say?"

"He said he would. He said he planned to tell you, but I couldn't push him into it. He didn't want to lose you again."

"And he still couldn't tell me."

Carly sighs heavily. "I think he spent the day in bed with a migraine when I was through with him. He's loved you since you met, and because of his stubborn pigheadedness, he hurt you in a misguided attempt to protect you."

"I think I said the same thing to him," I say softly, looking up.

"He fired her." Her lips twitch. "He forced her to sign the divorce papers in front of us and our lawyer. Then he signed the papers that transferred ownership of Stone to him while she watched. And he fired her."

Smugness fills me. She was holding out for more, hoping he'd get the company before the divorce was settled, and he did it all right in front of her.

"She lost while she thought she was winning."

"Couldn't have put it better. She got the settlement she was after, but not what she truly wanted. She wanted some of the company, but my boy is smarter than that. He refused until it was done. That was something that was made more important when he met you again. She had to be out of his life completely."

I pause before asking, "And is she?"

Carly tops up our glasses. "My son is no fool. When you have the best lawyer in the city, you can slip anything into a contract."

"Like what?"

"Like if Naomi contacts him in any way, except in business situations which are unavoidable, the agreement will be null and void and she'll have to pay him fifty percent of the settlement."

My smile mirrors hers. "He really did cover everything, didn't he?"

"When you left, all he was focused on was doing whatever he could to get you back. That meant rushing his business in Paris, canceling his London trip, and finalizing his divorce before coming to Seattle. He's just taken control of a multimillion-dollar, worldwide company, but all he wanted was you."

I open my mouth, but no words come out.

"He messed up. He messed up hugely, Dayton, but that doesn't have an impact on the way he feels for you. As well as inheriting his stubbornness from his father, he also got his capacity and ability to love. I can see it in Aaron's eyes when he looks at you. There isn't a mountain he wouldn't climb or a sea he wouldn't cross if it meant making you happy. I don't know where you two are now, but I can see how very much he loves you."

"He could try telling me sometime. I might like him a little more then."

She laughs. "I've loved Brandon for thirty-five years, but I've liked him for only a handful of those. It's something you carry with you, I'm afraid." She winks then drops her smile and takes my hand. "There's a hollow kind of sadness in his eyes, but he's still happier with you than I've seen him for seven years. If you can forgive him for keeping her from you, please do it."

I squeeze her hand lightly. "I think I already have. I just don't plan on telling him so anytime soon."

Aaron takes the seat next to me when his mom joins his dad at the bar. He turns to me and rests his hand on my knee. Heat sears through the dark material of my dress, and I feel the resounding sparks as he trails his fingers up my thigh. They skim my hip, and I turn to him instinctively, raising my eyes from the table to meet his.

They're startlingly blue. Clear and honest. I see how he feels. I see that guilt and remorse, but this time, they're wrapped in hope. A hope that tugs at my stomach, because we're hoping for the very same thing but in different ways.

He's hoping I'll forgive him, and I'm hoping he'll tell me what I need to hear.

We're both hoping for the kind of happiness that can only be found intricately threaded into love.

I lean forward and kiss him softly. It must surprise him because he stills for half a second before curving his hand around my hip and pulling me closer to him.

The satin of his jacket is soft beneath my fingers as I run them across his shoulder and down his body. His chest heaves beneath my touch, and he rests his forehead against mine, our noses next to the other's, our breaths mingling in the whisper of space between our mouths.

He takes my hand in his and squeezes it tightly. "I'm sorry," he whispers.

I close my eyes at the sound of those words. I told him that they were important, but I never realized just how much until now. With them hanging between us on a delicate thread, the words validate every ounce of regret I've felt in his touch and seen in his eyes.

"It nudged it," I whisper back, tightening my own grip on his hand.

"Good."

He pulls back and brings our hands to his mouth. Gently, he presses a kiss to each of my knuckles then flips my hand over and kisses my wrist on my pulse point. I can feel his lips soft against my skin and the way my pulse increases at the intimate touch. I can feel the way my heart speeds up, threatening to break through my ribs with the sheer force of it. With everything I feel for this infuriating man.

"Nice talk with my mom?" His smirk cuts through the intimate moment, and I'm almost glad as some of the heaviness lifts. I can breathe again. Only just.

"Oh yeah. What did you see in Naomi?" I raise my eyebrows.

He laughs, but it more closely resembles a growl. "She's never going to let it go."

"She won't. She's a woman. We hold our grudges, even when you think we've let go."

"Good to know." He grabs his drink from the table and sips the amber liquid. "We've already discussed her. I don't want to talk about her anymore with you, Day. She's my past, and right now, sitting here with you, the most beautiful woman I've ever laid eyes on, she's nothing. The time we spent together is a blur of nothing. She's barely even a memory, but you? You're everything."

"I seem to remember you saying you were everything."

"I am everything, but only to you. That doesn't mean you're not everything to me, because you are."

I run my fingers down the lapel of his jacket. "Did you really rush your business to get back to the US?"

"I condensed a week of meetings into a few days. I had no choice but to attend them, but the second I could leave, I was on the plane back to New York."

"Why?" I swallow and look at him.

His mom might have told me, but I need to hear it from him. My crazy mind, the insanity he makes me feel, needs to hear it. It needs to hear something to validate the relationship he believes he pays for but is so very real.

Aaron's lips curl slightly at the corners, and he brushes some hair from my face. He leaves his hand cupping my head and draws our faces closer together.

"Because I couldn't be away from you for any longer than I had to be. I couldn't stand by and not fight for you when you were back here. There wasn't a single part of me that would let me do that."

"Your fighting could use some work." I tap his nose. "Pinning a girl to her front door and kissing the shit out of her isn't exactly a way to win back her heart."

"But you're so stubborn," he teases. "You wouldn't listen to what I had to say, so I had to make you feel it instead. Of course, I ultimately decided you were going to listen to me anyway."

I narrow my eyes. "Men."

His parents rejoin us, and I slide back along the booth seat. Aaron clasps my hip and slides me back into him, and he digs his fingers into my skin in a warning. *Don't move.*

A light is shining in his mom's eyes, and the way his dad is smiling tells me that they were watching from the bar. At least his mom was.

"So, son," Brandon begins after checking we all have enough to drink, "are you all ready for London?"

I stop, raise an eyebrow, and slowly turn my face to Aaron. "London?"

He parts his lips then closes his mouth again, instead choosing to wet his bottom lip.

"Aaron! You didn't tell her?" Carly scolds him.

"No, no he didn't," I answer for him. "Evidently we need to work on the talking part of our relationship."

Aaron's eyes widen in a move so slight I'm sure only I noticed it. His grasp on me tightens even more, like he wants to hold on to my last two words and not let them go in case he's imagining it.

"Yes," he says slowly. "Evidently, we do."

"I'm sorry. Did I say 'we'? I meant you." I smile sweetly and lay my hand on his chest.

"I guessed as much. You talk enough for the both of us, sweetheart."

"And apparently you should tell me to shut up once in a while." I jab him with my finger.

Aaron sighs and looks at his father. "Thank you, Dad. If you don't mind, I think Dayton and I will call it a night. Apparently, we have an upcoming trip to discuss."

We say our goodbyes, all the while my eyes cutting to Aaron in displeasure. Is this something he's conveniently declined to mention yet again?

I get into the waiting town car without a word to him, and his sigh drifts across the car to me.

"Are you mad at me again?"

"I haven't stopped being mad at you. I just got better at hiding it." I spin in my seat. "When do you go?"

"In three days."

"And when were you going to tell me?"

"I wasn't. I was obviously planning to kidnap you in the dead of night, sling you over my shoulder, and hoist you off to London for ten days." He grins.

"Cor, don't hold back. Romance me, baby." I roll my eyes. "Why didn't you tell me?"

"You're really mad I didn't, aren't you?"

"Yes, I'm mad! Is this how it's always going to be? Am I always going to be finding these kind of very important things out from other people?"

He rubs a hand down his face, and I follow him from the car. He doesn't reply as we walk through the lobby and step into the elevator to take us to his penthouse apartment. Silence lingers through the journey, the only thing between us is my anger and his rapidly developing annoyance.

I can always tell. His hand twitches and he flexes his fingers when it's building in him, and his eyes take on this heated hardness. I'm sure the heated part is only for my benefit, but angry looks good on him.

"No," he finally says when we enter the apartment. "It honestly slipped my mind until Dad mentioned it tonight. I would have remembered when I arrived at the office tomorrow and seen it on my schedule."

"Then you would have called me right away, correct?"

"No. I would have gone to my scheduled meeting then called you."

I huff and stalk into the spare room. Dammit, I don't even want to be here tonight. I want to go home and sink into the comfort of my own bed. I want to cocoon myself in my blankets and just breathe.

The floorboards creak as Aaron follows me. I slide my fingers beneath the shoulder of my dress, ready to push it down, but his hand stills the movement. His breath cascades over my bare neck, making the tiny hairs stand on end.

"Is this how it's always going to be?" he whispers, repeating my own words back to me. "I do something wrong and you get mad at me?"

"There's no getting." I shrug his hand off. "I'm never not mad. We've covered this several times."

He pulls me back into him, tilting my head to one side. His fingers splay on my stomach and hold me in place, trapped against the hardness of his body. "Even when I make you come?" His finger slips beneath my dress strap and slides it over the curve of my shoulder. "Are you mad at me then?"

"Deliriously so." I sigh when he kisses the part of my neck where it meets my shoulder, that tender, erotic spot that seems to be connected to every nerve in my body.

"I like your deliriously mad." His lips brush across the bottom of my neck, and he gathers my hair in his free hand, exposing the other side of my neck. He lets the dark locks fall to the side as he slides the other side of my dress down. "I wanted you in this dress the second I saw it, but now I believe I'd much prefer you out of it."

Everything in me comes alive. My nerve endings tingle animatedly until the deep ache of my clit overshadows it. I curve into him instinctively as he stands before me. His skin is hot as my hands find his waist, but the connection lasts only seconds before he steps back. My hands fall to my sides, and he moves to me again.

"No touching," he murmurs, the low, demanding growl in it making me shiver.

His fingers trace the neckline of the dress, ghosting over the curve of my breasts, and his fingers are soon replaced by his hot mouth as he drags the material down my body. It's so effortless for him, peeling the tight outfit from me, even as he lavishes attention on my breasts.

My nipples harden almost painfully inside my bra as he continues his journey down. A gentle breeze caresses me when the dress is pulled over my ass. It pools at my feet, my body finally free from its restraints.

Aaron's tongue licks a lazy path just above my thong from hip to hip. I push my hips into him, reaching forward to steady myself.

His hands shoot out and grasp my wrists. He bends my arms around my body and pins my hands to the bottom of my back. I can't move despite my best efforts. His grip is too strong and steadily certain.

"Let's make you deliriously mad, baby."

Chapter Nine

He brushes his nose across my mound and flicks his tongue against me. The sensation is rough through the lace of my thong, and it makes me jerk and whimper at the same time. He flattens the end of his tongue over my clit and rubs repeatedly in slow circles. The lace grazes over me, heightening the pleasure he's giving me.

My knees give out, bending a little at a jolt of pleasure shooting through my pussy. Aaron lets go of me with one hand and cups my ass, righting me.

"Stay standing." His voice is raw.

I lock my knees in place. He slides my thong down my legs, leaving it hooked around my ankles, and encourages me to open my legs a little. I do it, unable to do anything but what he wants.

Unable to do anything but release the low moan in my throat when his mouth covers my pussy completely.

My hips push into him, pull away, thrash, and twist. He continues his gentle onslaught against me with his tongue. No part of me is unexplored, no part untouched by the gentle swipe of his tongue.

He squeezes my ass in time with every movement his tongue makes. My legs bend again at the heat building inside, and his squeeze becomes a sharp slap.

"Stand!"

I moan in pleasure and frustration as I fight my natural response. I shouldn't be standing as this pleasure ripples gently through me. I should be collapsing, ready for the final hit. The leg-trembling hit that I'm not supposed to be standing for.

I explode on that final thought. I cry out, only held up by Aaron holding me in place. His tongue continues to work against me even as my hips thrash against him. My eyes close, and my whole body is tight. He keeps his mouth on me until the final wave sweeps through me and leaves me quivering against him.

He lowers me to him and wraps my arms around his neck. His arms go around me, strong and assured, and he carries me from the room.

"What are you doing?" I say against his neck. Unable to resist his pulse pounding before my eyes, I close my lips over the throbbing spot and suck lightly.

He groans, his body going taut, his step faltering. I smirk at it. I love eliciting that response from him. I love bringing him to his knees.

"I'm not fucking you anywhere other than my bed."

He drops me on it unceremoniously, and I scramble against the soft sheets, wearing only my bra and my heels.

"Nowhere else?"

Aaron removes his clothes, keeping his eyes on mine, and stalks toward me. With his hands either side of me, he leans forward on the bed until he's right over me.

"Just for tonight. There are plenty of surfaces in this house just waiting for me to lay your gorgeous body back on while I fuck you senseless."

He unclips my bra, and after sliding it down my arms, he whips it from beneath me. It flies across the room, hitting the wall with a small thud before falling to the floor. I pull my gaze from the bra and find the pools of unadulterated lust staring down at me.

"Even that wall?" I whisper.

He trails his hands to my thighs. "Even that wall."

"What about the kitchen side?"

"All of them."

"The sofa?"

"Every cushion."

He pushes the end of his cock inside me, and I feel the pull in my muscles as they stretch to accommodate him and let him in farther.

"And the desk?"

Aaron reaches behind his back and hooks my ankles together. He leans over me slowly, lowering his body on top of mine, and bites my bottom lip gently. "Especially the fucking desk."

He fills me in one swift thrust. I throw my head back at the exquisite feeling of having him inside me, of being fully around him and connected to him. Of having his breath hot against my cheek and the tightening of his jaw as I tilt my hips up, letting him drive deeper into me.

His thrusts are hard, each withdraw as slow as the last, and the mixture of them repeatedly begs my body to respond. He sinks deeper until he hits the end of me. A strangled cry filled with pleasure and pain escapes me, and Aaron growls in his throat.

He slides his hand to the small of my back and holds my hips up as the slowness of a moment ago dissipates into a frenzy of hard pounds that pushes a moan from me with each one. I grip his back, my whole body lifting from the bed aside from my shoulders.

My muscles clench as the orgasm approaches. As my deliriously mad oblivion creeps up on me, ready to explode and shatter any semblance of rationality into nothing.

"Dayton. Fuck!" Aaron growls against my jaw.

"Fuck!" I arch into him, and he takes my mouth roughly. My

nails drag across his skin, and he takes my bottom lip between his teeth and tugs in payback.

That undoes me.

Muscles I didn't know I had constrict with the sheer force of the pleasure assaulting my body. I vaguely hear Aaron's curse as he comes through the pounding of my heart in my ears. He's buried in me to the hilt, and my pussy is clenching and clenching and clenching, drawing everything from him, drawing my own out.

His lips take mine tenderly, and he kisses me this way until my body goes limp beneath him.

Without a word, he lifts me and carries me into his bathroom. Somewhere in the back of my mind, I register the same neutral tones that are prevalent throughout the apartment, but I'm more interested when he sets me on the side of the bath and starts to run the taps.

I'm too tired to ask what he's doing. Why he's running a bath at whatever time it might be.

I watch the tub fill up with hot water, the bubbles steadily growing. Aaron kills the taps when it's half full and steps in. He swings my legs over the side, making me smile, and pulls me in with him.

He sits in front of me, my legs resting over his, and I lean into him. I wrap my arms around his waist and close my eyes, focusing on the beating of his heart beneath my cheek.

The rhythmic beat is as soothing to me as the water. The feeling of his body against mine is as comforting and grounding as submerging myself in the depths of the bath. It's more freeing than swimming endless lengths of a pool.

Because it's real, and it's tangible, and it's something that won't slip through my fingers if I hold tight enough.

"What are you doing?" I mumble when I feel him tying my hair up.

"I don't want to get it wet," he answers.

A few seconds later, the sound of a bottle squirting reaches my ears, and I feel the cold shock of the shower gel against my back. I squeal and squirm.

Aaron laughs, his chest vibrating, and rubs his hands over my back. It warms instantly, and I smile as he washes my body. Every part of me is washed, even my submerged legs. He grabs a sponge and trickles the water over me, washing the soap from my body, the whole time without me moving.

The man is magical. And really quite wonderful.

"Come on, Bambi," he says softly, easing me back.

I slide from him, letting him get out, and stare up at him. He wraps a towel around his waist and grabs me. I giggle quietly at the ease he lifts me from the tub with and grab a towel for myself.

I sit on the bed and watch as he dries himself. And as the little water droplets cascade down his silky skin. Each one is gradually soaked up by the towel, and a pair of boxer briefs hangs low on his hips.

He towels me off tenderly, making sure every part of me is dry, and instructs me to lift my arms and legs until he's certain there isn't a drop of water left on my skin.

"Wait here." He disappears into his closet. I'm sitting naked on his bed, the only light the city lights flooding through the window, and I've never felt more comfortable.

He emerges from the closet, a pair of panties in hand.

"Is that...?"

"I ordered more." He hands them to me with a knowing smirk.

"That's impossible. It was like"—I glance at the clock on the nightstand—"six hours ago."

"And I called while you were getting ready and had some stuff delivered. My housekeeper put it away."

"Your *housekeeper?*"

Holy crap. Someone else touched my panties.

Someone who isn't Aaron.

He pulls them up my legs, making me stand, and lightly smacks my ass. "Don't worry. She only comes in when no one is here. Her schedule will be different now."

I roll my eyes and climb into his bed. Soft. Warm. Sex-smelling.

Aaron-smelling, rich and musky and woody and masculine.

He gets in next to me and pulls me into him. Our legs tangle. His arms go around me and he holds me tight. I press my face into his neck, breathing him in.

"How am I doing on the making it up to you?" he mutters after a long moment of silence.

"Not bad." I smile against his skin.

"Not bad?"

My smile widens, but I say nothing. If I justify it, I'll let him in further than I need to. I'll tell him what he doesn't need to know yet. He still has work to do. He still has to prove everything to me, make me know we're solid and that everything we have is secure. That it's really for real this time.

"Thank you for looking out for me tonight," I whisper, snuggling in even farther. I could be under his skin and it wouldn't be close enough.

"Oh," he breathes, kissing my head. "I'll always look after you, Dayton. Always."

Aaron opens the car door and lets me climb out. "You could stay at my apartment."

"I need to be here. I need to pack," I remind him, patting his chest. "Besides, I don't want to put any crazy moving ideas in your presumptuous little head."

"God forbid." He drops his head and brushes his lips across mine. "I'll be back when my meetings are over to pick you up."

"What if I want to stay at my place tonight?"

"Then I'll make sure to get some spare clothes before I come over."

I raise an eyebrow. "Did I invite you to stay over?"

"You don't need to," he mutters, running his thumb along my jaw. "I'm going to anyway."

"Is this part of making it up to me?"

"No. This is part of making sure you can't walk away again."

"By being together almost all of the time?"

"Yes. Get used to it, sweetheart. It's not changing anytime soon."

He kisses me chastely and moves me to the side. He climbs back in the car with a wicked smirk, leaving me standing on the sidewalk as it pulls away.

"Bastard," I mutter, pulling my keys from my pocket and unlocking the door. My voicemail blinks at me, and I jab the button as I walk past.

"*Dayton? Call me when you get this. We need to talk.*" Aunt Leigh's voice is sharp and to the point, as always, and I sigh. Talking with my aunt right now is the last thing I want to do.

I reach for the phone when it rings again. Her name flashes on the tiny screen.

"Hey," I answer. "What's wrong?"

"Oh good. You're in. Where have you been?"

"Uh…"

"Dayton."

I cringe as I answer. "With Aaron."

"Mmm. Monique called. Will you be at home in ten minutes?"

"Yes. I just got back."

"Good. Stay there. I'm coming over."

Fantastic.

The line cuts before I can say goodbye, and I drop the phone with another sigh. There isn't a single part of me looking forward to this. I know what she'll say, what she'll remind me of. This conversation is unnecessary.

I don't care and I don't want to hear it.

Besides, it's a little late to *not* fall in love, isn't it?

I hear the rumble of her Audi outside as I pour myself a cup of coffee. She lets herself in without as much as a single knock. Her heels click almost formidably against the wooden floors as she walks through to join me in the kitchen, and I hold an empty mug over my shoulder.

"Coffee?"

"Sit," she demands, knocking on the island.

"I guess not," I mumble, setting the mug down and turning.

I sit opposite her. Her lips are pursed, her eyes narrowed, and her nails rap against the marble countertop repeatedly. I reach over and smack her hand down. *Fucking irritating sound.*

"So. You're off the books." No questions. A simple statement that sounds so final.

"Temporarily," I correct her. "For now."

She unwinds her lightweight scarf from her neck and lays it on the island. "So, what? You're going to spend however long with Aaron Stone then just go back to your job? Or is he the kind of man to let you continue fucking other men every day and not let it impact your relationship?"

I stare at her flatly.

"Because that's what they all are, honey. They're all good with it until they're not and they leave you in the dust as they speed away to something better."

"My aunt, always the cynic."

"Realistic, Day. I'm realistic."

I get back up and pour my coffee. "You would know, right? One marriage accounts for all the men in the world."

"It accounts for all the men with an ounce of self-respect. You and I both know Aaron won't stand for you escorting if you're in a relationship."

My fingers curl around the lip of the counter, and I take a deep breath. "I know. He's made that crystal clear several times."

"So he should. Call girls don't have relationships and—"

"They don't fall in love. Yeah, I know."

"In theory."

"Theory is bullshit without reality."

My aunt's lips curve into a smirk that is identical to mine. "Precisely, Day. Theories are just that. They can be tossed aside as easily as the one before them."

I chew the inside of my cheek and study her. The hardness has gone from her eyes. All the tension has seeped from her shoulders, and she almost looks relaxed. Alarm bells ring in the depths of my mind.

"Where is this going?"

Aunt Leigh pauses, nibbling on her bottom lip. "Will you give it up? For him? If it's him or your job, will you step away from the escorting world and give him everything you have?"

"Yes," I whisper without a thought. "If that's what it comes to, yes. I'll walk away for him."

"Good."

My eyes shoot up to hers. "What?"

"Good," she repeats, her voice firmer than a moment ago.

The stool scrapes against the floor as she stands and turns away from me. She looks out the doors that lead to my backyard and briefly rests her forehead against the glass.

"Good," she says yet again. "Do it. If you have the choice, take the escape. Take the way out. Don't let your job ruin your relationship."

Silence lingers as I process her words. They're soft and heartfelt. They're tinged—no, they're saturated—in regret. They hit where it hurts.

"Aunt Leigh?"

"You know I didn't. You know I chose escorting over my marriage to Luke. You know it killed the five years we'd spent together." She exhales heavily. "I chose the power and control over the love I had for him, and it destroyed us."

"You've lived with that for six years? Why didn't you say anything?"

She turns, a wan smile on her face. "I gave it up six months later. Do you remember?"

I nod.

"It was simply six months too late. If I'd left when Luke told me he was leaving, we could have saved our marriage. I didn't. We didn't."

"Why are you telling me this? After all the times you've told me call girls don't fall in love, why now?"

She crosses the kitchen to me and cups my cheeks in her hands in a rare show of her maternal side. "Dayton, I'm telling you so you don't make the same mistake I did Call girls don't fall in love…until they do. Don't choose power and control over love because, when you lose that control, you have nothing else left. With love, at least you'll always have something."

"You're telling me to leave Monique." Now it's my turn to state a fact.

"I'm telling you to do whatever you need to, to stay true to yourself." She pats my cheek softly and steps back, grabbing her purse. "Whatever that might be."

I watch as she strolls from my kitchen, completely dumbfounded by that conversation. Never did I imagine she felt that way—that she regretted her lifestyle.

Would that be me? If I don't give Aaron everything, will I look back in five years' time and regret it?

Is not giving him everything even an option?

I sink into the stool she just vacated. My head is spinning. First, my agent tells me to believe in true love. Then, my cold and cynical aunt tells me to pick love over the job she so adored.

I feel like I've entered the Twilight zone.

I drop my head to the table and turn it to the side. And stare right at Aunt Leigh's scarf. I reach for my cell on the other side of the island and dial her number. It rings to voicemail.

"Hey, Aunt Leigh, you left your scarf—" The rumble of a car outside distracts me. "Oh, never mind. You're here."

I drop the phone, grab the silk scarf, and walk to the front door to meet her.

But when I open it, it's not my aunt.

"What the hell are you doing here?"

Naomi stands in front of me, her blond hair pulled back in a bun, and her long, fake eyelashes fanning out as she blinks at me. "We need to talk."

She moves forward to enter the house, but I step in front of her, pulling the door shut behind me.

"Is that so?"

"Aren't you going to invite me in?"

"You're the ex-wife of my boyfriend. What do you think?"

Her lips curl into an evil smile. "It's really in your best interests to invite me in, *Mia*."

Fuck.

Chapter Ten

I step back silently, allowing her to pass through, and follow her into my living room. She walks around it, her eyes examining every last detail, her heels snapping against the hardwood floor.

I fold my arms across my chest and pin her with my stare. "What are you doing here?"

"You're a hard woman to find, Dayton Black. Or is it Mia Lopez? I'm not sure if there's a difference between the two."

"Don't fuck around, Naomi. Say what you have to say or get the hell out of my house."

She pushes her bangs back from her face and perches on my sofa.

"Please, take a seat. Make yourself at home." I wave to her. "Perhaps you'd like to remove your shoes and have a coffee while you're here?"

Naomi smirks. And it's not a kind one. It's a malicious twist of her lips that makes my skin crawl. "Does Aaron know?"

"Does Aaron know what?" I ask, feigning ignorance.

"That his precious Dayton is a common whore."

"Oh, please. Give me some credit. I'm at least an upper-class whore."

Her tongue flicks across her bottom lip. "I'll guess he does."

"And this matters why?"

She sighs and stands again, resting her hands on her hips. "I'm wondering how problematic it would be for you if your little…alter ego…was forced to step from the shadows."

I straighten. Every nerve on my body is on high alert at her discreet threat. Adrenaline is buzzing through my veins, and I hit Naomi with a sharp stare that would make any other woman shrink back.

"What exactly are you insinuating?"

"Could you imagine the repercussions of your identity being revealed?" She runs a fingertip along my windowsill. "The effect that would have on Aaron and the business… The CEO of Stone Advertising dating a call girl." She tsks, shaking her head.

I step toward her, anger making my hands tremble, and stare at her dead-on. "I'm not sure what kind of manipulation and mind games happen in the modeling world, but you should be aware that I'm not a face-scratching or hair-pulling kind of girl. If I were you, Naomi, I'd get to the point quickly. I'm not the most patient woman in the world, and you're wearing what little patience I do possess down rather fast."

"The fashion world is fickle. If it was to be made public that Aaron was dating an escort, virtually every designer in existence would boycott the company. That would be followed by their remaining clients. You're a taboo subject, Dayton. Your existence is a cause of disgust for many people… Including me." She looks at me with that disgust written over her face in the curl of her lip.

"I can safely say the feeling is mutual."

That smirk appears back on her face.

"Your point, Naomi?"

"My point? Ah, yes." She walks around me, swaying her hips like the model she is. "The outcome of our marriage wasn't exactly what I was hoping for. And signing the Stone contract in front of me? That was underhanded." She sighs. "That's by the by… But like I said, the settlement was less than I was hoping for. Before he took over Stone, he was worth twenty-five million alone from his stake in the company, various investments, and smart business decisions. By the end of next year, he'll push the company over the billion-dollar threshold. Seven and a half million isn't nearly enough, don't you agree?"

I purse my lips. "Oh, I agree. It's far too much."

She holds my stare for a moment. "We signed an agreement that, in the case of a divorce, I would be entitled to half of what he was worth on the day we married. That was ten million."

"So you already have more than you should."

She ignores me. "That agreement was ridiculous, but the marriage was a clever move for us both, so I agreed. Of course, when he increased his worth exponentially throughout our marriage, five million was a meager amount."

"My underwear lasts longer than your marriage did."

She ignores me. "I was pushing for fifteen, but I would have been happy with ten. He only signed the amount he did to get it over with. I had no choice but to sign it if I didn't want it to go to court." She sighs again and taps her finger against her lips.

"My patience is close to exhaustion, Naomi."

"I want the final two-point-five mil. I want what I helped him achieve."

A sick feeling settles in my stomach. "And if you don't get it?"

"Aaron is very good at keeping his private life away from the media. I have the contacts to expose every dirty secret you have, Dayton, and take several others down with you. Aaron and the business would be an unfortunate fall, I admit, but sometimes you can't avoid these things." She smiles, but there isn't an ounce of friendliness in it. Just malice and spite and greed. Everything Carly said to me last night has been proven true by the woman standing before me.

"Are you threatening me?"

"Do you think I am?"

I walk to her, once again stopping in front of her. "Get out of my house."

"I'd prefer Aaron didn't know about this, so I'll give you a month." She looks me up and down. "I'm sure you can fuck enough guys in that time to raise the money."

I step closer to her again. "Get the fuck out of my house. Now. Or I'll throw you out."

After a long second of her staring into my eyes, she turns on her heels and leaves, slamming the door behind her. I stare at the empty doorway she just passed through, my chest heaving with each ragged breath I take.

Angry tears burn the backs of my eyes. I don't doubt her for a second. I know in my gut she'd go to the press just to spite us—to spite me.

I collapse on the sofa next to me. Do I even have anything close to that kind of money? I have savings, sure, and I know there's a lot of money in there, but nothing close to what she's asking for. And there's no chance of me going out and working for it.

Shit! Am I really considering paying that bitch off?

Yeah. Yeah, I am. Because of Aaron. Because if it means protecting him and the business, the business he and his father grew together, then yes. I'd pay her off.

I'd do just about anything to protect him.

My first thought when my financial planner informs me that there's four hundred and forty thousand dollars sitting in my investment account is why the hell I haven't paid off my mortgage yet.

My second is a resounding *Fuck*.

That's also the first word I mutter when I leave the building, discreetly tucking the printed slip into my bra.

I can barely believe I'm considering this—that I'm here, getting the information I need to fulfill her fucked-up request. I don't think I've yet truly processed our conversation.

I mean, shit. The woman walked into my house and blackmailed me. In my own fucking house!

I lean against the wall and press my fingers to my temple, rubbing harshly. My head is throbbing from the events of today. Hell, it's throbbing from the events of the last few weeks.

I get into my car and pull out of the parking lot. The journey passes in a blur with seemingly no time passing at all when I arrive back at my house. Words and threats and promises and hopes swirl in my mind, each of them crashing into each other until the throb becomes a relentless pound.

I park and scramble into my house. My cell and keys hit the table with a clunk, and I run upstairs to the bathroom. I twist the bath taps until they're on full power and peel my clothes away.

There's barely any water in the tub, but I climb in anyway. The hot and cold water mingles at my feet. I watch as the level slowly rises, and I lean forward, hugging my thighs to my chest.

I can feel the thump of my heart against my legs, the hectic rise and fall of my chest. And the fear. The very real fear, racing through my body and taking hold of me.

The fear of losing everything.

Of losing my control. Of losing the relationship I have belief in. Of losing the man I love.

But if I leave him, Naomi loses her trump card.

If I leave him, he's safe. She can't hurt him or the business.

If I leave him, I'll slowly but surely destroy us both.

I dig my fingernails into the inside of my thighs. That isn't an option. We have things to work through and things to prove, but I can't walk away from how far we've come or how far we have to go.

I turn off the taps, lie back, and sink beneath the water. It sloshes around me as I move, and I lift my legs out of the tub and rest them on the edge. I lean up for a breath before dropping my face back down again.

Beneath the water, it's silent, and it quiets the crazy in my mind. It calms the beating of my heart until it settles to the steady rhythm I know so well, and the tension seeps from my body in the hot water.

Two hands grab my arms and lift me from the water. "Jesus, Dayton!"

Aaron pulls me into his chest. I'm still sitting in the water and he's still in his suit. His hands shake against my bare back.

"What the fucking hell were you doing?" he rasps into my wet hair, holding me tight.

"Relaxing," I whisper.

"You know most people watch TV or have a glass of wine, right? They don't ignore their calls and submerge themselves in water."

"I'm not most people." I wriggle from his hold and climb from the tub.

He hands me two towels. I wrap my hair in one and the other around my body before walking into my bedroom.

"I know that. Shit, Day." He grabs me again. "I've been calling you for an hour. I've been so worried about you."

"Wait. How did you get in? You didn't bash the door down like you did on the boat, did you?"

Aaron pulls back, a smile on his face despite the worry in his eyes. "No, I didn't break your door down, sweetheart. You didn't lock it."

I bite my lip. "Oops."

He raises his eyebrows but doesn't comment on it. "Why didn't you answer my calls?"

A thought crosses my mind. "How did you get my new number?"

"Irrelevant." He dismisses it with a wave of his hand.

I grab some underwear and walk back into my room to find him leaning against my headboard, his jacket discarded and his shoes kicked off on my floor.

"Mmph. Okay." I clasp my bra and slide my thong up my legs. "I was in the bath and didn't hear it ringing upstairs."

"For a whole hour?"

"Time ran away from me. I had a bad day." I rub my hair with the towel and grab the dryer from the top of the dresser. The bed creaks behind me, and a second later, Aaron's hand closes around mine.

"What happened?"

"Just stuff." I shrug and turn on the hairdryer. Aaron flicks the switch on the wall, cutting the hot air.

"Dayton."

I meet his eyes in the mirror. "I had a bad day. It sucked. End of discussion."

Something in my tone must tell him that pushing me won't work this time, because he backs off with a sigh. I lean over, turn the power back on, and perch on the end of the bed.

I can feel his eyes on my back as I blast my hair dry. The irony of this situation doesn't escape me. I'm holding out on him and berating him for keeping something from me, yet here I am doing the exact same thing.

And the same woman is at the center of both.

I should turn around and tell him. I should tell him about her showing up and blackmailing me—but that will do nothing except give her what she wants. I know that, when it comes down to it, Aaron will do whatever it takes.

He already said that there isn't a price he wouldn't pay for me.

Two and a half million is a steep price, but he'd pay it without blinking.

I don't want him to do that. I don't want her to have that control over him any longer. She held that for long enough, dictating and holding back on something that should have been sorted. She controlled far too much of his life for far too long.

Now, the only person who gets to have any semblance of control over him is me.

I place the hairdryer back on top of the dresser and run my brush through my hair. He's still sitting on the bed, and now his tie is sitting on my nightstand. The top button of his shirt is open, but my focus is on the material stretching across his shoulders and the way it clings to his body. It's on the smatter of dark hair peeking over the top of his shirt and the faint outline of his abs. It's on the pleasure and release I know he can provide. The release I know he will selflessly provide me.

The few seconds of pure nothing.

He rests his cell facedown next to his tie and peers at me through heavy eyelids when I crawl up the bed. His eyes darken, roaring with heat, when I straddle him and grab his collar.

"Dayton." My name is a low growl, a warning, a threat, a promise.

I roughly press my lips to his, and his hands slide up my thighs and curve round my ass. My tongue flicks against his lips, demanding they part for me, and I slide my hands in his hair. I tug a little, pressing my core against him, and he groans.

Our tongues meet in a heated desperation driven solely by me. If I've ever needed him, truly craved his touch, it's right now. I need the sweet release and spiral of bliss I know Aaron can provide for me.

His fingers dig into my backside, holding my hips to his. His erection presses against me and I rub against him, each gyration of my hips hardening his ready cock further. I make quick work of the buttons of his shirt and shove it over his shoulders. His skin is smooth and hot beneath my fingertips as I run them down his body to his belt. My knuckles brush my throbbing clit as I unbuckle it.

I shove his boxers down with his trousers, leaving them around his knees, and reach between us. I wrap my fingers around the silky pink skin of his shaft and stroke him almost roughly. Aaron groans again and grabs my hand, moving it so the head of his cock rubs against my clit.

My juices coat him in seconds, and when the first clench takes over my body, I ease myself onto him instead.

"Fuuuuck," he groans into my shoulder.

I wind my fingers back in his hair and move against him. My lips part and my breathing speeds at each movement. This isn't like before—even when it's been rougher. There was always endless passion and seduction.

This is pure, raw need. This is hard and fast, and when he grabs my hips, stilling me, and pounds into me frantically, it's almost brutal. There's nothing romantic or flowery about the way our skin slaps together, and my cries are swallowed by his rough kisses and nibbles at my lips.

There's nothing beautiful about this, except everything that shouldn't be.

I explode with a loud moan and my teeth sinking into his shoulder. He roars his own release, slamming into me one last time. He drops his hips to the bed, lowering mine with his, still buried deep inside me.

I press my face into his neck and tightly wrap my arms around him. His own hands stroke across my back, fingers splayed, one at the small of my back and the other resting between my shoulder blades.

Aaron kisses along my shoulder, each kiss softer than the last. Each kiss holding the feelings neither of us displayed just a moment ago.

"I'm sorry," I whisper. "I didn't plan to do that."

"Shh," he says into my hair. "You needed to let go. I was here. I don't begrudge you that."

I squeeze my eyes shut. Goddamn him for being so wonderful and understanding and *him*.

"My day was awful, and I just… I don't know."

"You needed control back."

I nod and sit up. I brush my thumb over his cheek and along his jaw, my eyes following the path of it. Guilt eats at me inside, but I batter it down. I kiss him once and get off him, heading into the bathroom to clean up. Aaron follows me in.

"Have you eaten tonight?"

I shake my head and throw my panties in the laundry basket. "No. I'm starving."

"I brought takeout, but it's probably cold by now." He shoots a wickedly sexy smirk my way, and my cheeks flush a little. "Blushing?"

I duck into my lingerie room and slip on another pair of panties before deciding to answer that. "You, Mr. Stone, are the only man in existence who can make me blush."

"I happen to enjoy making you blush very much, Miss Black. I'll strive to do it more often."

I roll my eyes and grab the cartons sitting on the kitchen side. "Baby, you can pin me against a wall and describe to me in explicit detail all the things you'd like to do to me with your tongue and your cock and I still wouldn't blush. I said you can make me blush, but I didn't say it was easy."

I set the timer on the microwave oven at the same time Aaron wraps his arms around me.

"Baby," he murmurs. "I have a soft spot for that."

"Even though I only said it originally to annoy you?"

"Yes." He turns my face to the side and brushes his lips against the corner of my mouth. "Do you usually dine in your lingerie?"

"Quite often." I spin and run my finger down the middle of his stomach. "Would you prefer I put some clothes on?"

"Don't even think about it."

I smile and turn back to the oven at its ping. Aaron sits down, and I set the Chinese food between us.

"So. London," I say after a few minutes.

Aaron nods. "You'll come with me?"

"Since you're asking, I suppose so."

His eyes light up. "If I had known asking would make you so agreeable, I would have tried it before."

"We both forget to ask sometimes."

"I like your demanding. A lot."

I throw a shrimp at him. "Watch it, baby. I'm more demanding than you know."

Aaron raises his eyebrows and leans forward on his elbows, his eyes hot and his voice silky smooth. "I'm ready for anything you demand of me, Dayton. Anything."

Chapter Eleven

Aaron gently shakes me awake, his breath cascading over my cheek. "Dayton, sweetheart? We're in London."

"Stupid time difference," I mumble, rubbing my eyes and sitting up.

He chuckles. "Come on. Dinner then you can go back to sleep."

"What? What time is it here?"

"It's around six p.m."

I blink at him, sitting up, and shake my head. I'm not even going to try and work that out. I grab my jacket, and he guides me out of the plane.

"On the bright side, you don't have to meet my cousin until tomorrow. Tyler is always a delight." His tone is dry, but there's an obvious fondness there.

"You didn't mention your cousin."

"I didn't mention London until my father reminded me three days ago. What makes you think I'd remember to inform you that we're staying with my cousin for ten days?"

I smack him lightly in the chest. "We definitely have to work on the conversational part of our relationship."

Yes, we do, don't we, Dayton?

Aaron laughs and wraps an arm around my waist. We're expedited through customs and swept straight into a waiting car. I stifle a yawn as I slide across the back seat and press myself against the window.

I've never been to London, and it isn't a place I ever envisioned myself visiting. After my parents died, I never imagined I'd fly again, but I have. I've conquered that fear, and now here I am. In London. With Aaron.

Nothing should surprise me anymore, but it does. At every turn.

"Where does he live?"

"Tyler stays in my aunt and uncle's house in Belgravia. They primarily spend their time in the US, so the house as good as belongs to him. It was passed to Aunt Kate from her parents as part of their restaurant business. She and Uncle Todd spent a couple of years in the US expanding the business when we were young and decided to move back when Ty and Tessa were older. Ty stays in Belgravia rent-free."

"Nice," I mutter. "Won't he take over the business, like you did with Stone?"

Aaron shakes his head. "He made it clear very early that it isn't something he's interested in. He's happier being a photographer and working for me. Ty's never been business-minded like me and his sister. Tessa manages the UK business and will eventually take over the US side, too."

I nod slowly. "Did you always know you'd take Stone over?"

"There was never any question. I inherited ten percent when I graduated from Columbia, and obviously the rest became mine a few weeks ago."

"I didn't know you went to Columbia."

"You never asked."

"When have I had time to ask you?" I turn to him and raise an eyebrow. "Really, Aaron."

He laughs. "Apparently your nap hasn't brightened your mood any."

"Shut up." I curl myself into his side and close my eyes again.

"Don't get comfortable," he whispers. "We're here."

We get out of the car and I look up at the house in front of me. The cream brick building is four stories high, with a black railing on the first floor surrounding a small balcony. The black wooden front door is sheltered beneath the same balcony, and two perfectly trimmed triangular bushes are above it.

"This is his house?"

"His parents'." Aaron leads me forward.

He pulls a silver key from his pocket and unlocks the front door. Then he gestures for me to go first, and I step into the gorgeous townhouse. It's the embodiment of opulence and elegance, despite essentially being a bachelor pad. The tiled floor of the hall stretches forward with several doors coming off of it. I wring my hands in front of my stomach.

Jesus. I thought my house was big.

"Come on." Aaron takes my hand when the suitcases are lined up in the hall. The small bag we took on the plane is in his other hand. "We'll freshen up before dinner then put those away."

He takes me up a winding staircase. Pictures of a young boy and girl adorn the walls as we go, and it's evident this was very much a family home at one point. As the pictures show the almost-identical children growing up, I turn to Aaron.

"Are your cousins twins?"

He nods. "Yes. Tessa will be getting married next week. We never really got along as kids despite our inclination for our parents' businesses. I'll be expected to attend the wedding since we're here."

"You sound delighted," I note, hearing the flat tone of his voice.

He laughs. "Ty and I were boys' boys. We were forever climbing the trees in the yard and playing soccer and getting all muddy. Tessa is a true lady. She was never seen with a hair out of place even when she was still playing dress-up with her mom's shoes."

I smile sadly and look down. Wasn't I that girl, too?

"This is our room." Aaron pushes open a heavy door and guides me into the room.

The furniture is all antique style, including the bed, and the sheets covering it are black satin. I groan at the sight of them.

"What's wrong?"

"Do you know how hard it is to sleep in satin sheets?"

Aaron smirks, and my heart skips a beat at the look in his eyes. "Oh, Day," he mutters, turning me into him and rubbing his thumb across my bottom lip. "Who said anything about sleeping?"

I smile at the touch of his lips to mine. "I wouldn't want to disturb your cousin."

"My cousin goes through women the way you go through Agent Provocateur's latest collection. It's impossible to disturb Tyler."

"Well then." I reach on my tiptoes and flick my tongue against his mouth. "That's a different story, isn't it?"

He slaps my ass. "Stop turning me on and get ready before I bend you over this bed and fuck you into tomorrow morning."

I take the bag from him and throw him a flirty grin. "Is that supposed to deter me?"

"Dayton." He growls my name. "The bathroom is next door."

I roll over in bed and stretch my arm out, expecting Aaron to be beside me. When it flops straight to the empty sheets, I force my heavy eyelids open and look at the clock on the nightstand.

Ten thirty. *Crap.*

My sleeping habits leave a lot to be desired.

Faint voices travel up the stairs and through the small crack in the door. One is Aaron's, and another one is distinctly British. The second voice has to be Tyler. The low hum of their conversation is broken by a bout of loud laughter. My own lips twitch at the outburst, and I climb out bed.

I haven't heard Aaron laugh like that in weeks. He has the kind of laugh that trickles through your body and warms your insides. It's infectious, and I have a burning desire to meet the person who can make him laugh this way.

I should probably get dressed though… I bite my lip as I stare at my suitcase. What do I wear? Doesn't it always rain in England?

A quick peek out the window proves me wrong. The sun is filtering through a smattering of fluffy white clouds set against a bright blue sky. Not even the ground is wet.

I slip on a simple dress and quietly push the door open. In the light of this day, the house is even more elegant than I thought it was. The frames holding the pictures on the stairs are ornate, and the rail on the staircase is just as fancy.

Clearly, I have simple living tastes.

I walk downstairs quietly. Aaron is standing in the kitchen with his back to me, his suit jacket slung over the back of the chair he's leaning against. The creak on the bottom stair gives me away, and he turns, a mug of steaming coffee in his hand.

The smile that spreads across his face makes my heart beat double-time. It's the kind of smile where no words are needed, because everything is said with the curve of your lips. This one says that he's very, very happy to see me.

"Good morning," he murmurs, wrapping an arm around my waist and pulling me into him.

"Morning," I whisper.

"Did you sleep well?"

"Apart from sliding around several times, yes, thank you."

"Tyler? Jesus. Where are you now?" Aaron looks around the kitchen. "C'mon, man. You can't eat cookies for fucking breakfast."

"Never stopped us before."

The guy who emerges from what I'm guessing is the pantry is almost a carbon copy of Aaron. The only differences are the lack of stubble dotting his jaw and that his eyes are dark brown, not the startling blue of my man's. His hair is also a little longer and wavier, but the grin that breaks onto his face is identical to Aaron's.

Tyler puts down the cookie bag and gives me the once-over. I raise an eyebrow, and I immediately understand Aaron's words from last night. The appreciative way he trawls his gaze over me would melt any other woman.

Aaron clears his throat, and Tyler snaps his eyes to him. "I know the words 'off-limits' aren't something you're used to, Ty, but look at her that way again and I'll see to it you're unable to entertain another woman again."

God. I love protective Aaron.

Tyler holds his hands up. "I can look and not touch, cuz. It doesn't happen often, but it happens." He flicks his eyes to me quickly. "Shame though. I'll just wait until she's done with your boring arse."

Aaron slaps him around the back of the head with lightning speed, and Tyler laughs, ducking away.

"I was going to introduce you, but a hotel is looking incredibly tempting."

I roll my eyes and step forward. "You must be Tyler. I'm Dayton. Excuse his possessive streak. We're working on reining it in some."

Aaron's hand connects with my ass, and I shoot a glare over my shoulder.

"Watch it, Mr. Stone. You're still on my *shit list*."

He smirks and lifts his mug to his mouth, hiding it.

"Dayton." Tyler shoots me a beaming smile that oozes charm. Yep. This guy knows how to melt panties right off. Fortunately, not mine. "It's a pleasure to meet you. Of course, I would have preferred to meet you a few weeks ago. Between you and me if I'd known you looked like this—"

"Tyler," Aaron growls. "Do you think you could behave yourself while I have to work today, perhaps? Or do I need to make other arrangements for Dayton? I'm sure she'd much prefer to explore London than be locked in a spa, but the latter can be arranged."

"I'll behave." Tyler holds three fingers in front of his body. "Scout's honor."

Aaron narrows his eyes, but I can see the amusement shining there. I get the feeling that Tyler is the only guy he'd let pull this shit and get away with it. No doubt anyone else would be in a very uncomfortable, painful position right now.

"Day." Aaron pulls me back to him. "I have to work all day. Apparently my company doesn't understand jet lag." He yawns as if to prove his point.

I smile. "Have fun with that."

"So sympathetic." He wraps his hand around the back of my neck and pulls my face to his. "Tyler's agreed to spend the day with you. I'm not sure how much of a good idea this is, but if he pushes his luck, put the little asshole in his place."

"Don't worry. I will." I pat his chest.

"I have to go or I'll be late. I don't think I'll be home for dinner, so make sure Ty takes you somewhere expensive. On my tab," he adds, looking at me pointedly.

I chew my lip. "Yes, sir."

"Promise?"

"Promise."

"Good girl." He kisses me, his lips soft against mine. "Now I'm going. See you tonight."

"See you later, baby." I wink and kiss him quickly.

"Hey, Aaron?" The cookie bag rustles as Tyler picks it up.

"Yes?" Aaron looks at him, shrugging his jacket on.

"If any of the models at the casting today are any pop, send them my way, would you? The last is getting a bit clingy and I need to fend her off."

"You know I can't do that, Tyler. You'll have to go out and find some poor woman to use by yourself." He buttons his jacket and pockets his cell, then looks at me. "Remember, woman. My card."

I stare after him, and Tyler flicks a switch behind me.

"Fuck that. I'm not taking a woman to dinner on his card."

I turn.

"If I take you for dinner, I'm paying. He just wants to make me look like some cheap bastard."

"What is it with you men? Women are perfectly capable of buying themselves—and a man—dinner." I sit at the table in the center of the room and nod when he points to the coffee machine. "Please. Black."

"Jet lag is a bitch." He puts some beans and water in the machine and starts it. "And it's not that we don't think you're capable of buying your own dinner. You just shouldn't."

"Really? We *shouldn't*?"

"Day—I can call you that, right? Cool." He continues before I respond. "Look at us. Aaron runs a multimillion-dollar company, and I'm the technical heir to another. He breathes tailored Armani suits, and I live and die in my designer jeans. If either of us took you to dinner and you paid, we'd look like nothing more than trophy husbands."

I raise my eyebrows as he places a mug of coffee in front of me. "Are you saying I look old?"

"No. Fuck no. Shit." He rubs his hand down his face. "You're fucking gorgeous, and I have no problem saying so. Trust me, if you weren't my cousin's girlfriend, I wouldn't be serving you coffee on this table. I'd be serving you me."

"Apparently subtle isn't a word in the vocabulary of the Stone men."

"Not in mine, love. Cookie?" He thrusts the package in my face, and I take two. "Finally. A woman who will eat something I wouldn't feed to a rabbit."

"That's what happens when you sleep with models." I take a bite and wipe crumbs from the table.

"Don't forget the gold-diggers with pussies bigger than my wallet. They're even worse."

I pause for a moment, staring at the man in front of me. "This conversation is perhaps a little too personal for a first meeting."

Tyler's lips twist in amusement. "If you can't get personal on a first meeting, you're definitely not the kind of girl to be sitting in my kitchen."

The irony of that statement isn't lost on me, and my lips twist. If only he knew just how many personal first meetings I've had in my life.

"And I believe that sentence tells me everything I need to know about you, Tyler Stone."

He grins wolfishly, mischief twinkling in his dark eyes. "You're a smart woman, Dayton. What are you doing with my cousin?"

"That is a very good question."

Chapter Twelve

The look on Tyler's face when I told him I wanted to see Buckingham Palace was hilarious. It was a cross between exasperation and helplessness.

I promised myself years ago that, if I ever got to London, the palace would be the first place I visited. Now, sitting in the back of a black cab and driving to Tyler's favorite restaurant for an early dinner, I'm glad I saw it.

And despite his initial grumbling, Tyler didn't exactly hate trying to make a guard laugh.

"One of those hats would suit me. What do you think?"

I look across the car at him and shake my head. "Really? No."

He pouts. "I'm not sure I know what to do with a woman who doesn't fall at my feet."

"You act like a gentleman."

"Is that what they do nowadays? Bloody hell. I'm not a door-opening kind of guy. Unless it's to my bedroom, of course. Then I'm as close to a gentleman as they come—if you ignore the rough bits around the edges." He winks and hands the driver some money, telling him to keep the change.

I rest my hand on the door handle, but he shakes his head and jumps from the car. My eyebrows shoot up, and he appears at my window a second later with a cocky smile on his face. I shake my head when he opens the door and holds out his hand.

"M'lady."

I laugh and take it, stepping from the car. "You're an idiot, Tyler."

"I'm being a gentleman. Aaron would hold good on his threat to render my cock useless if I were anything less than one. And"—he pauses as he opens the restaurant door—"I have to admit to being rather attached to it."

We're immediately led to a table when the host recognizes Tyler. But not just any table—the best available table. It hits me now that, despite his relaxed, carefree attitude, Tyler is in London what Aaron is in Seattle. Well-known. Respected. The upper class.

Our drinks are served within a minute of us taking our seats, and there's no great long wait for food like I'm seeing for some others. There's a mix of both familiar and unfamiliar faces here—the familiar ones being people I've seen on the insides of glossy magazines and once or twice on television.

Holy shit. London is the British L.A. It's celebrity central in this place.

I somehow manage to make it through dinner without drooling over my plate. Tyler sits opposite me, completely unaffected.

My job has taken me to places I never imagined I'd visit and introduced me to people with a standing so high I shouldn't rightfully be alongside them, but there's rich and then there's *rich*.

Watching Aaron's cousin so at home in this obviously exclusive restaurant, I know what bracket he and Aaron fall in.

Stinking fucking rich.

I know Naomi said that Aaron would be the one to tip the business over the billion-dollar mark, but I don't think it sank in. I don't think it's hit me until now how much money he really does have.

How dangerous it could be if the knowledge of who I am, who I *was*, was made public.

"Dayton?" Tyler waves his hand in front of my face. "Are you okay?"

I blink harshly and turn to him. "Yes. Sorry. I was just thinking for a moment."

"Would you like pudding, or…?"

"I'll have a dessert." Aaron sits on the seat next to me and adjusts his tie. "I'm starving."

"Well, hello." I shift my body so I'm facing him. "How did you know we were here?"

"I'm Aaron Stone. I can find out anything." He winks and grabs the menu. "Has Tyler been behaving himself?"

I wink across the table at the man in question. "He's been a real gentleman. Even opened doors for me."

"Is he sick?"

"If we weren't in such an exclusive establishment, I'd have a few choice words for you," Tyler retorts. "And I'm perfectly healthy, thank you."

"Perhaps there's hope for you yet, my man." Aaron turns to me. "I think I'll have the chocolate fudge cake. What about you?"

"I'll have the same."

"Ty?"

"Not for me. I'm going to end my dry spell." He stands and brushes his shirt off.

"Dry spell." Aaron snorts. "Forty-eight hours?"

"Thirty-six. I'm never going the extra twelve again." He motions to a waiter. "I likely won't be back home tonight."

"Don't forget you have a shoot tomorrow," Aaron looks up at him.

"Lingerie, isn't it? With Jenna Kelly?"

Aaron nods. "For Catalina. In the office studios."

"Shit. I hate shooting in those. I'm sending in my own lights this time. Last time, we had to rebook." Tyler runs his hand through his messy hair and looks to me. "Wanna tag along?"

"Am I allowed?" I look between them both.

"You're the boss's girlfriend. You can do whatever the hell you want," Tyler answers.

Aaron smirks. "You can if you want to. I'm working all day."

I narrow my eyes and tap his arm. "Is this a setup? The last time I went to a shoot, I ended up *being* shot."

"Photographically, I hope." Tyler laughs. "No setup. I promise."

"Sure. I'll go."

"I'll pick you up at ten." He takes his jacket from the waiter. "See ya."

Aaron orders our desserts and places his hand over mine on the table. With his other, he pours me a glass of wine and accepts the whisky he's offered. His thumb slowly rubs along the side of my wrist, tickling the tender skin there, and when I look up, his eyes are on mine.

"What?" I ask softly.

"How do you manage to look so beautiful when you're barely wearing any makeup?"

"Your mind is blurred by all the models you've seen parading before you today."

He leans into me and runs his nose up my cheek. "And every single time, I was wishing it were you."

"I know where this is going."

"You considered it before. Will you again?"

I pull back and suck my bottom lip into my mouth. I did. I would. I have. I can't. Our dessert is placed between us with two forks, and Aaron nods his thanks.

I take my hand from his and grab a fork, stabbing it into the cake. This is too soon to have this conversation. It's too soon to have any kind of conversation about anything past right now.

I forgive him, but I don't know if I fully trust him. And this is the funny thing about trust. You can love and forgive, but you don't necessarily trust. Broken hearts and promises can be fixed so easily because they break in a different way than trust. When trust is broken, it's shattered into a thousand pieces. And sometimes, it's never put back together the same way.

Aaron takes the fork from me, resting it in the bowl, and sighs. "Dayton."

"We're not having this conversation. Not here and not now. If I decide to leave Monique, we'll discuss this."

"It really doesn't matter to me if you leave her or not. You'll belong to me either way."

I look into his eyes, forceful and determined. "Aaron, I'm not going to say this again. Working for you isn't something I think I can comprehend. I don't want to be the girl who got an 'in' because she's fucking the boss. If I ever decide I want to model, I'll do it because it's my decision, and I'll carry the weight of it on my own shoulders. I won't roll over and be signed by you just because I can be."

"You want to prove yourself." He brings the cake-laden fork to my mouth, and I open my mouth.

I nod and swallow the cake. "For me."

"I understand that." He takes a bite himself. "But for the record, Day, you're not fucking the boss. You're in a serious relationship with him. There's a very big difference, sweetheart."

"The level of our relationship depends on your ability to prove yourself to me." I swallow the bitterness of my own secret down, my whole body screaming at my hypocrisy. "There's a long way to go, baby."

He puts another forkful of cake in my mouth and follows it up by covering my lips with his. I pull back, swallow my mouthful, and tilt my face back for his kiss. His lips are sweet and woody at the same time, the chocolate fudge sauce mingling with the whisky in a strangely alluring and delicious mix.

"Can I show you something?"

"We've been here before."

He smiles. The waiter appears and Aaron hands him his card without glancing at the bill. I choose not to look at the slip of paper on the table. I'd probably have a heart attack.

"Trust me," he whispers, pulling me to standing and wrapping my cardigan around my shoulders.

"Honestly?" I look up at him. "That's what I'm a little afraid of."

His eyes flash with another indiscernible emotion. He swallows, taking his card from the waiter with a nod, and then he leads me outside. A sleek black car pulls up and Aaron opens the door, guiding me in.

"To Soho." His words are short and sharp, and I can hear the underlying pain in them. My stomach twists.

How can I do this to him when I'm no better? Fuck. Guilt riddles my body, and this is by far the most fucked-up situation I've been in for a long time.

I open my mouth but no words come out. Not even a squeak.

We travel in silence. The twenty-minute journey across London is coated in tension and regret and a tinge of heartbreak sneaking its way through.

What am I doing?

Aaron doesn't look at me when the car stops and he helps me out. He links his fingers through mine and leads me through several streets. The heavy air is still hanging between us, but when we stop, his words slice through it.

"You want to prove yourself?"

I nod slightly, narrowing my eyes.

"Walk around that corner, look at the billboard, and tell me you don't see a woman who has proven herself."

"What?"

He motions to the corner. I look between him and the street uncertainly. People mill around us, completely unaware of the turmoil surrounding us and seeping in.

I swallow hard and take the few steps around the corner. We're the first thing I see. My hand on his waist. His at my jaw. My head tilted back. My lips parted. His eyes boring into mine. The gorgeous Australian background.

Aaron rests his hands on my waist. "I see a woman who's already proven herself. I see a woman so worried about what the rest of the world thinks that she's afraid to take the step her heart really wants to. I see a woman held back by an irrational fear she doesn't know she possesses. But most of all, I see a beautiful woman standing in front of and in the arms of the man who would burn bridges and build cities if that's what it took to make her happy."

I blink several times as the tears build in my eyes. Aaron spins me in his arms and cups my cheek with his palm, brushing his thumb across my temple.

"I own a multimillion-dollar company, Dayton, but I'm not rich. I could buy anything I wanted without blinking, without seeing the dent in any one of my bank accounts. I could buy another company if I wanted. Another car. Another plane. A whole estate of houses. I could buy an island if I truly desired, but I'm not rich. The one thing that would make me rich, I can't buy. Unless I have your love, given freely and wholeheartedly, I'm just as poor as the man you see on the corner of the street. All I can do is buy the time to convince you that I'm worth it. That we're worth it. I can use that time to make you believe in us. To trust in us." He brings his forehead to mine. "And I truly won't stop until you do. I won't stop fighting until you're standing in front of me and telling me you love me with everything you are and you give that to me."

He takes my mouth in a raw and heartfelt kiss I feel right down to my toes. They curl in my shoes, and the tears sneak from my eyes and down my cheeks.

Aaron pulls back and wipes them from my face. "Every time I kiss you, I taste the rest of my life. I won't stop fighting for you until you taste yours, too."

I wrap my arms around his waist and bury my face into his chest. He envelopes me in his arms, holding me against him in a desperate way. He lets out a long, shuddery breath that snakes across my neck and leaves goose bumps in its wake.

I taste it, I want to say. I've tasted it since the moment he first kissed me. Every brush, every tease, every deep, probing kiss and sweep of his tongue through my mouth has been filled with the taste of forever. I feel it in his touch and see it in his eyes.

In the same way I wish he could tell me that he loves me, I wish I could tell him everything.

Chapter Thirteen

"Dayton? Are you ready to go?" Tyler's voice echoes through the house, and I grab my coffee mug.

"Hold on." I down the rest of the mug in one gulp and leave it on the counter. I'll clean it up later. I grab my purse from the table and meet him in the hallway. "Ready."

"Come on. I'm already late."

"Hot date last night?"

"More like animalistic. She was a dream." Tyler leads to me an Audi R8 and presses a button on the keys. "In you get."

"This is your car?"

"Nah. I stopped by the dealership this morning and stole it." He opens his door and stares at me. My lips twitch up on one corner, and I get in the passenger's side.

"It's gorgeous."

"It gets me laid."

"I have no doubt."

I sit almost stiffly. I've never been in a car so expensive or...pretty.

"She won't blow up if you sit back or actually touch the seat, you know." Tyler smirks. "I guess you haven't seen Aaron's baby."

"I didn't even know he had a car in his possession. He's driven everywhere."

He laughs. "That's because my cousin is a particular bastard who won't let anyone touch his Ferrari. I could count on one hand the amount of times he's driven that."

What? "He has a fucking Ferrari?"

"A 458 Italia. Boyhood dream car."

"Even I know what car that is."

"His apartment block has an underground garage. There's a private section for his apartment, and it's under lock and key. Make him show you when you get back. Then, for the love of bloody God, please drag your finger across it."

"Why?"

He sighs. "Because getting it dirty is my fucking dream, and you're the only person that could touch it and get away with it. He'd kick my ass."

"He'd kick mine too, no doubt."

"He wouldn't."

"How are you so sure?" I twist and look at him.

Tyler flashes a card to a security guard and drives into an underground parking lot. "I see how he looks at you. He never looked at Trouty that way."

"Trouty?"

We pull up, and Tyler cuts the engine. "Yeah. Naomi. You know, those lips? It's a trout pout."

I think back to the last time I saw her. Anger builds in me again, but I somehow fight it down along with the sliver of fear tingeing the edges.

"I suppose you're right. She does rock the fish face a little."

Tyler winks and places his hand on my upper back, leading me into an elevator. "I'm pretty sure there's an Anti-Trout group in this building. I'm even more certain Aaron is the president."

I cover my mouth with my hand. "No, that would be his mom."

Tyler laughs loudly. "Oh, Aunt Carly. Yes, she'd be the founder." He sobers when he sees the receptionist looking at him pointedly. "Don't laugh. Don't speak. Don't do fucking anything remotely human while she's around," he whispers.

I frown but stay silent as he leads me to the desk.

"Mr. Stone. I trust you know where you're going."

"I do. Thank you, Darla. Is Jenna here?"

"She's waiting for you."

Tyler turns and takes me to another elevator without responding. I feel the receptionist's eyes following both of us and burning into my back. I turn, and her eyes are filled with annoyance and hatred.

"You fucked her, didn't you?"

Another laugh leaves him. "How did you know that?"

"The sharp voice and eyes that could kill might have given it away."

"Damn. She was a clingy bitch. I'm not into that shit."

I raise my eyebrows at his back, following him down a long corridor. "What are you, a sex addict?"

He doesn't answer, just pushes open a door and hits me with a shit-eating grin that answers my question. I don't believe he and Aaron could be any more different if they tried.

"Sit over here on the sofa," Tyler directs me. "This is a boudoir and lingerie shoot, so we'll be using the bed and the window." He points to the large window that overlooks London. I peek out as I walk past, noticing Big Ben standing tall across the river, and take my seat on the bright red sofa.

Tyler runs back and forth across the room, adjusting lights and setting up his camera. Other people run around as much as he does, and a girl with a clipboard offers me a coffee. I accept and sit back in the plush cushions, enjoying the anonymity. None of these people have any idea who I am.

That stops the second a tall, raven-haired girl walks into the room wrapped in a thick robe.

"Who is that?" she asks, pointing at me.

"Jenna, it's lovely to see you again." Tyler kisses her cheek.

"Keep your charm in your trousers, Tyler Stone. Who is the girl on the sofa?"

"That would be the boss's girlfriend."

Jenna looks at me, and I smile.

"Does that mean he's finally divorced from Naomi?"

Tyler nods.

Jenna sighs. "Thank god for that. I couldn't stand her. Coming into shoots and acting like she was in charge because she was hot in America for, like, six months. She thought she was Naomi *Campbell* or something." She snorts.

"See?" Tyler turns to me. "She has her own little fan club."

Jenna approaches me and holds out her hand. "Jenna Kelly."

I stand and shake her hand. "Dayton Black."

"You're not here to direct my shoot, are you?"

"No." I laugh. "I'm just watching. I won't say a word."

She nods and smiles with nude lips. "Perfect." She turns to Tyler. "Tyler Stone, stop looking at my arse. You're only entitled to do that through a camera, you lecherous git."

Something tells me that Tyler Stone has a much, much bigger reputation than either he or Aaron has let on.

$\mathcal{C}\mathbin{\text{\large)}}\mathbin{\text{\large (}}\mathcal{D}$

Modeling is a funny business, and it's easy to see where the incessant bitchiness comes from. Unless you're someone familiar with the jealous flicking of eyes and thinning of lips, you wouldn't notice the way the girls tending to Jenna were looking at her.

I spent the majority of the shoot watching and wondering why they were looking at her that way—until I realized. She's beautiful, she's confident, and she's not afraid to show it. It's a lethal combination. A recipe for jealousy and hatred.

"Dayton?" Tyler calls through to me from the front room in a pained whine.

"What?" I reply, strolling into the room. "What's up?"

He sits back on his heels and looks at me. "I have no fucking idea what I'm choosing here."

I look at the vast spread of photos in front of him. "Why aren't you doing this on the computer? There's what, one hundred photos here?"

"Hundred and fourteen."

"I thought you guys only printed when you had them narrowed down."

He sighs and leans back. He winces when his ass hits the floor. "These are the narrowed-down images."

"Well, shit."

"Mhmm. Be a love and get me a beer."

I raise my eyebrows.

"Please."

"That's better." I walk into the kitchen and uncap a bottle for him. Damn, I might as well get myself a glass of wine. I know I'm going to be kneeling on that floor for fuck knows how long.

I pour mine and stroll back into the front room. Tyler has his laptop open on the sofa now, music pouring softly from the speakers. I hand him the beer and sit next to him, adjusting my sweatpants as I do.

"Jenna is the best and worst kind of model to work with. It's impossible to pick her final images because they're so fucking good."

"And you have a crush on her."

"I'm not denying I'd love to rip these blue panties off her. Fuck me." He shoves a picture in my face. "Seen this, Day? She's sexy as shit."

I snatch the photo and throw it onto the floor. "Focus, you douche. Thinking about having sex with your model isn't going to help you in this situation."

Tyler shifts. "You're right. Help me."

"Fine." I sift through the photos with him.

He's right. Jenna is beautiful, although not in a classical way. Her nose is a little on the large side, her eyes may be too wide for her face, and her forehead is a little small, but combined with her porcelain skin, naturally pouty lips, and black hair, it works.

She also oozes sex and temptation. Sultry looks beneath her lashes, lips parted just the right amount, her back arched perfectly.

No wonder Tyler wants to fuck her.

"How do you do this job? In front of girls like this, dressed like this, and stay sane?" My eyes find his brown ones.

He looks at me seriously. "I wank a lot."

"Wank?"

"I spend an unhealthy amount of time in my room getting myself off."

I stop and stare at him. *Shit. Is he serious?*

He is. He fucking is.

"Way too much information, Ty."

"You asked." He shrugs.

"I'm sorry, how old are you again? Was it twenty-six or sixteen?"

"Twenty-six with the sexual temperament of a sixteen-year-old."

I asked for that, really. I shake my head and filter through the last of the pictures, handing a small stack to him. He takes them and flicks through him.

"Thanks. You're amazing at this. Ever thought of working in Stone?"

I push up onto the sofa, wine glass in hand, and sit back with a groan. "Not you, too."

Tyler holds up a finger and packs the photos away. He puts his laptop on the floor between us, grabs his beer, and sits at the other end of the sofa. "Aaron being a pushy knob again?"

"If by 'knob' you mean 'asshole,' then kind of. He wants me to model for them."

He looks at me like I'm crazy. "What's the problem? I saw your pictures. You have it, Dayton."

I shake my head and tell him what I explained to Aaron last night. I won't ride his coattails. I won't be somebody just because I have the easy road in.

Tyler stares at me for a long moment. "Would you let me shoot you?"

"What?"

"Hear me out." He holds up a hand. "And fuck, don't tell Aaron. You want to do it by yourself—let me shoot you. I'll compile your portfolio and send it to some agencies in Seattle." He shrugs like it's so simple. And it is. If you're not dating the CEO of Stone Advertising and Modeling.

"He'd kill both of us. I don't know if I could."

"Think about it, all right? You're here for another week, so don't dismiss it just yet. One of the upstairs rooms is a studio."

I can't help the way my lips tug to one side. "I don't think I want to ask."

"I'll clean through before you use it." He winks and takes a drink. "Will you think about it?"

Because it wouldn't be awkward or anything. For some reason, though, I find myself nodding in agreement. I find myself promising that I will.

"Great. Now you can tell me what had you spacing out last night at dinner."

I look away. "I have no idea what you're talking about."

"And why you freeze every time someone says Naomi's name."

I say nothing.

"I'm a photographer, Dayton. *Body* is my second language."

"I don't like her. Would you?" I turn back to him, a Mia-mask on my face. Unaffected. Not caring. "She's Aaron's ex-wife and, by all accounts, a total bitch. That's all there is to it."

"You're a bloody awful liar."

"I'm not lying."

Tyler shrugs a shoulder and grabs the remote. "Suit yourself, love. Don't forget I know her. She's more than just a bitch on steroids. She's a bitch on crack."

He flicks the top of his laptop down with his foot and turns on the TV. Some English drama I don't know blares out, and I stare blankly at the screen.

I can't tell him. I could ignore him now, watch this stupid show where they drop half of their letters when they speak, and let the evening pass by until Aaron returns from a late meeting.

But I don't want to. It's barely been a week and already it's eating me from the inside out. My conversation with Naomi is burning away at me. The guilt is going to coil tighter and tighter in my stomach until I'm sure it'll unwind, taking everything else I have with it, and I won't just admit the secret. I'm afraid it'll go so far that the only way I'll be able to get it out will be by screaming it until my throat is raw.

"She came to my house last week." I rub my thumb across my top lip harshly, looking everywhere but at Tyler. "She knows…something about me not many people do. I don't know how she does, but she does. She's not happy with the divorce settlement, and she's using that against me."

"She's blackmailing you?"

I nod slowly. "Aaron doesn't know, and I don't want him to find out either." I bring my eyes to Tyler's. "Please don't tell him. I don't know why I'm telling you, except that it's killing me."

He says nothing for a long moment. Then he jerks his head in agreement. "She wants money?"

"A lot of it."

"How much?"

"Too much. That's how much."

He reaches over and rests his hand on my shoulder. "How much?"

I close my eyes. "Two and a half million."

Tyler draws in a sharp breath and withdraws his hand. "What could she know that's worth that much money?"

"Something that could destroy everything Brandon, and now Aaron, have ever worked for."

"I don't believe it's that bad."

I put my glass on the side and stand, turning my back to the man who looks so much like the one I love. The one I'm trying to protect.

"Dayton."

"This is ridiculous. I've known you for two days. I have no idea why I just told you that. Forget it. I'm going to bed."

Tyler grabs my arm before I can leave the room. "You told me because you need help, and I'm guessing I'm the closest thing you have."

I don't reply. I don't know if he is or not. He's just so easy to talk to and someone who makes you want to tell him everything.

"What could possibly be so bad it would destroy Stone?"

My mouth goes dry, along with my lips, and I make a vain attempt at wetting them with my tongue. My throat constricts around the sudden lump in it, and my heart pounds so hard that it's threatening to break free of the restraints of my chest.

"I can't help you if I don't know everything," Tyler says softly.

I clench my hands into fists. My nails dig into my sweaty palms, and I squeeze my eyes shut. "Promise you won't think any less of me."

"My cousin, my best friend, loves you. I thought the world of you before I knew you."

I take those words and I hold on to them with everything. I can't believe I'm about to do this—tell him who I am. What my job is.

Am. Were. Is. Was.

I don't know the difference now.

My eyes sting with tears. "Naomi knows the truth about who I am."

"I don't get it."

"I'm a call girl."

Chapter Fourteen

Silence lingers heavily after my words. The only faint sound is that of my heavy breathing as my chest heaves.

"An escort. A whore. A prostitute. Whatever you call it. I get paid for sex on a regular basis."

My words seem to echo in the large living room. They bounce off the walls and ring out in my ears. I cover my face with my hands, frozen in place, the repercussions of my revelation flooding my body.

Shock. Disbelief.

Utter fear.

I expect Tyler to push me from him in disgust. To tear his hand from my arm and recoil from me. But he doesn't. He puts his other hand on my other arm and steers me back into the room, sitting me on the sofa.

He holds up a finger and disappears into the kitchen, returning with my wine bottle and a bottle of vodka. "Thought this was needed," he mutters, shaking the vodka bottle.

I smile weakly and watch as he pours me some wine. "Surprise, right?"

"Aaron knows?"

"How do you think we met again so coincidentally after seven years?"

"You're the girl from Paris? Fuck. That puts a new spin on things."

I look at him, and he's rubbing his chin contemplatively. His eyes are narrowed, his lips pursed.

"How does it?"

"Naomi despised the girl from Paris. She knew she could never be that person. She never knew you, but you were her worst enemy. She truly believed if you never existed, Aaron would love her."

"She loves him?"

"In her own way. I think it's more possession than anything. She wanted him, but you always had him." Tyler shrugs and takes a swig from his beer. "Any idea what you're going to do?"

"I wish. I don't know how I'm supposed to get that kind of money."

"You'd pay her off?"

"It's paying or losing Aaron. I can't do that." I hug my knees to my chest as the idea stabs through my heart.

"Tell him."

I shake my head. "No. I still have three weeks to try and do something about it. If I haven't by then, I'll tell him."

"You could just go to the police. I don't know about you guys, but blackmail is illegal here." He looks at me pointedly.

"That's too easy." I run my finger around the rim of my glass. "She'll have guessed that would be my first move and will have some bullshit plan in place. She's probably not even in America anymore. She's not stupid."

Tyler meets my eyes, and in his, I see the brutal reality of this situation. I'm fucked. I have so many options, but none of them are possible or plausible. That doesn't change the fact I feel a little lighter from telling him.

"Dayton, Naomi isn't stupid, but she isn't exactly smart either. She's fucking with your head, and when Aaron finds out, he's going to go apeshit. People don't fuck with the people he cares about."

"He said that to me once," I whisper.

"And they especially do not fuck with you. I was there when he fired her. Believe me—they don't fuck with you and get away with it."

I swallow. "I'm going to bed."

Tyler downs his beer and stands. "I'm going out. I saw Aaron's schedule earlier. He'll be back late. Go get some sleep, and we'll both wake up tomorrow like this conversation never happened. Agreed?"

I nod.

"Good. Now I'm going to find some poor girl to bang this shit out of my system with."

The front door closes with a bang, and I sink my fingers into my hair. *Fucking hell.* Why do I feel like I've just made my clusterfuck of royal fuckery worse?

❦

The feeling of kisses being peppered across my shoulder draws me from my heavy sleep. Aaron's hand sliding up my stomach, his fingers splayed, ignites a red-hot desire my body recognizes before my drowsy mind does.

I smile and roll onto my back, blinking up at his gorgeous blue eyes. "Morning."

"Morning." He kisses along my jaw, shifting his body closer to me. His erection presses against the side of my thigh, hard and ready, and he wraps his arm around my back. He flips me onto my side easily, his hand sliding down to my ass.

My hips are pulled into his as he touches his lips to mine. I slide my hands up his chest and wind my fingers in his hair, savoring the feel of his lazy yet deep kisses. I hook my leg over his, and Aaron guides it up over his hip. My center is fully against him now, and I can feel his rock-hard erection rubbing me through the material of our underwear.

I ping his waistband. He nips my bottom lip in response, sucking on it lightly before taking it between his teeth once again and tugging. Each tug of it evokes a tug in my lower stomach, one that reaches my clit.

"Take 'em off," I mutter through kisses, flicking his waistband again.

He smiles against me. "Patience."

He unclasps my bra before I can respond and takes one of my breasts in his hand. He rubs my nipple until it hardens beneath his touch then pulls it lightly. I gasp and grind my hips against him. *Sweet Jesus.* He repeats this several times before moving my bra away and sealing his lips around my nipple.

The roughness of his tongue against the tender flesh there and the hardness of his cock rubbing my clit make me moan loudly. Aaron tastes my nipple almost aggressively, leaning me back just so he can give the other the same treatment. I arch into him, needing more of his touch.

His fingers slip beneath my panties and he slides them over my ass. I move my leg so he can remove them and kick them off when they reach my ankles. When he moves to pull my leg back over him, I grab the band of his boxers and tug hard.

"Fuck no. Lose 'em, baby."

He laughs quietly. "Go ahead, woman. Take them off."

I do—with a little too much vigor. Aaron smirks at my enthusiasm. Something I quickly wipe off his face when I wrap my hand around his cock.

"Something funny?" I ask, rubbing a drop of pre-cum around the tip with my thumb.

"Yeah." He pulls my hand away from him, loops my leg over his waist, and positions himself at my entrance. "How you think you have a semblance of control in this is beyond me."

"Is that so?" I take his lips with mine.

He puts two fingers between our mouths. "We can finish this two ways, Dayton. You can cooperate and we'll go nice and slow, or you can push it and we'll go hard and fast. Understood?"

A smirk curves my lips and I wriggle against him, fighting back the moan that wants to leave me at the sensation. "I'm not feeling very agreeable this morning, Mr. Stone." I reach down and gently cup his balls with my other hand, slowly dragging my hand to his cock and along the underside of it.

Aaron snatches my hands away, grabs my hips, and pushes me down onto him in one swift movement that makes me throw my head back. My muscles tighten around him at the sudden intrusion, but it's more pleasure than pain. It's more complete and utter fulfillment than it is an invasion.

"You asked for it," he whispers in my ear, tangling his fingers in my hair. He tugs on it, pulling my head back a little farther. Slowly, he eases himself from me until only the tip of him is inside me.

My chest heaves as I wait. I know what's coming. I know his hard and his fast and I fucking love them both.

It surprises me despite my expecting it. The angle he enters me from ensures that he's buried right to the hilt, hitting the end of me, and I don't fight the cry that leaves me. He sucks lightly on my pulse point as he moves inside me with the ease of a man who's memorized every inch of my pussy. He flexes his hips at the right time and hits the right spots, eliciting desperate cries from me.

My fingers dig into his back. "Fuck. Aaron."

He tilts my hips slightly and gets deeper than I thought possible. "What's the matter, baby? Can't take it?"

I half-moan, half-laugh a response. "I can take you. Oh, god." I close my eyes briefly as my whole body jerks in pleasure.

"What were you saying?" His teeth graze across my neck, and I shiver as he stills inside me to let me speak.

I bring my lips to his ear. "Asking. I was asking."

"Mhmm?" He flexes inside me, rubbing that tender spot that sends a wave of heat through me. "What for?"

"Harder. Faster. Deeper." I pull my body against his. "*Please.*"

He flips me onto my back and lifts my hips. His eyes are an odd mix of electric and smoky blue when they find mine. He says nothing as he leans over me, my hips still in the air, and thrusts into me powerfully.

"Like that?"

"Mmm."

"Is this how you want me to fuck you?"

"Yes."

He kisses along my jaw, still moving inside me, never letting up his pace. His breathing is as heavy as mine, but I can feel the tightness in his body as he holds back. As he gives me what I want.

"You want me to fuck you so deep there isn't a part of my cock not inside your gorgeous, tight cunt? Is that it, Dayton?" My name rolls off his tongue in a husky tone that makes my body hyperactive. "You want it so all you can feel is the way I move inside you?" He slides one hand between us and presses his thumb to my clit. "So when you come you see stars and take me with you?"

"Yes!" I don't know what I'm yessing. It could be his words or the orgasm threatening to wrack my body.

"What was that? I didn't hear it."

"Fuck!" My whole body goes rigid and I push myself against him. My hips are still as I give myself over to the orgasm washing over me.

He still pounds into me, pushing it to the very edge of pleasure until he finds his own with a deep groan of my name.

I cling to him like a koala, my limbs wrapped completely around him. Both of us are covered in a sheen of sweat, and I can feel his cock twitching inside me. Aaron takes a deep breath, and I push against him before he can collapse on me.

"What the…"

I grin down at him. "What if I'd told you I wanted it hard from the moment I woke up?"

He narrows his eyes.

"Then who had the control over that, hmm?" I drag his bottom lip between my teeth. "Don't ever give me the choice, because I'll choose hard and fast every fucking time."

Aaron slaps my ass, his hand connecting with my bare skin in a sharp sound that rings out around the room. "You're a bad girl, Dayton."

"You haven't seen anything yet." I climb from him and he slaps my other butt cheek. "What? Was that one feeling left out or something?" I hit him with a glare, rubbing it.

Fuck. That shit hurts.

His eyes flash dangerously and he pulls me back down on top of him. He slowly rubs my stinging skin, his fingers tracing the curve of my ass and dipping between my legs, making me clench them together.

"Next time you pull this shit, you should remember that I'm not averse to spanking you."

My lips part at the force of his kiss, and I watch him as he drops me off him and saunters into the adjoining bathroom. *Damn, he really does have a nice ass.*

"What if I like spanking?" I call after him, feeling like I need some payback for those two slaps.

"Do you?"

"Depends if you're fucking me from behind or not."

He appears in the doorway, still naked and still with an erection. "Is there a preference as to where you'd like to be fucked from behind?"

I raise an eyebrow. "Are you seriously planning this?"

"Planning to surprise you."

I sit up and study him. He's deadly serious. Fine. After another moment of looking into his eyes, I get up and stroll into the bathroom after him. He watches me, never taking his eyes from me.

"Well?"

I turn on the shower and step inside. The tiles are cold against my hands as I flatten them against the wall and stick out my ass. I look over my shoulder at him and give it a wriggle, shooting him a wink when his eyes take on that dark, smoldering heat.

He joins me in the shower, and after rubbing his hand over my butt, he pulls me into him. I rest my hands on his chest and look up at him.

"We'll see," he murmurs, lowering his face to mine. "Until then though…"

He pulls the door shut and turns up the water temperature, spinning me into the wall.

Oh boy.

Chapter Fifteen

"Tyler! Where the bloody hell are you, you ignorant bastard?" a woman's voice shrieks through the house. It's followed by the slamming of the door.

I jolt, sitting straight up on the sofa and placing my Kindle down next to me. *What the...?*

"Tyler!"

"Jesus, Tessa!" Tyler yells down the stairs. "What did I do this time?"

"You slept with my bridesmaid, you absolute knobhead!"

Oops.

Tyler appears in the hallway in my line of sight, wearing a pair of jeans and a T-shirt. His hair is still dripping wet, and I watch as he runs his tongue across his bottom lip.

"Did I?"

"Yes! Two nights ago!"

He stops for a moment and scratches his jaw. "Shit. What was her name?"

"Tyler!" Tessa steps forward and shoves him in the chest. "One thing. That's all I fucking asked of you. Don't sleep with my bridesmaids! It was all you had to do. The only damn thing and you couldn't even do that."

"Now, Tess—"

"No. No. Don't 'Now, Tess,' me, you prick."

"In my defense, sis, you have, like, ten bridesmaids and they all look the same."

I feel the heat of her stare from here.

"They do not all look the same! And her name was Lilly!"

"Lilly, Lilly…" Tyler claps his hands once. "Oh, Lilly!"

Tessa smacks her hands over her eyes. "Why couldn't I get a normal brother? Why did my parents have to give me one who can't keep it in his pants for his own sister's wedding?"

"It's not that bad."

"Not that bad? Not that bad?" Her voice rises a few octaves. "I get married in five days, and Mum and Dad don't fly in until tomorrow. I have a thousand things to do, so imagine how delighted I was to travel across London this morning and find one of my bridesmaids crying because my brother didn't call her back."

"Hey. I never promised to call her."

"Oh, you are such a giant arse, Tyler!"

The front door opens and closes. "I should have guessed you'd be here when I heard the shrieking a block away," Aaron says dryly.

I cross my legs Indian-style. So I'm enjoying the drama. Shoot me. It certainly beats my book.

"Aaron. Fantastic. Does it get better?" Tessa cries.

"Jeez, Tessa. Do we need to call someone to calm you down?" Tyler asks.

"No need, man. London Zoo put out a call earlier. Their Bridezilla escaped," Aaron retorts.

Both of the guys laugh, and I frown.

"You two are utter assholes."

Everyone stops and turns to me. Tessa's eyebrows shoot up, her lips parting.

"Ooh, is this…"

"Tessa, meet Dayton." Tyler waves an arm between us. "Dayton, meet my lovely twin sister."

Tessa springs forward and wraps me in a hug. Oh okay. Okay.

"I'm so happy to meet you! I've heard so much about you from Mum, who heard it from Aunt Carly... But yes." She coughs and sits next to me, her earlier anger seemingly dissipated. "Gosh, you're pretty. Aaron, why didn't you tell me how beautiful she is?"

My cheeks flush. Geez, this family has a thing about making me blush.

Tyler stuffs his hands in his pockets, reminiscent of the cocky teenage boy he obviously was. "Yeah, Aaron. Why didn't you tell her?"

"You." Tessa turns on him and points a stern finger. "Shut it. I'm not done with you. Aaron?"

"Tess, the last time we talked, you were telling me my wife was an utter bitch who had more Botox than brains." Aaron shucks off his jacket and drops it over the back of a chair before sitting. "That was two and a half years ago. You've avoided me ever since."

"I've avoided you and my brother," she sighs. "Individually, you're professional businessmen. Together? You're knobs. Utter knobs."

Tyler frowns. "I took it earlier because you were pissed but watch your mouth, Tess."

"The day I watch my mouth is the day you watch your dick."

I disguise my snort with a cough. Tessa winks at me and turns back to Aaron.

"I'm glad you divorced her, by the way. If you'd tried bringing her to my wedding, she would have conveniently ended up in the river that runs in front of the house." Tessa sniffs. "A place my brother may just end up."

"What did he do now?"

Tessa launches into an explanation, much quieter than before but just as passionate. I can see the ire in her eyes. The anger is practically vibrating around her, and she takes a deep breath when she finishes.

Tyler scuttles from the room and reappears a minute later with a bottle of wine and two glasses. He sets them on the table in front of us, his smile tinged with shame.

"I'm driving," Tessa snaps.

"I'll take you home and you can get your car tomorrow."

"Believe me, Ty. The last place I want to be right now is in a car with you."

"I'll have a car collect you," Aaron butts in. "For the love of God, Tess, just drink the wine and calm down."

She takes a deep breath, and I hand her a filled glass. She shoots me a small smile, taking it, and downs half of it in one go. I raise my eyebrows at Aaron, and he smirks in response. Yep. I see what he meant when he said she was a proper lady.

Wine-glugging aside.

"Ty, can you just try not to sleep with any more of my wedding party, please? I'm going crazy here without Mum to help me, and I just don't need any more stress."

Tyler sighs. "I'm sorry. But next time, can you make sure they all wear badges saying 'Tessa's bridesmaid' so I don't do it?"

The look she gives him is so heated it could set ice on fire.

"Okay, okay." He holds up his hands. "I'll behave."

"Thank you." She closes her eyes and sits back.

"Hey!" he cries after a moment. "I've got an idea."

"God no," Aaron mutters.

"Why doesn't Dayton help you? With the wedding?"

No no no no no. My eyes widen. "I, uh, um…"

"Oh! Would you?" Tessa turns to me, her eyes pleading. "It's just until Mum and Aunt Carly get in tomorrow night."

"I really have no idea what I'm doing with a wedding," I admit. "I'd be in your way."

"So? It'll be good practice."

I look at Aaron, my eyes even wider, but he just smirks. *What. The. Fuck.* No. No marriages. No nothing.

"Please!" Tessa takes my hands.

I meet everyone's eyes in turns, finally resting on Tessa's brown ones, and sigh in defeat. "Okay. I'll do my best."

"Thank you!" she squeals and hugs me again.

I pat her back with one hand and point in Aaron's direction with the other. "Don't get any ideas, buddy," I warn him.

He smirks again.

I drop onto the velvet seat at a table in the bar. Never again. Never again am I helping anyone iron out wedding details.

Shit. Today makes me want anything *but* marriage. Not that the thought has crossed my mind, but still. From finalizing flowers to a last-minute buffet change and a meltdown over the fact that Tessa's shoes still haven't been delivered, I'm all wedding-ed out.

I rub my fingers against my temples and let out a long breath.

"Don't tell her I said this, but there's a reason we waited until now to fly over." Carly sits next to me and places a glass of wine in front of me.

"When I get back, I'm going to string Tyler from a streetlight by a very private part of his anatomy." I sip the wine. "I mean, she's lovely, but wow."

Carly smiles and pats my thigh. "Don't worry, honey. I have it on good authority that you'll barely be able to finish… Oh, never mind."

A hand rests on my neck, and I turn, staring straight into Aaron's face. "What are you doing here?"

He smiles slowly. "I'm coming to steal you."

I raise an eyebrow. "What if I'm happy here?"

"Then I'm stealing you anyway." He leans over the back of the chair and kisses Carly's cheek. "Mom."

"Son." She beams at him. "Go on, Dayton. Tessa won't mind." She winks, and I shrug.

"If you're sure?"

"Positive."

I nod and finish the glass of wine. Aaron rolls his eyes, and I pause before putting my jacket on. "What? It's rude to leave wine in a glass if you're leaving."

His lips curve slightly, and he wraps an arm around my waist. "See you at the wedding, Mom."

Aaron leads us from the bar and straight into a waiting car.

"What are we doing?"

"You'll see." He takes my hand and rubs his thumb across my knuckles. I watch him as he brings our hands to his mouth and kisses my fingers one by one.

"Aren't you supposed to be in a meeting?"

"Yes, I am. I canceled it."

"Why?"

He cups the side of my face. "Because, beautiful woman, I missed you. I have all day tomorrow free, but I want you right now. The meeting wasn't important, so it can wait. You can never wait, and it's not an option for me where you're concerned."

I turn my face into his palm with a smile. Sometimes he says the right words in the right way and they warm my whole body. They give me a glimpse of the feelings he's yet to say outright, and it's comforting. It solidifies my reasoning for being here, for forgiving him, for staying in the place my heart cries so desperately for.

And now I have him to myself for just over a day.

"Did you miss me?" he asks, leaning into me.

"*Tu me manques,*" I whisper, kissing his wrist.

Aaron's cheek is soft as he rests his face alongside mine and curls his fingers around the back of my neck. I breathe in his scent, woody and so very masculine. So distinctly him. It wraps around me in a cocooning blanket, making my heart pound and my blood rush through my veins in the most comforting way.

"I have a surprise for you."

"I hate surprises," I mutter.

"Not this one. I promise you'll love it."

The car stops, and he pulls me out after him. I stop him before he starts walking and bring my hands to his neck. I undo his tie, sliding the silk around his neck until it's balled in my hand, and tuck it into my purse.

"You're not working now." I flick open his top button and brush my fingertips across his chest. "No tie."

He smiles and kisses the end of my nose. "No tie. Come on, Bambi. I want to show you something."

He links his fingers through mine and tugs me after him. I look around us, noting the River Thames to my left. A small gasp leaves me, and I pull my hand from Aaron's, walking to the wall that separates the river and the embankment. I rest my arms on it and lean forward, looking down the river at the reflections in it in the night.

London is still buzzing with life at eight p.m. There are still bright slivers of white and yellow in the building opposite me, casting an eerie glow that's so beautiful onto the water. The face of Big Ben is lit up like a beacon high above the buildings surrounding it.

"That's the Houses of Parliament." Aaron points at the building I was just looking at. "If you walk just down from it, you'll be at Downing Street, where the Prime Minister lives. If you go in the other direction and walk a little, you'll arrive at Buckingham Palace."

I nod. "Tyler took me to see it. I wish we had more time to see everything else though. I'm kind of greedy. I want to see it all just in case I never get to come back."

Aaron takes my hand. "I promise you. You'll be back. More times than you can count."

I smile and bring our clasped hands to my cheek. "Really?"

"I promised, didn't I?" He half-grins and walks backward. "And we have all day tomorrow. We'll start early and go wherever you want to go, okay?"

"Really? Anywhere?"

"Anywhere. But now, I want to show you it all."

"All of London?"

He nods, and I raise my eyes to the majestic wheel behind him. The London Eye.

"Oh!"

His half grin becomes a full one. "Surprise."

"It definitely is!" I cover my mouth with my hand as he leads me to it and we step into one of the clear pods. "Oh, I've always wanted to go on this."

I shrug off my jacket and leave it on the bench in the middle, walking to the edge of it. I press my fingers against the thick glass in front of me as we move around slowly, eager to see everything. I do—I want it all. I want to see this gorgeous city spread before me in the night.

"We came to London right after we'd been to Paris," Aaron says out of the blue. His words cut through the easy silence that descended between us in the wake of my excitement.

"Really?"

"Yes. Dad had an important meeting I couldn't attend, so Mom asked me if I'd accompany her shopping. I agreed, and at the end of the day, after dinner, she brought me here. It was marginally lighter on our journey, but I hated every second of it."

I turn to him. "Why? How could you hate this?"

He crosses the pod to me and brushes the backs of his fingers down my cheeks. "I spent the whole time thinking of you and how much you would have loved to have seen it. I spent the whole time wondering what it would be like to hold you in my arms and stare out at the city with you the way we did at the top of the Eiffel Tower."

I take a step to the side, into his hold, and relax into the familiar way his arms wrap around my waist from behind. "Now you can find out."

His lips brush my forehead. "Finally. I can finally take you to all the places I thought I saw you in and do everything I wanted to all those years ago. But most importantly, I can take you home at the end of every single day and know you're not going anywhere."

I can't bring myself to respond to it. I don't know if I'm ready for that, no matter how natural it feels. It doesn't matter that we've barely spent a night apart the whole time we've been together—that's a final thing I can't commit to. Not until the past is fully behind us.

"This is beautiful," I whisper, changing the direction of the conversation.

And it is. London, stretched out before me, completely uninterrupted. Lights upon lights in winding patterns of crazy interconnecting streets. I can see everywhere. There's Camden and Soho and Piccadilly. The colorful lights of Piccadilly Circus are perhaps some of the brightest I can see despite how small they are from our place in the sky.

It's beautiful. More beautiful than I imagined it would be, and far more beautiful than it would be had I seen all of this from the ground. The bird's-eye view is breathtaking.

"I haven't been on this since," Aaron says softly into my ear, brushing his nose against my cheek.

"Really? How many times have you been here?"

"More than I care to count. I could never come back on here though. I was always too afraid it would make me think of you. It's exactly why, whenever I went to Paris, all I really did was work. I haven't been up the Tower since the day you left."

I wet my lips. "Do you think we'll ever go back?"

Aaron spins me in his arms and looks down at me, his eyes full of raw emotion that reaches out and takes hold of every part of my body. "I will take you anywhere you want to go, whenever you want to go. I can do that, and I will. All you have to do is ask me, Dayton. I'll never say no to anything that will make you happy."

"But Paris seems to be both a blessing and a curse to our relationship." I run my thumb along his jaw, his stubble lightly scratching it. "Twice it's made us and twice it's broken us."

Aaron brings his hands from my back to my face and tilts my head back so my eyes are on his. He looks at me with a scary kind of certainty, the hold of his gaze too strong to even consider looking away.

"Dayton, nothing can break us. It can crack us, but it can't break us. What you feel—what I feel—is far too strong for anything to tear it apart. If it weren't, neither of us would be here. We would have been able to walk away and forget everything we've shared. This isn't two people clinging on to the past and what might have been. This is two people propelled into the here and now *because* of the past, and it's them looking to what could be in the future. There isn't a day that passes that I don't think of my life with you. And every thought makes me more determined to have it." He covers my mouth with his in a warm, honest kiss that sends tingles through my body to my toes. "The next time we go to Paris, I promise you, we'll be leaving stronger than ever."

I gaze at him with wide, wet eyes. "You promise?" My words are a whisper.

"I promise. There's a reason they say the third time's a charm."

"Maybe we just needed a couple of tries before we got it right."

Aaron smiles, one that lights up his whole face and brings a sparkle to his eyes. "And this time, it won't go wrong, sweetheart. I won't let it."

I squeeze my eyes shut as he takes my mouth again and wish. I wish for him to be right. I wish and hope that this time it won't, that this time it will be the kind of perfect we've been holding out for. The kind of perfect little girls dream of after watching too many Disney movies and, later, too many chick-flick movies where the guy always wins the girl.

But the threat nudges at the back of my mind, and I know that, if we have any chance of making it this time, it's going to cost me.

Chapter Sixteen

I slip my hand into Aaron's and curl my other around his arm, leaning into his side. He smiles down at me and kisses the top of my head, pulling me into the hustle and bustle of Camden market.

It's not the kind of place I ever imagined him to go. With its endless stalls of vintage clothing, designers no one knows, and knickknacks, it doesn't fit in with his M.O. Oxford Street? Yes. A thousand times, yes. Camden market? Never.

There are people everywhere. And I mean everywhere. I push myself right into Aaron to avoid being shoved from every direction. He shakes my hands off his arm and wraps it around my waist, curling me right into him.

It doesn't make a bit of difference, but I definitely prefer it. The warmth from the sun beating down on us is nothing compared to the warmth that emanates from his body.

"You surprise me."

Aaron leans down and speaks over the various levels of chatter around us. "Why?"

"I was expecting you to whisk me off to a ridiculously expensive store and force me into a fitting room like you did in Italy."

"Do you want me to?"

"Hell no." I laugh. "Nice try though, Mr. Stone."

"Perhaps. Although we will be going somewhere later where I intend to spend a lot of money on you."

I look at him from the corner of my eyes. "Where?"

"There's no need to sound so suspicious. I can guarantee it's a place you'll be completely at home in."

"Where?"

He taps my hip. "You're a little small without heels. Do you know that?"

I smack his stomach. "Aaron! Don't change the subject! And I am not short."

His lips spread into a grin. "I know, but you're a good few inches shorter."

"This isn't the conversation we're having. I want to know where you're taking me later. And I want to know now."

"Is that a demand, Miss Black?"

"It's a requirement I know, Mr. Stone. Or I'm not walking another step." I stop and put some extra oomph into stamping my foot down.

Aaron chuckles quietly and stands in front of me. I put my hands on my hips and stare him down.

"God, you're sexy when you get that fire in your eyes," he murmurs huskily, cupping my chin.

"Don't try and seduce me."

"I thought you didn't get seduced."

I run my finger down his chest. "Don't play dumb with me, baby. Now tell me."

His blue eyes bore into mine for a long moment, and he sighs. "Come on. We'll go now."

That's not telling me. Still, I let him link his fingers through mine and tug me after him and back to the car. He pulls out his cell and informs someone that we'll be there early as we drive through the streets, and I press myself against the window, trying to work out where we're going.

"Oxford Street?" I squeak. "You said no Oxford Street."

"Incorrect. I said no ridiculously expensive store. This time," he adds under his breath. "The store I'm taking you to is here."

I narrow my eyes and grab my purse before slamming the car door. Aaron takes it from my hand and throws it back into the car.

"You won't need that, Dayton."

"I might want it."

"Don't be so fucking difficult. You don't need it. Want it or not. Now move your sexy little ass or I'll be forced to haul you down this street over my shoulder."

"Is that a demand?"

He spins me so forcefully that I fall into his hard body. "You're pushing it, woman. Move. Now."

I smirk. "I don't know where I'm going. Remember?"

"You're sure earning that spanking. I'll tell you that much." He flattens his hand on my back and forces me forward. I smile to myself as he steers me to wherever we're going.

I take in each storefront as we stroll down the iconic street. I recognize hardly any of them—and I especially don't recognize the one we stop in front of.

But I do recognize what it sells.

"You're bringing me to buy lingerie?"

Aaron places his mouth by my ear. "And the whole store is yours for one hour."

I raise an eyebrow. "You think one hour in a lingerie store is enough? Oh, baby. You have a lot to learn."

He pushes the door open and we step inside the empty store. One wall is covered in baby dolls and chemises, one with bras and panties, and another holds a doorway to a section at the back labeled "18+ only."

Well, it doesn't take a genius to work out that that's where the toys are.

The bright colors assault my senses and a streak of excitement fizzles through my body. Lingerie shopping is my favorite thing ever, but in a store I've never been in? This is a whole new level of heaven.

"Go wild," Aaron whispers in my ear, lightly squeezing my ass.

I walk to the wall of bras and trail my fingers across a few different styles. T-shirt, balconette, push-up... There's lace and frills and trims, and oh, God. I can't.

I turn back to Aaron and shake my head.

He raises his eyebrows. "I'm not taking no for an answer."

I shake my head again. "I can't. I don't know if you realize how financially destructive I am in this environment."

He walks to me and pulls me close. "It doesn't matter. One day, everything I own will be yours, so you might as well spend it now."

My breath catches. "You have to get me to move in with you before anything remotely close to that happens."

He smirks and puts his hands on my shoulders. He turns me so I'm facing the underwear again. "For the record, I like that turquoise bra with the black lace. And the matching panties. They have my mind spinning with all the ways I could take you out of them." His lips brush my earlobe. "Just in case you were so inclined."

I look at the set he's picked out and my heart flutters a little. So it's pretty. Really pretty, actually. And it would look good on me. And it would replace the turquoise set I have to throw out.

I make a sound somewhere between excitement and defeat and hold my hand out. "Get me a basket."

Aaron releases me and hands me one. I skim through the hangers until I find one in my size and grab the bottoms to match. I prod Aaron in the chest.

"You better make it good, Mr. Stone. Real fucking good."

My hair flicks over my shoulder as I turn away from him again and peruse the underwear. Damn him. He knows how to work me and manipulate me into doing what he wants. Not that I need much convincing in a store like this, but I'd really rather be handing over my card at the end of it.

Soon enough, I've exhausted the bra-and-panties section and I'm swapping baskets with Aaron. He hands me an empty one with a smug smirk curving his lips and takes the full one. He sets it on a chair next to the register and combs through it.

"What are you doing?" I pause, holding a red basque in front of me.

"You didn't think I'd let you buy anything without prior approval, did you?"

I raise an eyebrow. "Well, don't let me stop you from combing through my choice of underwear yet again."

He laughs at my subtle dig. "Dayton?"

My eyes find his.

"Put that in the basket."

I check the tag. "It's a lot of money for something that will just come off."

His eyes darken. "That one won't be coming off."

A quiet cough comes from beside him, and I flick my eyes to the woman behind the register. She's in her mid-forties, at a guess, and there's a light flush on her cheeks.

"Mr. and Mrs. Stone. Can I help you at all?" Her crisp British accent doesn't betray her embarrassment at having walked in on our conversation.

My eyebrows take up residence somewhere behind my hairline. *Mrs. Stone?*

"We're not married," I correct her politely. "Much to Mr. Stone's chagrin."

He gives me a look that says I'll regret that later.

"Oh, I'm ever so sorry." She places a hand on her chest. "That's what one gets for assuming."

"It's okay." I smile. "I doubt you'll be the last to."

She returns my smile. "Can I help you in any way?"

"Hmm…" My eyes find the tiny strings I saw Aaron eying contemplatively earlier. I pick up the white one beneath a matching basque and show her it. "Do you have this in any other colors?"

Aaron clears his throat and shifts when I look at him.

"We do. They're just over here." She waves me over and shows me a section of the wall with the exact pair of panties in an array of colors.

"Well," I say, glancing back at Aaron and grabbing a couple of them, "would you look at that?"

"I warned you."

"Do I look like I'm remotely bothered about the amount of money that just cost me? I love spoiling you."

"Aaron, you and I both know that lingerie isn't exactly spoiling me. You get far more pleasure from it than I do."

He pulls my feet onto his lap and massages them. "But in the end, we both get the pleasure, so does it really matter?"

I lean my head against the seat and smile. "I suppose not."

I really did warn him. After one long hour of wandering back and forth through the shop and trying on a few items I wasn't so sure of, he handed over his card and a few hundred pounds. Despite my cringe at the time, I've accepted that it wasn't my fault.

He made me do it with talk of pulling me out of and fucking me in it all.

And after sitting in a restaurant with him for two and a half hours, I'm more than ready to see if he'll make good on his promises. But first…

"Can I ask you something?"

"It sounds serious."

"It is… Kind of. Did you mean what you said earlier?"

"About fucking you in that devil-sent red outfit? Absolutely."

I climb from the car after him and follow him into the house. "No," I say slowly, kicking my shoes off at the door. "The other thing."

"I said a lot of things to you earlier, Bambi. You're going to have to elaborate a little more than 'the other thing.'" He raises his eyebrows in amusement, and the movement tugs his lips up with it.

I sit on the edge of the kitchen table and watch as he maneuvers his way around it. He's certain in everything he does, even if it's only throwing a teabag in a mug and pouring water over it. If I've noticed anything, it's that he never falters in his movements. There's never a tremble of his hand or a slip of his fingers.

That's something reflected in the rest of his life. He never does something unless he wholeheartedly means it, and the same goes for his words. He never says something he doesn't mean.

"When you said that one day everything you have will be mine." I swallow, and he freezes. "Did you mean that?"

"Does that scare you?" he asks without looking at me.

"Will that make a difference to your answer?"

"No. I'm just curious."

I put my hands in my lap and look down, uncertainty swirling in me. Right now, we're polar opposites. "Yes. It does—a little."

A mug hits the countertop, and he appears in front of me. One of his hands creeps up my thigh, opening my legs, and he slips between them.

"Why does it scare you?"

I shrug one shoulder. "It just does. It's a big step."

"Now tell me the real reason." He hooks two fingers under my chin and lifts my face until our eyes meet. "Dayton."

"It's something I can't control," I say softly. "I can't control whether or not you want to ask me, and I definitely can't control whether or not you do. And I wouldn't ask you to wait until I definitively said I was ready because I might never be ready."

"I would wait until you said so if that's what freaks you out."

I shake my head. "I wasn't ready to go with you to Vegas. I wasn't ready to say yes when you begged for another chance. I wasn't ready to come here. It's when the best things happen. Sometimes you want the exact thing you think you're not ready for because you actually are."

"Look at me."

I keep my eyes down.

"Dayton, look at me, sweetheart." He brushes a thumb across my cheek. "I'm not answering your question until you do."

Reluctantly, I meet his gaze—his raw, emotion-filled, honest gaze that tugs at a part of me buried deep down.

"Did I mean what I said? Absolutely. I meant it with everything I am. One day, you will have everything I have. One day, you'll walk into a store, they'll call you Mrs. Stone, and you won't have to correct them. You'll smile and nod instead." He swallows audibly and cups my face. "But only when you're ready. If I have to wait ten years until you're ready to say yes, then I will. You're mine anyway. I know in my heart you belong to me. I don't need the validation of a piece of paper to tell me you're mine for the rest of my life. But it will happen, Dayton. There's nothing I want more than to see you walking down an aisle toward me knowing you're giving me everything."

"But you've done it before." My words are a mere whisper.

He touches his lips to my forehead and lets them linger for a long moment. "My body might have, but my heart hasn't. My heart has always been married to you."

I wrap my arms around him and bury my face in his neck. His go around me just as tightly, and I take a deep breath. I just need him to hold me.

This conversation wasn't supposed to happen for a long, long time. It's just one more wrench in the works of my life right now.

Except that this is the kind of wrench that sets my heart beating frantically with both excitement and fear.

"You still have to convince me to move in with you first," I mumble against his skin.

Silence.

"Aaron."

Silence.

"Aaron!"

I pull back and study his smirking face. It's the same look he had earlier when I mentioned it. It's the look that says he knows something I don't, and it sets my body on red alert.

"Aaron," I put a warning in my voice this time, and he laughs.

"Don't worry. I'm not doing anything ridiculously impulsive or drastic. Not right now." He covers my mouth with his before I can respond, and I lightly punch his chest.

"What have you done? Are you doing? Going to do? Whatever it is. What is it?"

"Nothing. I'm messing with you. I haven't done anything. I promise." He drops another kiss to my lips.

"Yet? There's always a yet with you. Always."

"I'm not promising I won't, but I haven't done anything at this moment in time."

"Oh, because that makes me feel so much better," I scoff, rolling my eyes. "You scare me. Do you know that?"

He pushes away from the table and grabs his tea, watching me over the rim of the mug with amusement. "Yes. I'm terrifying. I'm amazed you haven't run from the room screaming yet."

I grab a grape from the bunch in the fruit bowl behind me and throw it at him. "Shut up. You scare me because I can tell you not to do something and you'll go and do it anyway. Why do I bother?"

"Yes, Dayton, why do you?" His eyes twinkle.

"Because I have an insane, evidently naïve idea that I can ask you not to do something and you'll actually follow my wishes. Gasp! Imagine how beautiful that day would be."

"It would be very beautiful and even more unlikely."

"So what we're saying is the whole conversation we just had about the rest of our lives was a total waste of my time."

His effort to keep a straight face is admirable but wasted. "I'll maybe give you six months. A year if you catch me on a more amicable day."

"Presumptuous, pushy bastard."

"Seems like she's got you all worked out, cuz." Tyler strolls through the door and puts his camera bag on the table next to me. "What's he on about this time?"

I sigh. "Don't ask. Just don't ask."

"Suit yourselves. By the way, Tessa said she'll pick you up at ten tomorrow. She needs someone to help her decide her final hairstyle or some bullshit I don't care about."

"But your mom is here now."

"I know." He grins. "Have fun."

Chapter Seventeen

Bridezillas make the best brides.

After standing for so long, watching Tessa say her vows, I know this to be true. She may have been a nightmare for the past few days, but so far, her day has gone off without a hitch.

It's absolutely perfect. From the figure-hugging white dress that flares into a full skirt at her hips to the powder blue of her bridesmaids' dresses and the matching bouquets of flowers everywhere. I can't begin to imagine the work—or the cost—that's gone into this day.

I've been to more weddings than I care to count, but none of them hit me the way Tessa's has. Perhaps it was the raw honesty in her voice when she promised to give Michael the rest of her life. Perhaps it was the way they looked at each other, so in love, and sealed it all with a kiss.

Or perhaps it was the way Aaron held my hand tightly throughout the ceremony or the way my emotions were running rampant in my body, still raw from our conversation about this very topic a few days ago.

"Dayton!" Tessa shouts my name and waves me over.

"No." I shake my head. "These are your family shots."

Several pairs of eyes turn to look at me. Tessa's, Tyler's, Carly's, Brandon's, Tessa's parents', and Aaron's. Aaron's are the hardest as he approaches me and takes both my hands in his.

"You are family," he says softly. "And Tessa wants you in these pictures."

"I..." I look at her pleading eyes and let him pull me forward. "Okay."

Everyone smiles as I join them, and Aaron tucks me into his side.

"Whoa. Don't crease the dress," I mutter, much to everyone's amusement.

"Excuse me," he responds, his own laughter in his voice. "Was it expensive?"

"I wouldn't know. I wasn't allowed to see the price." I grin and slip my arm around his waist as the photographer shouts for us all to smile.

I'm passed from here to there and back again over the next fifteen minutes. In and out of photos. In and out of Aaron's hold. By the time they're all done, I'm glad to have a chance to sit down for dinner.

"I didn't see the price either, but it was worth every cent," Aaron says as he takes a seat next to me. "The dress," he says at my questioning look.

"Oh!" I smile. "What do you mean you didn't see the price?"

"I rarely see my accounts. My accountant is aware of all my finances and he watches them carefully. I only see them when something isn't as it should be."

"Oh, to be so rich."

He brings my hand to his mouth and brushes his lips across it. "You know my feelings on this."

"I do and I acknowledge them, and I refuse to take this discussion further." I punctuate my last words with a raise of my brows as the entrées are brought out.

As I suspected, the meal is incredible. One of the best I've ever had by a million miles. The wine is crisp and fresh, and you don't need to be familiar with the label to know that they're expensive bottles. I wonder how much this cost.

"You'd pass out with shock," Aaron whispers.

Crap. Did I say that out loud?

"You whispered it."

"Dammit. I need to stop thinking." I pick up my glass and drink before I say something else.

"I won't give you an exact figure, but it was comfortably in the six-figure bracket."

I choke as I swallow my wine. "Six figures?"

"Did you expect anything less?"

"On a wedding?"

"That's what we're attending."

"Oh my God."

Aaron smiles. "I love how shocked you get at money."

"Money doesn't shock me. I have plenty myself, but I don't understand the frivolity, I guess. Spending just because you can. It baffles me."

"This, from the woman who almost snapped my bank card two days ago?"

I hold up a finger. "We all have our exceptions, Mr. Stone. That's mine. Besides, that will all get used."

"I can guarantee it." He touches my back and kisses the corner of my mouth. "Now eat."

"Yes, sir."

We spend the rest of the dinner in silence before we all step into the gardens for drinks while the tables are cleared away. I engage in casual conversation with Tyler, doing my best to keep him away from yet another of Tessa's bridesmaids.

"Come dance," he says, dragging me back into the room.

"Your sister has to have her dance first, and I think Aaron would likely kill you."

"Tomorrow, maybe, and he's not here right now. Let me steal one." He winks, his grin oozing boyish charm instead of sexuality, and I find myself giving in.

"Fine. Okay. But I'm not being held responsible for this."

"I'll take the blame."

We stand by the side and watch as Michael takes Tessa in his arms. A smile teases my lips as they move elegantly across the floor, never taking their eyes from the other. Their parents join them on the floor, followed by the wedding party and their dates, and Tyler grabs my hand.

The grip is broken, and Aaron presses himself against the back of me. "Nice try, Ty. Better luck next time."

He sweeps me away onto the dance floor and envelopes me in his arms. I wrap mine around his neck and look up at him, unable to hide the smile on my lips.

"What? No one is dancing with you tonight except me," he murmurs, lowering his face to mine.

"I'd be offended if you let them."

We slowly move around the floor, in perfect sync, our bodies swaying together with ease. Like we've always danced together.

"Do you remember the first time we danced together?" Aaron asks quietly, his fingers twitching against my back.

"Do you think I'd forget?"

His mom's birthday is in the middle of the summer, and his dad threw her a party. Aaron insisted I go along with my parents, and I protested at dancing. I wasn't a dancer. I never have been, but he made me do it anyway.

"I never wanted that song to end," he admits. "I could have danced with you all night."

"You did." I smile. "I think you would have tried again the next day if I hadn't have jumped on you to make you stop."

He laughs. "Yes. I suppose you're right." He kisses me softly as the song ends, and I feel his cell vibrate in his pocket between us.

"Aaron!"

He slides it out and glances at the screen. "I have to take this. I'll be right back."

He kisses me quickly and disappears out of the large doors behind us. I watch him, shaking my head. Unbelievable. Can he not leave work at home for one night?

"Looks like I get my dance after all." Tyler appears in front of me.

"Let's not anger him. How about a drink instead?"

He motions for me to lead the way, and we both take a seat at the bar. I sigh. Fucking phone.

"Have you thought about what I said?"

"About the pictures?"

Tyler nods. "No pressure. I'm just wondering since you leave again in a couple of days."

"I don't know. Do you come to Seattle much?"

"I will be now that Aaron lives there. I split my time between here and there."

"Can we come back to this? There's still a lot to...work through...before I make any decisions."

He studies me for a second. "He still doesn't know?"

I shake my head. "I'm going to figure it out when I get home. Somehow. And no," I snap when he opens his mouth. "Don't even go there, Tyler Stone. Don't you dare."

He holds up his hands. "Okay. Okay. I'm just throwing it out there though, Day. If."

"No. This is my problem, and I'm going to deal with it. Now let's talk about something else."

"Let's talk about why Aaron is walking toward you with a face like thunder."

I spin and stare into angry blue eyes. "Uh-oh. Tyler, what did I do this time?"

"We're leaving," Aaron snaps, grabbing my arm. "Tyler, are you back tonight?"

"Nope. Not now, anyway."

"Excellent. Dayton." He pulls me from the chair and after him, dropping his hand to mine so it doesn't look like he's fucking manhandling me.

Oh fuck. What if he's found out somehow? What if he knows about Naomi?

I'm too afraid to ask as he deposits me in the car and gets in after me. He orders the driver, whose name I've never learned, to take us back to Tyler's. Then he turns his back on me. I take a deep breath and wring my fingers in my lap. Jesus.

I can feel his annoyance and frustration like it's my own. It's an awful feeling, one I want to scrape off my skin and shake away. One that clings to me.

"Inside." One word. Short. Sharp. Controlled.

I follow him, knowing that a smart answer won't help me from whatever has him so annoyed.

He opens a cupboard in the front room, pours two fingers of whisky, and drinks them in one. The glass slams against the side and his fingers curl around the side of the bar so tightly that I can see his knuckles whitening.

"Care to explain why three payments to Monique were declined?"

Every bit of tension oozes out of my body. *He doesn't know.*

I drop my purse on the sofa and pull off my heels. "I told her to cancel them."

"She hasn't had a dollar off of me."

"That's the idea of me telling her to cancel them."

Aaron turns, questions now filling his eyes where his annoyance just was. "Why? Why would you do that?"

"Because I needed to be with you without that."

"Why the fuck didn't you tell me, Day? This whole time I've thought you've been here because you've been forced to be. And you haven't. You've been here because, what? You've wanted to be?"

I nod slowly and meet his eyes. "I needed to be with you without the obligation that comes with the money to figure out how I feel. I needed to know I could decide what I want without knowing it was there and forcing me to decide. I needed to do this as Dayton the person, not Dayton the call girl."

"And? Have you decided?"

I cross the room to him and undo his tie. I leave it on the bar next to us and untuck his shirt, sliding my hands beneath it and around to his back as I lay my face against his chest.

He lets out a heavy breath and holds me to him. "You're not answering my question."

"I'm going to call Monique when we get back to Seattle."

"And?" He cups my face and pulls me back from him when I don't answer. "And fucking what, Dayton?"

"And I'm going to tell her I'm done. I'm leaving. I quit."

His lips crash into mine with a ferocity I never believed possible. They stoke a fire deep in the pit of my belly with each hard and forceful movement across mine.

"Does this mean you forgive me?"

I nod against him. "I do."

"I don't know how you do, but I'm… God." He kisses me again. "I'm the luckiest bastard."

"I know," I mumble.

He buries his face into my hair and takes a deep breath. "You're incredible, you know that? I am so very, very lucky to have you." He presses his lips to my collarbone, and the words tumble from my lips before I can stop them.

"Why won't you say it?"

"Say what?"

I swallow and step back from him, closing my eyes. "Why won't you tell me you love me?"

"I have. So many times."

"No. No, you haven't." I turn back to him. "You've said you've never stopped loving me. You've said your heart belongs to me. You've said you've never loved anyone else, but you've never actually said it. You've never looked me in the eyes and told me you love me."

"You know I do, Dayton. And if you don't, I want to know why."

"I do. I know it, but I need to hear it. I just stood here and told you that I'm giving up my life to be with you and you still haven't said it."

Silence lingers between us, growing steadily heavier until Aaron finally speaks.

"That's what you've been waiting for, isn't it? That's what you wanted in my office—when you said you wanted me to strip myself bare and tell you how I feel."

I nod and close my eyes. "It's stupid, so stupid, but it's like hearing those words will make me realize that I've made the right choice in choosing you over my life. I don't care if that makes me weak or pathetic. I wish you would say them, but not because I'm standing here asking you to. I want you tell me because you want to. Because they're—"

"True," he finishes. "They are. I haven't said them because you are this crazy independent woman who fights me at every turn. I can't do anything without you pushing back at me, and your independence is one of the best things about you. You don't hang on to my arm and beg me for things. You don't look at me like I can buy you the world. You look at me like I'm a pain in your ass half of the time, and that's why I haven't told you. You balk every time I talk of something more serious than a night together."

His palms are warm as they close over my cheeks and tilt my face up to his. I open my eyes and stare into his.

"But I do, Dayton. Don't ever doubt for a second that I love you. I love you when you wake up in the morning, your hair is a mess and your eyes all misty from sleep. I love you when you're spilling soda on your shirt and brushing crumbs from your lap. I love you when you're glancing at me, thinking I don't notice, and I love you when you're asleep and you're whispering my name." He rests his forehead against mine. "I love you every second of my life, and that love is so strong that it encompasses everything else I feel."

I hiccup as he folds his arms around me. His heart is pounding inside his chest, thumping against my chest, and I know mine is doing the same. They're beating the same, right down to the same rhythm. Like they were always meant to. Like there's no other rhythm they could possibly beat to except for the one reserved just for us.

"It scares me how in love with you I am, Dayton. I think I love you even beyond love itself. You're my obsession, and there's nothing I wouldn't do to keep you. You have to know that."

I nod again, fisting his shirt.

"There," he whispers, walking back with me. "I've told you. Now let me show you."

Aaron sweeps me into his arms and carries me upstairs, unzipping the back of my dress before setting me on the edge of the bed. His fingers are soft against mine as he slides the sleeves over my shoulders, exposing the turquoise bra he loved so much.

He ghosts his fingertips over the curve of my breast. "So I get to take it off after all."

I smile at him, and he dips his head. His kiss is slow and languid, an exploration of my mouth that's filled with revelry and adoration. It reverberates throughout my whole body, a sweeping caress that touches every part of me.

"This isn't fair," I whisper when he kisses my jaw, tugging at his shirt.

He smiles against me and straightens. His fingers work the buttons and he shrugs it off, leaving it to drop to the floor behind him.

My fingers, like they have a mind of their own, sweep over the taut muscles of his stomach. They trace each shadowed indent of skin, finally following the shape of the 'v' muscle and resting on his hips. I lean forward and kiss the patch of skin above his pants, his skin is scorching hot beneath my lips.

Aaron leans me back on the bed and slides my dress down my legs. His mouth travels down my body and over my breasts, leaving a blazing trail of seduction as he goes. His hand slips beneath me and unclips the bra, which is gone a second later.

This is different. This time, as he explores my body, there's no rush, no hurry, no desperation. There are no whispered words of naughty promises that send my body into overdrive. There's only his breath coating my skin in murmurs against me I can't decipher.

And when his mouth reaches the apex of my thighs, the removal of my panties is slow, and the journey back up my legs is accompanied by a thousand peppered kisses. It's joined by a crazy anticipation of what's coming, of a silent beg from me for the show he's promised.

His tongue's strokes are as slow and easy as his kisses were earlier. His hands are wrapped around my legs, keeping them open, and he sucks lightly on my clit. He slides his tongue between my folds and inside me and over that tender bundle of nerves until I come apart beneath him in a way that's crazily intense.

His pants hit the floor with a clunk of his belt, and he leans over me, his lips covering mine. "You taste good on you," he whispers.

I smile. "Like your own personal heaven and hell all in one, right?"

"Exactly like that, beautiful woman. Exactly like that."

Aaron pushes himself inside me slowly, so slowly that I feel the stretching of all my muscles as every inch of him finds its home. Each stroke is deeper than the last, long and sweet, deliciously erotic. His heavy breath in my ear is seductive, and I don't remember ever feeling this way.

Like right now, in this moment, it's just me and him and the love that's finally out in the open.

Like everything is perfect.

"Aaron." His name is a desperate plea from my lips as I feel the orgasm inside, coiling and sculpting deep in my belly, sending red-hot shoots of pleasure out.

"Easy, baby." He kisses my neck, lingering on my pulse point.

"Please… I need…"

He pushes right into me, hitting the right spot, and pulls back out. He does this again, still slowly, still gently, still with a remarkable amount of restraint. I push my hips into him when I feel his cock swelling inside me, and as soon as he presses his thumb against my clit, I feel the first red-hot spurt of his come inside me and let myself go.

It hits me so intensely, so incredibly strong, that tears spill from my eyes. When it's all over and Aaron's tucking us into bed, they're still falling, leaving wet patches on the pillow.

He pulls me into his chest and wipes the tears away with his thumb. "Sex and crying is a habit with you."

I choke a laugh, covering my mouth with my hand, and nudge him. "Shut up. I just…"

"Just what?"

"Love you," I whisper, tilting my face back to look at him. His lips curve on each side, a light sparking in his eyes. "I love you. That's all."

"That's all, she says. Like it's so simple."

"It is, remember? You told me it's simple."

"So I did." He presses a gentle kiss to my tender lips. "I love you, too, Bambi. I love you so much."

Chapter Eighteen

The grey skies and heavy rainfall in Seattle are a stark contrast to the early summer sunshine we left behind in London some sixteen hours ago.

"I want to go back," I mutter, putting up the umbrella the flight attendant just handed to me before I get off the plane. Thunder rumbles overhead. Of course we'd land back in the middle of a rare frigging thunderstorm.

"Come on, woman. Stop complaining." Aaron nudges my back and I sigh.

"Okay, but if I ruin these shoes in all those puddles…"

"I'll buy you another ten pairs. Now go."

I laugh and walk down the steps, the damp air making me shiver through my thin cardigan. Note to self: check destination weather before getting on a plane.

Aaron rests his jacket over my shoulders with a kiss to my cheek. I smile gratefully at him and lift my umbrella for him to come under. He raises his eyebrows, but I give him a hard, no-nonsense look.

Not that I'm averse to that white button-down shirt getting wet, of course. I'm just not prepared to deal with the inevitable man flu if he gets soaked.

We hurry into the airport and speed through our checks. I shake off the umbrella before lowering myself into our waiting car and drop it by my feet.

"Well, that's my shoes ruined."

"From a little rain?"

"That's not a little rain. If I'd have known it was raining, I wouldn't have worn these." I lift my leg and flash him my black Louboutins, the iconic red underside showing as I do.

Aaron's strong fingers grasp my lower leg and he lifts my foot higher. I slump back in the chair, pursing my lips, unimpressed, and he kisses my ankle.

"I like these. I'm definitely replacing them. They'll match that red thing you bought."

I roll my eyes. "You and the red thing."

"I like you in red. You look like the temptation you are."

"Like a great big chocolate cake in front of a dieting person?"

His lips quirk. "If you say so, Dayton."

I smile and tug my foot from his hold, righting myself in the seat. Arriving back in Seattle is a blessing and a curse. The blessing falls in knowing that we're both on the same page about this relationship. Well, mostly, anyway. We know it's real. There's no money, no obligation, no forcing. Just very real, very consuming feelings.

That's not to say that this will be easy. Obvious things aside, a relationship is based on more than sex and love. Those things can't make a relationship. They can make it better, oh yes, but they can't make it something strong enough to go the distance. Sex and love don't make a relationship something real enough to last forever.

It's the little things that do that. Like Aaron said in Vegas, it's the little things that mean the most. The things you pass on by because they're seemingly irrelevant although they're really the most important things.

Love is how the other person likes their coffee on a morning. How long they put their toast in the toaster for. How they like their throw pillows on the sofa to be arranged. How hot they have their shower water. How many bubbles in the bath.

How they always leave empty glasses on the bar in the kitchen, and how they know exactly how you take your coffee. How they know how many candles to light around a bathtub before you get in, and how chilled your wine has to be before it's an acceptable drinking temperature.

We still have so much to learn about each other, and while I know there's no rush, I want to know these things. I want to know if he prefers butter or jelly on his toast on a morning and if really he prefers tea over coffee, which I suspect he does.

I want to know if he changes the temperature of the shower water to my preference of red hot instead of a normal hot. I want to know every little thing I don't.

Because at the end of the day, when it gets hard and you're in the middle of the room shouting at each other over something trivial, you won't remember the huge declarations of love. When you're sitting against your bedroom door crying because you hate fighting, you'll remember the way he smiles at you over breakfast and the way he trails his thumb down your spine to make you shiver.

You'll remember all the crazy little things that remind you that, no matter what, no matter how difficult or impossible it may seem, there's no one else in this world more perfect for you than he is.

"What are you thinking?" Aaron strokes the inside of my wrist with his thumb.

I roll my head to the side and smile. "I'm thinking I'm really glad you hired Mia Lopez."

He leans forward and kisses me with his own smile playing on his lips.

And I am. In all honesty, I'm completely glad he hired me that night. Regardless of the events since, staying and seeing it out was the best thing I could have done.

I can't control love. I know this. But I can control how much of an impact it has on my life. I can control whether or not I choose to let it *be* my life. And that's what I'm doing. Instead of letting it spiral crazily inside me, instead of fighting it, I'm embracing it.

I'm giving Aaron my all, and he's giving me his.

I look out the window. "Um, this isn't the way to my house."

"I know. You're staying with me tonight."

"Demanding again, Mr. Stone?"

"Requirement, Miss Black."

"You're getting awfully requirement-happy lately. Are you aware of this?"

His eyes crash into mine, the lust there tugging at my own desire, and his lips curve into a dangerously sexy smirk that makes me want to kiss it off him.

"Oh, I'm very aware. My cock is also aware of its numerous requirements. Requirements you will be finding out more about very, very soon."

"Sounds promising."

"I never joke about fucking you, Miss Black."

"Is that so?" I run my tongue across my bottom lip. His eyes follow the movement, and he cups my chin, pulling my face to his.

"There's nothing funny about making you come, Dayton. Nor is there anything funny about having my cock so deep inside you that you can't feel anything but me."

My desire flares like a lit match. It engulfs my body as his words strike up any number of thoughts about the way he moves inside me, and I swallow hard like it'll counteract the aching in my core.

"I agree. It's a very serious matter," I manage, trying to keep a straight face.

Aaron stares at me until we reach his apartment building and we get out. He places a hand on either side of my waist, steering me toward the elevator, and lowers his mouth to my ear.

"A very serious matter I intend to take care of tonight. Perhaps twice."

My mouth goes dry. *Holy fuck. Yes. Please do.*

The elevator doors open and he unlocks his apartment door, pausing slightly before opening it. I look at his hand then him. As if my eyes on him flicks something, he pushes the handle down and the door swings open.

I step in before I realize that anything is different. And freeze when I see it.

My coats are hanging on the hooks in the hallway. Some of my throw pillows are strewn across the large U-shaped sofa, and my books have filled the bookcase that curves behind it. I stroll into the bathroom without speaking, and sure as shit, my stuff is in here too. My toothbrush. My shampoo. My soap.

I yank open the cupboard doors beneath the sinks and find all my of my beauty products lined up—exactly the way I had them in my own bathroom. My towels are hanging on the rails next to the bath, and my favorite Yankee candles are sitting in the windowsill.

What. The. Fuck?

Slamming the door behind me, I walk into Aaron's bedroom, ignoring my other candles on the side, and shove my way into his closet. My clothes are hanging next to his. My shoes are lined beneath them, from boots to heels to sandals, and the box holding all my nail polishes and extra makeup is sitting on the shelf above the rail.

The large canvas of us he showed me in his office apartment is hanging on the wall in here, and when I walk next door to his office, there are another two pictures. One framed on the desk, one on the wall.

I cover my eyes with my hand, my chest tight. It takes a lot for me to take a deep breath and not scream at him when I walk back into the main room.

"Either someone who has belongings exactly the same as me has taken residence in your apartment or you've moved me in."

"I'll ease your mind and confirm the latter."

I put my hands on my hips. *Don't shout. Don't freak. Don't go—*

"What the fuck, Aaron? You said you didn't do anything stupid! Jesus! I told you I wasn't ready for this! I can't fucking believe you've moved me into your apartment without even asking me!"

So much for not going crazy.

"I wasn't lying when I said I hadn't done anything impulsive. I did it after."

"Oh, and that makes it all better, does it? It's totally fucking okay because you didn't lie to me about it. Oh my god!" I run my fingers through my hair. "How the hell did you even get into my house?"

"Your best friend has a spare key."

"You roped Liv in on this?"

"I may not have been completely honest when I told her you'd requested some of your belongings be moved here."

I exhale through pursed lips. "You and I? Not fucking talking right now."

I spin on my heels and stalk into the spare bedroom, ready to face-plant the bed and scream into the pillow. But of course, I can't. Because of course he's turned that into a lingerie room. My lingerie room. With space for all my new stuff.

And it's organized perfectly. Just how I had it. As if he'd been in and taken photos before everything was transferred.

I leave the room again. Aaron's leaning against the bar, a steaming mug in hand, his eyes following me.

"What do you expect me to do with my house? Am I supposed to sell it now?"

He shakes his head. "No, absolutely not. Without meaning to bring up our previous conversation, my apartment isn't exactly where I imagine living with you in the future."

Ah, yes. That conversation.

"So, what? I'm supposed to pay a mortgage on a house I'm not even living in?"

"You'll find that an amount covering the rest of your mortgage repayments was deposited into your account this morning for you to pay it off."

"Fuck no." I stalk across the room and jab my finger in his chest. "That is *my* house, and I'm not letting you pay it off. I'm calling the bank tomorrow and having it sent back to your account. I will pay it off."

Great. Now there's another one hundred and twenty-five thousand I have to find for Naomi.

Aaron curls his fingers around my wrist and lowers my hand. "By all means, sweetheart, have it transferred back to my account. You'll find it'll be back in yours within the hour."

"You're not paying off my house," I say through gritted teeth. "I don't need or want you to."

He leans across the bar, his mug hitting the surface of it with a gentle clunk, and tugs my face toward him. "And one day that will be *our* house, just like this will be *our* apartment, and *our* company, and *our* money. I know you like to do things yourself, but start getting used to me doing them for you because it's going to happen a lot more often."

"I am so mad at you right now that I don't even know what to say." I knock his hand from me and walk into the bedroom, letting the door slam behind me.

The bedroom.

Our bedroom.

I kick off my shoes and leave my clothes in a heap before climbing into bed.

Our bed.

Huh.

A mug of coffee is waiting on the nightstand when I wake up. I steal a look at the clock on Aaron's side, blinking when it reads eight thirty p.m. I've slept all afternoon?

Damn jet lag.

I inhale the rich scent of the coffee before taking my first sip. It's still piping hot, and my eyes flit to the open bedroom door. I can't hear anything—no television, no music, no low rumble of his voice.

I place the cup back on the side and grab some shorts and a tank from the closet. Seeing my clothes next to his is a little surreal, and now that I've cooled off thanks to my unplanned nap, I can't deny the flutter in my stomach at the sight.

I can't deny that a part of me loves the fact I really do get to wake up next to him every morning and fall asleep in his arms each night.

When I find him in his office, he's sitting at the desk, hunched over, his fingers moving at lightning speed across the keyboard. He must be totally engrossed in what he's doing, because he doesn't move as I curl up in the corner of the sofa.

I open one of the books I took from the front room during my search for him and drop my eyes to it. As I turn the pages, I know that he's registered my presence. He can't not—unless there's someone else who comes into his office on a regular basis and reads while he works.

Still, he doesn't turn. He continues his tapping, clicking, whatever he's doing. So I don't speak either, and we settle into a comfortable silence that somehow kills the remaining tension between us.

And this is…nice. Both of us here, not speaking, doing our own things. It's comforting in the oddest kind of way, not least because I'm not used to being in the same room without interacting with him in some way. Whether it's talking, touching, kissing—we're always doing something. But here, we're individuals together.

After several chapters, I hear the click of the laptop closing. I peer over the top of the book, and Aaron joins me on the sofa. His black shirt stretches over his shoulders, and his hair is all mussed like he's been rubbing his fingers through it repeatedly.

I turn my attention back to the pages to finish the chapter, feeling his eyes on me the whole time. I slip the bookmark from the back cover and use it to mark my page.

Aaron reaches out and runs his hand down my thigh. "Did you sleep well?"

"Your mattress is awful," I reply. "If you were going to bring my stuff over, you could have brought my mattress."

He smiles. "I agree. Your mattress is much comfier than mine. I'll rectify that tomorrow."

"Good." I nod and set the book on the floor next to me. "When did you do it? Move my stuff here?"

"The day after Tessa's wedding." He moves up the sofa and lifts my legs over his. His arm settles across the back of the cushions and he threads his fingers into my hair, gently running them through to the ends. "I know you told me you weren't ready, but then we had that conversation about the future about the things you're not ready for being the things you want the most."

"And you're using that as an excuse."

"No. Not an excuse. The first reason."

"And the second?"

He runs his fingers down my cheek. "The look in your eyes when you told me how much you needed me to tell you I love you. I didn't realize it was so important to you until then, and it was that moment that made me realize it's important to me to tell you every single day. The only way I can do that—and show you at the same time—is if you live with me."

Well, how the fucking hell am I supposed to argue with that?

That's right. I'm not. So he's going to get away with it.

Goddamn it.

"Do anything like this ever again and I might just have to kill you," I murmur when he leans in for a kiss.

"Understood." He sweeps his mouth across mine. "Liv only packed the basics, which is apparently more than I imagined considering your whole closet is here…"

I smirk.

"So if you want to, we'll go back tomorrow and get anything else you need."

"Does anything else include food? Because, y'know, if I'm living here, I'm gonna need some real food."

"Empty your cupboards if that's what you want to do." He grins. "It'll save me from having to go grocery shopping."

"I don't believe for a second you go grocery shopping."

"Occasionally. As proven by the lack of food in my kitchen."

I make a 'hmph' sound. "That will change, Mr. Stone. We're going to set some ground rules."

He sits back, his lips twitching. "Fire away."

I sit up straighter and tick off on my fingers. "Grocery shopping happens once a week, with both of us. Ah, ah! We're in a relationship now, and multimillionaire or not, we're going to do relationship things. Understood?"

He nods.

"Good. And that also means that, unless there are unavoidable circumstances, not including deliberately scheduled meetings, you will be home for dinner every single night because I will be cooking it."

"You can cook?"

"No, I've survived for the last three years on water, raw meat, and Cheetos." I roll my eyes. "Of course I can cook. I spent my childhood in the kitchen with my mom."

"Why haven't you cooked for me before?"

I look at him blankly. "You've never asked me to."

"Fair point. Can you cook tomorrow?"

"I suppose. And back to the rules." I give him a pointed stare. "Living together does not give you the right to hide my shorts. Yes, I found them in the closet, and yes, I'm keeping them. They're comfy. No arguing."

"I like it when you go all bossy on me."

"Well I can't have you making all the decisions, can I? If I did, I'd be married and pregnant by the end of the month."

His lips twitch again.

I hold up my left arm and tap my skin. "Implant. Don't get any ideas."

"No ideas."

"Good. Let's keep it that way."

He leans in again. "But you know about that being ready thing—"

I press my finger against his lips. "The implant has a year left, and perhaps if you don't piss me off too much, we'll revisit this then. So for now, tuck those little dreams back in their little box, because it is not up for discussion. Are we clear, Mr. Stone?"

"Crystal, Miss Black." He slides his hand beneath my shorts and tugs on my bottom lip with his teeth. "Now, are you done with your requirements—uh, rules?"

"Uh, um, yep." I breathe what passes for words as he brushes his nose down my neck.

"Good." He stands and lifts me. I wrap my legs around his waist, and he walks in the direction of the bedroom. "Because my cock has a requirement you need to fulfill. Right now."

Chapter Nineteen

My house feels empty despite everything but my clothes being here. I mean, my sofa is still next to the window in the front room, and my mugs are still lined on the shelf in the kitchen, but it feels different.

Maybe it's because I'm here alone. Where this was once my sanctuary, it's now a building that's almost unfamiliar. Uncomfortable.

The fact that the last time I was here was with Naomi is irrelevant.

I grab the pile of mail from behind the door and drop it on the island in the kitchen. An envelope with a handwritten address on it catches my eye.

Shivers snake their way down my spine when I pick it up, and I swallow hard. The only things I get in mail are bills and lingerie catalogs, and I don't like what my gut feeling is telling me. It's a shame that ignoring it won't make it go away.

I slide my pinkie finger under the flap and pull out the piece of paper inside.

Tick tock.

I fold the note over and shove it in a drawer with a bang. Because I needed the reminder. Because I really needed a shitty little note to tell me that I have two fucking weeks to come up with a miracle.

I lean against the side and take several deep breaths, letting the tension roll off my shoulders. Bitch. Absolute bitch.

There's nothing I want to do more now than get all my things and leave this house. I don't want to wait for Aaron. I don't want to sit here in this house trying to figure out what I have to do.

I don't want to spend my time thinking about how such a beautiful love carries something so ugly.

I fill a suitcase with everything else necessary, photos, books left behind, the half-full can of hairspray sitting on my dresser. Downstairs, I fill two bags full with food and leave them on the floor by the door.

And I grab my cell. I speed-dial Monique and pace until the line clicks.

"Dayton."

"Monique. Can we talk?"

"Unnecessary. I already know what you're telling me, don't I?"

I nod. Stupidly. She can't see me. "If it's…" I swallow, my stomach coiling, and screw my eyes shut. This is harder than it should be. "If it's that I'm leaving you, then yes. You already know."

"I expected you would. I'm sorry to see you go, Day."

"I'm sorry I have to. Truly, I am."

"But as sorry as I am, I'm much happier for you. Although you tell that man if he hurts you, I'm coming after his rich motherfucking ass and I'm going to slice off his balls."

I laugh. "I will. Don't worry. I promise."

"Good. And, Dayton? If you ever need anything, even as a friend, call me."

"Why, Monique. Are you going soft in your old age?"

"No. You and your aunt bring out the worst in me," she laughs. "I have to go. The girls are here for the weekly meeting."

"Tell them bye from me, will you?" I ask as something pangs in my chest.

"Of course. I'll see you, honey."

"See you," I whisper, hanging up.

I close my eyes and press my hand to my stomach. I never expected leaving that world to be easy, but I never thought it would hurt either. For five years, it truly was my life. But just like a book has different chapters, life has different stages.

This, me and Aaron, is a new stage in my life. One I can fully only embrace by saying goodbye to the previous one.

Two sharp raps at the door echo through the house, and I jump. I don't want to answer it—just in case. What if...

Aaron strolls into the kitchen and I let out the breath I was holding. Stupid woman, jumping to conclusions. Of course it's Aaron.

"You're back early." I lean back as he kisses me.

"I have senior staff for a reason. All they needed was a handful of signatures on contracts after they'd been to the lawyers. Why they couldn't wait, I'll never know." He looks at the suitcase and bags. "Do you have everything you need?"

I nod. "Including food."

He smirks. "You and your food."

"It's a basic need." I flatten my hands against his chest, loving the feel of the solid muscle beneath my fingertips. "I called Monique."

"You did? Already?"

"Yep. I'm a free woman," I whisper.

He sweeps me his arms around me and plants a hot kiss on my lips. "No, baby. You're not a free woman. You're *my* woman."

I smile against him and kiss his cheek. "Like I have any other choice."

"Damn right you don't." He releases me. "Can I ask you something about this place before we go?"

"Sure. What?"

"When my assistant came here with Liv—"

"Your assistant was here?!"

"—she said there was an extension, but it was locked and Liv wouldn't let her in."

I suck my bottom lip into my mouth. Would you believe I totally forgot about my extension? With everything...it just faded from my mind.

"Why is it locked?"

"I built my extension to...work in." I hold my hands up when his eyes widen. "It's not uncommon. Some entertain in their bedroom, but I never did."

"Thank fucking god for that."

"I wasn't comfortable with it, so I had the extension built. There're two rooms. A normal bedroom and something a little...kinkier."

Aaron's shock soon changes to an amused curiosity. "Kinkier?"

"Um, yes. Whips and the like."

"You were whipped?"

I shake my head. "No. It wasn't—it isn't—my thing. I'm all for a bit of kink, but that doesn't appeal to me. There were some clients who preferred it that way... Who preferred being dominated."

"Is it wrong that the thought of you head to toe in black leather is turning me the fuck on right now?"

"That's awfully stereotypical of you, Mr. Stone. I didn't always wear leather. Sometimes I didn't wear anything at all."

"Dayton," he growls in the bottom of his throat, the huskiness of it hitting me square between the legs. "Can I see?"

I drop my gaze to his pants and the bulge there. "Do you think that's a good idea?"

"I'm not planning on laying you on a bed and whipping your ass or asking you to do it to me. I'm just...curious."

"Curious? About whips and chains and kink?"

"Chains?"

"They do the same job as your tie, but I much prefer the tie." I grin sexily and take his hand in mine. "Come on."

I grab my keys and pull him through to the back of the house. My key clicks in the lock, and we enter a small hallway.

"Which side first? The normal room or the kink room?"

"I've seen your bedroom, sweetheart. I don't need to see it again."

I put my hand on the doorknob and smile at him. *Oh, dear.* "Aaron, this is nothing like my bedroom. Trust me."

I push it open and step inside. Nude photos line the walls, and thick red curtains are draped over the window. The blankets on the large, black cast-iron bed match them, and the black throw pillows break up the red somewhat.

Aaron's eyes skim the whole room, including the leather chair in the corner and the fluffy rug at the side of the bed. "You're right. This is nothing like your bedroom."

"It's not supposed to be." I drop his hand and cross to the curtains, pushing them open a crack. "My bedroom is my space to relax. This bedroom is for seduction and pure, hard fucking."

"And the kink room, as you put it?"

I drop the curtain and lead him into that room. The coloring is mostly the same, the décor not much different at all, with the exception of the leather chair now being a thick wooden one.

Oh, and the fact there are whips, floggers, and paddles hanging on one wall. Aaron stops when he sees them, and I walk to them. I pull a whip down and run it through one hand, gazing up at him through my lashes.

"Crack in your armor, Mr. Stone?"

"No." He takes it from me and hangs it back up. "As sexy as that look is on you, I'm struggling to imagine a situation in which I'd rather smack your gorgeous ass with a bit of leather instead of my hand."

"I would be offended if you preferred the whip over your hand."

"I'd be offended if you *wanted* the whip."

"Well, would you look at that? Something we both agree on." I pat his cheek with a grin and leave the room.

The thought that I won't be using this room again is happier than I imagined it would be. Truth be told, this room was never my favorite, but they were big players because of the taboo that goes with the dom/sub arrangement. Absolute anonymity was required because they were the guys with the most money. The most powerful ones.

"You know the interior of these rooms will be ripped out, don't you?" Aaron asks softly behind me.

I twist the key in the lock and nod. "I know. And I'm okay with that. It's my past, and that doesn't matter anymore."

His kiss is soft. "Good, because those rooms are the perfect size for—"

"An office and a playroom." I laugh the words and he pauses. "Hey, you were about to say that exact thing."

"I was," he agrees with a smile and pulls me into his side in the kitchen. "Come on, Bambi. Let's go home. I'm hungry."

I smack his stomach and grab the food bags. "I hope you can cook. I don't intend to."

"When are you in Seattle?"

"In two days."

"Got a couple of hours to spare for me?"

Tyler chuckles down the phone. "Finally come to your senses and realized I'm the better cousin?"

I laugh into my hand. "Yes, that's it. Since leaving London, I've realized I'm madly in love with you and I can't be without you any longer."

"Ah, well, it was coming."

"You're an ass, Ty. No. I was wondering if I could…take you up on your offer."

"You're going to let me shoot you?"

"As long as we're talking cameras and not guns, yes."

He clicks his tongue. "I suppose I can go easy on you. Of course I have time for you. I'll call you when boss man has given me my schedule."

"Text me. This is going to be a…surprise."

"A surprise, huh? Is that what they call a shock these days?"

"Shut up. He already moved me into his apartment. I'm not giving him the further satisfaction of knowing he's getting his way with this too."

Chapter Twenty

His shirt is open, showing every perfectly sculpted pack of muscle on his chest. A blue tie is tucked beneath the collar, hanging undone around his neck, and a cell phone is perched precariously between his ear and his shoulder as he buttons his fly.

"No…. Jesus, Derrick, I said no…. Working with them last time was less than desirable… Set up a meeting if we must, but the probability of a contract is next to fucking nothing." Aaron sighs. "You'll have to speak with Dottie. She has my schedule on hand… No, she won't be in the office for another hour… I'm positive Mr. Dawson won't combust if he doesn't have an answer within the next ten minutes. Call him back and tell him you'll touch base during office hours… That's my final say on the matter, yes. I'll see you later." He throws his cell across the room, and it bounces off the sofa and onto the floor. "Fucking incompetent bastard. Who calls their boss at eight in the morning unless it's life or death?"

My lips curve, and I lift my coffee mug. My eyes roam shamelessly over his exposed body, and if the spark in Aaron's eyes is anything to go by, he's caught it.

"Like what you see?"

"Do you?" I meet his gaze and flick the collar of one of his shirts.

"I'm not sure. I can't see all of you."

I tilt my head to one side and put my mug down, standing slowly. His eyes darken as they coast over my body the way mine just did his, and he clenches one hand into a fist when he realizes I'm wearing nothing beneath the shirt.

"Is this going to be a habit, Dayton?"

"Is what going to be a habit? My being up early enough to see you off to work?" I raise an eyebrow. "I wouldn't count on it, baby. I don't do mornings."

He leans across the bar, wrapping his hand around my neck, and pulls me into him. "Oh, I know you don't. You're a little night owl. Do you know how exhausted I am?"

"Perhaps you should reconsider changing your schedule. A ten a.m. start may be more fitting for your current lifestyle."

"The lifestyle in which I take you to our bed every night and fuck you until you see black?"

A spark of red-hot lust shoots through my pussy, dissipating into a heavy ache at his words. "Or we could go with the one in which I flip you onto your back and fuck *you* until *you* see black—like I did last night."

A growl rumbles deep in Aaron's throat. "Are you trying to send me to work with a raging hard-on?"

"Are you going to be going with one?"

"Unless I lift you onto this counter and sink inside you and make you come in ten minutes, yes, I am." He buttons his shirt slowly, his eyes never leaving mine.

I shake my head with a rueful smile. "Not going to happen. I'm actually rather offended at the idea that you'll come in ten minutes of sex with me. That's a hit to my ego, you know? I know for a fact I can work you for longer than that."

"Dayton, sweetheart." Aaron rounds the bar and slips between my legs on the stool. "That's not an insult. It's a compliment. You're so fucking sexy you're lucky I don't come the second I slide inside you."

"You're lucky you don't, you mean." I grab either side of his tie and knot it for him. "If you did, I'd be really fucking mad you denied me of an orgasm."

"Trust me, if that ever happens—which it won't—I'll slide down your body and taste you until you come several times over to make up for my incompetence."

The thought of Aaron being incompetent in the bedroom is seriously laughable.

I flatten his collar over the neck of tie and pat it down, making sure his tie is perfect. "I'll remember that."

He threads his fingers into his hair. "Look at you, dressing me. Can I count on that being a rarity, Miss Black? I much prefer the alternative."

"Dressing yourself? There's no fun in that."

His lips curl in the smirk that always gets me, the one that sets a dangerous spark off in his eyes and tightens my muscles. "I can safely say getting dressed is the least favorite part of my day. Especially since you moved in."

"Since I was forced to," I correct him, lightly pushing on his chest. He straightens, his mouth twisting in annoyance. "Oh, don't pull that with me. We both know I had no choice in the matter. I chewed your ass out and now I'm all good with it. Kind of. Sort of."

Aaron takes my coffee and finishes it. *Bastard.* "Lose one of the sugars. Makes the coffee taste funny."

"You know, there's a reason I made two mugs. One for me and one for you."

He glances over my shoulder to the coffee machine and winces when he sees the second mug. "Dammit. Still, lose the sugar. I prefer stealing yours."

Of course he does. Why would he have his own when he can

just steal mine? He obviously thinks I make it for shits and giggles. I don't. Coffee is serious stuff.

"I'm going to start making myself two mugs every morning so that when you steal one, I still have one for myself."

"You do that, sweetheart." He kisses me softly. "I have to go to work. What are you doing today?"

I shrug a shoulder. "Probably the same thing I've done for the last few days. Not very much."

Guilt flashes in his eyes for half a second. "Why don't you call Liv?"

"She's working."

"You'll think of something, I'm sure. I'd invite you to come into the office with me, but I can guarantee I wouldn't get a great deal of work done." He flicks his eyes to the space between my breasts that's exposed by the open front of his shirt. "Make that none."

"Go to work before I suddenly make plans for my day and call you in sick," I warn, seeing the heat clouding his eyes.

Aaron smirks, pulling me into him again and sweeping his lips across mine. "I fail to see how that sentence is supposed to convince me to leave you here alone."

I kiss him hard and shove him off me, standing. "Go before I make good on my threat."

"You drive a hard bargain." He slaps my ass and grabs his jacket. "Behave yourself, and no DIY orgasms."

I gasp, turning and walking backward toward the bathroom. "How did you know what I was thinking?"

He winks and disappears out the door. A smile curves my lips. All the bullshit aside, being with him is so easy. Living with him is so easy.

His blue eyes are the first and last things I see every day. His arms around me is the first and last thing I feel every day. His voice is the first and last thing I hear.

If it weren't for the bullshit simmering beneath the surface courtesy of his ex, this would be pretty much perfect right now.

If perfect existed, that is. It doesn't, but true love is the closest thing you'll get to perfect. And despite everything, all the fights and the time that's passed, I know this is true love.

Nothing but true love can make you feel as if you're walking on air, even during the bad shit.

I shrug off his shirt, drop it in the laundry basket, and run naked back to the second bedroom. My lingerie room. My fingers brush across the endless fabric until my eyes fall on that turquoise bra I fell in love with in London.

Briefly, I glance at the red outfit Aaron loves. I discard the thought just as quickly.

I have no idea what his response will be when he finds out that Tyler is taking my portfolio shots, but I bet it won't be pretty if I wear that one.

No, I'll leave that for another day.

I grab some black panties, slide them up my legs, then slip into the bra. My lips curve at my stupidly when I stand in front of the mirror and jiggle my boobs in the cups to make them sit right. Inside-bra-boob-adjusting: necessary but idiotic, and something every woman does.

A knock sounds at the door as I tie the belt of my robe, and I cross the apartment to answer it. I open the door to Tyler, and he ruffles his hair and grins.

"I'm still amazed you're up."

"Shut up." I step to the side and let him in. "Coffee?"

"Tea, thanks. You can keep your bloody coffee." He hangs his jacket on the hooks in the hall and follows me into the kitchen, looking around. "I see you've added some femininity to this place."

"Believe me, it was by force," I reply dryly and hand him his tea. "Here."

"Thanks. Did you tell him yet?"

I shake my head and lead him into the front room. I sink onto the sofa and tuck my legs beneath me. "What am I supposed to say? 'Oh, hey, baby, I forgot to tell you that your conniving, gold-digging bitch-whore of an ex-wife dropped by my place three weeks ago and threatened me unless I pay her two and a half million'?"

"It pretty much sums it up." A smile teases his lips, and I smack him with a throw pillow, narrowly missing his tea.

"It's just so good right now, like we're finally where we're supposed to be, and I'm scared it'll ruin everything. I know I have to though. I think she's keeping tabs on me."

Tyler looks at me, a frown marring his features. "What do you mean, keeping tabs on you?"

"It's totally irrational, but when I went home the day after we left London, there was a letter from her in my mail. All it said was, 'Tick tock.' I bet she knew I wasn't home. There was no postmark and it was handwritten. And it was sitting on top of the pile. It had only just been delivered."

"Are you sure it wasn't a couple of days old?"

I shake my head. "No. The mailman had already been by when I went back to my house. It was definitely delivered that day."

He runs his fingers over his lips, looking away thoughtfully. "That was what, a few days ago now?"

"Yep. And now there's only one week until she'll go to the press with who I am."

"She might be bluffing."

The look he gives me tells me that even he knows it's farfetched.

"No. She'll go, and she'll expose me, and she'll get paid a stupid amount of money for breaking the story about the whore Aaron Stone is dating."

Now he hits me with a pillow. "Don't call yourself that. You're not a whore."

I smile wryly. "Maybe not now. I was though. Don't argue with me, Ty," I add when he opens his mouth again. "I'm not sugarcoating shit. You're one of the few people who know what I did for a living, so please don't wrap it in fluffy crap either. It's the blunt and ugly reality of my existence. It's who I was. I'm not ashamed of it, but I'm ashamed of the fact it could destroy Stone."

"Stone is a huge company, Dayton, and even if your past got out, it would take a lot to bring it down."

"A lot Naomi could do. I don't know her half as well as you do, yet you're the one underestimating what she could do. She won't stop until she's destroyed the company and exposed every last one of my skeletons all because she wants to get to Aaron."

"You really think Aaron will let that happen?" Tyler puts his mug on the table and shifts to face me. "Aaron will protect you as fiercely as he'll protect the company, maybe even more so. You have to tell him."

"I know." I run my fingers through my hair and sigh, resting my elbow on the back of the sofa. "I just… I gave him such a hard time about keeping her a secret and now I'm doing the exact same thing. That makes me a raging bitch, Ty."

"No. It makes you someone who's afraid of hurting the person you love. Just like he was."

I swallow. "I guess you're right. I have a week left and no idea how I'm supposed to pay her off, so I don't have a choice. I'll tell him when he gets back from work tonight."

He reaches over and squeezes my knee. "Good choice. Now, let's go shoot you and put together some shit-hot pictures that'll get you a superstar agent."

I watch as he grabs his bag and stand. "Doesn't it make you feel awkward, shooting your cousin's girlfriend?"

"Do you feel awkward with me doing it?"

"A little, yeah."

"Then don't think of me as that. You won't see my face anyway. I'll be behind a camera. Pretend you don't know me and this will be fine." He points to the canvas on the bedroom wall. "See that? You're a natural. Now take off that robe and let's get to work."

⁂

I don't know if I'll ever get used to looking at pictures of myself. If I'll ever accept myself the way the camera sees it.

And it's not even confidence. It's…strange. Twenty-four is an old age to get into modeling—okay, so I'm three days away from twenty-five, but let's not think about that right now—but I don't look twenty-four. I've always looked a couple of years younger, and right now, that's something that could work in my favor.

"I don't know why you didn't do this before."

"Because it wasn't my thing. It still isn't, I don't think." I swipe my finger across the laptop screen and the picture flicks to the next one. I'm kneeling on the bed, my back to the camera, and my robe is sliding off my shoulder. I'm glancing over it and looking down, and I kind of get it.

I can do sexy pretty well. I'm just used to sexy-between-the-sheets.

"These are brilliant. At least the ones after you killed your giggles are."

I laugh again at the memory. So the awkwardness was more awkward than I'd anticipated, and I spent the first hour in and out of random fits of giggles. There are a few shots of me laughing in various positions, and they're probably my favorites because of how natural they are.

"Can I see those again?" I ask.

Tyler nods and taps the screen a few times. We sectioned them off and went through the images in batches, and when the folder comes up, I smile. I flick through them to find my favorite.

My knees are bent and I'm leaning forward, laughing. One hand is on my thigh and the other is curved around the neck of my robe and it's tugging it down, exposing my bra on one side.

"Can you edit this and print it?" My cheeks flush a little. "I mean…"

"It's a gorgeous photo and you want it for Aaron."

"Um, yes." I laugh. "Look at me, all shy. That man is ruining me."

"That's far too much information." Tyler snorts, shutting the laptop down. "It'll take a few days to edit these, but when they're done, I'll email you them so you can pick the ones you want for your portfolio. Then I'll put it together and email it out. A different name, right?"

I nod. "I don't want anyone at the company recognizing my name. I've never met any of the agents, so there's no chance they'll recognize me. Is that crazy?"

Tyler shakes his head. "Nope. Perfectly sane. Until you have to explain you're not Maria Espinoza Barielles."

"Yeah, I'll pass on that one. I'll think the name up myself, thank you very much." I grin and grab the ringing phone. "Hello?"

"Miss Black? There's a letter downstairs for you. It was just delivered," Jasper, the guy on security, says.

"Oh. That's strange. Do you know who delivered it?"

"No, ma'am. I'm sorry. It was delivered by a courier."

My heart pounds dangerously loud in my chest, and I close my eyes. "Can you have it brought up?"

"Of course."

"Thank you, Jasper."

I set the phone on the cradle and wrap my arms around my stomach. My hands are shaking, and I barely hear Tyler asking me what's wrong. I just shake my head and open the door when there's a knock before taking the letter from Jasper.

I drop it on the bar in the kitchen and stare at it. The handwriting is the same. No postmark. No stamp. Just a scrawling mass of letters that makes up my name and my address.

"Dayton?" Tyler rests a hand on my shoulder.

"It's another letter. She knows I'm living here now."

"Fuck." His fingers flex and he drops his hand. He rounds the bar and stands opposite me, clenching the countertop. "Are you going to open it?"

"What choice do I have?" I ask weakly, picking it up and flipping it over. I slide my pinkie beneath the flap just like I did last time and pull out the scrap of paper.

> *One week. Doesn't time fly when you're having fun? It's a shame you told Tyler… I'll let it pass. You're getting desperate, after all. But if you tell Aaron…the world will meet Mia Lopez.*

I drop it like it's burning my fingers and squeeze my eyes shut. "Fuck. Fuck, fuck, fuck, fuck, fuck!"

The volume of my voice rises until the word echoes off the walls. Fear and anxiety run rife through my body, constricting my throat and sending my heart into a dangerously crazy rhythm. My eyes blur with unshed tears, and as I gulp for air, I feel two hands rest on my upper arms.

"Dayton. Calm down. Day, Jesus. You have to breathe, love. Come on."

I shake my head, rubbing my hands across my arms to stop the cold. The room is spinning. I can't breathe and I can't think and all that's real is the frantic rushing of blood through my body. It's coupled with adrenaline and a fear so strong it consumes me.

Until his voice breaks through and the touch of his hand on my cheek bats it away.

"Dayton. Breathe for me, sweetheart," Aaron says softly. "Come on now. Breathe."

I take a deep breath in.

"That's it. And out. And back in. That's better." He wraps his arms around me, and I realize we're on the floor.

How did we get here?

How did *I* get here?

Aaron kisses my forehead as I continue breathing steadily, and I brush tears from my cheeks. He holds me until I've calmed down and my heart is beating somewhat more normally.

"I'm glad you were here," Aaron says over his shoulder to Tyler.

"Sorry I pulled you from your meeting, cuz."

Aaron shakes his head. "Fuck the meeting. The contract will still be there tomorrow morning." He turns to me. "What's wrong?"

There's nothing but compassion and worry in his eyes, and a stab of guilt hits me in the stomach. Jesus. I should have told him. I should have been honest. I never should have kept this to myself. I've been so fucking stupid.

"I have to tell you something," I whisper.

"What is it? What's wrong?"

I glance up at Tyler, holding my breath, and he nods. "Naomi came to see me just before we went to London."

Aaron's whole body tenses. "What?"

I rub my hands over my face and stand, leaning on the bar. "She wasn't happy with the divorce settlement, and she came to ask me for money."

Tyler snorts, and I see Aaron's eyes flit between us.

"You knew about this?" he directs at his cousin.

Tyler nods, and I see anger wash over Aaron's features when he faces me.

"She asked you for money? Why didn't you just tell me?"

"She didn't…ask…so much as blackmail me," I finish in a small voice.

"How much?"

"Two and a half million."

"What the fucking hell, Dayton!"

"She gave me four weeks to get it to her, and I have one week left."

Aaron takes a few deep breaths and waits for me to continue.

"When I went home after London, there was a letter waiting, and today, there was one delivered here." I look accusingly at the paper in front of me. "She's keeping tabs on me. She knows Tyler knows and she said if I told you all bets were off."

"All bets for what? What could she possibly know about you that she could hold over your head?"

I hand him the paper. "She knows I was a call girl. If I don't pay, she's threatening to expose my past and destroy your business."

Aaron's eyes skim over the words in front of them and close briefly. When they open again, I see nothing but pure anger. It's a rage so fierce that it scares me a little—and even more so from knowing that some of that is directed at me.

Because I did what I condemned him for.

But I did it worse. I put his whole life on the line because of my own fear.

He drops the paper and walks out without a word. The apartment door slams behind him, the sound ricocheting around the room with a finality that settles deep inside me.

I look at Tyler. "Go," I whisper. "He needs you more than I do. I don't deserve to need you."

He looks at me uncertainly, but I merely nod my head. I don't want him here. I can feel the pressure building in my chest, and I don't want him here when it bursts. He crosses the room and kisses the side of my head before following Aaron out the door.

The door closes again, and I sink to the floor. I let the pressure run free, and a sob escapes my lips.

Yet again, there's a part of me inside that's broken. But this time, I have only myself to blame.

The mattress dips next to me, and I curl myself tighter into a ball. My hands fist the sheets covering me, and I screw my eyes shut. Uncertainty is all I feel, when all I want to feel is—

His arms wrapping around me, pulling me into his hard body.

Aaron buries his face in my neck as he holds me close to him. His chest rises and falls, and I can feel the pounding of his heart against my back. He slips his knee between my legs and kisses my shoulder.

"What are you doing?" I whisper, my words thick with unshed tears.

"I'm holding you, baby. What else do you think I'm doing?"

"You shouldn't be. You should hate me."

He urges me onto my back and leans over me. Even in the darkness, his eyes are bright blue, shining like a beacon through the blackness surrounding us. But they're not angry, not at me. They're soft and forgiving and everything I don't deserve.

"I could never hate you, Dayton. Not ever." He wipes away a tear that escapes. "So don't say such ridiculous things."

I lift my hand and cup his face, feeling the roughness of his stubble against my palm. "Why aren't you mad at me?"

"Because you didn't keep it a secret to spite me. You kept it to protect me, and yes, it was a little misguided and unnecessary, but you did it because you care."

"But you did that, too, and I left you."

He drops his face to mine and kisses me. Certainly. Strongly. "I'm not leaving you, beautiful woman, so get that thought right out of your pretty little head. I'm not going anywhere and neither are you."

"But you did. Earlier. When you found out." My bottom lip quivers and I bite it gently. "You left then."

"Because I was a kind of angry I never want you to see. But it wasn't at you. Not entirely, anyway. Most of it was at her, and if you hadn't sent Tyler after me, I just might have found her apartment and done something incredibly stupid."

"I'm sorry." I wrap my arms around his neck and squeeze him tightly.

His arms go around me equally as firmly, and he rolls me onto my side and into his body. He brushes my hair from my face and looks at me, tugging the sheet up over us.

"I know. We'll talk some more in the morning, okay? Get some sleep now."

"Never go to sleep on an argument," I murmur. "That's what my mom always taught me. You sort it out first."

"Bambi, we're not arguing. Not even close." He brushes his thumb across my eyelid, forcing me to close my eyes, and sets one of my arms over his waist. "Now we're going to go to sleep together and wake up the same way, today and every day. Understand?"

I nod and push my face into his neck. "I don't deserve you."

"And I don't deserve you, so I guess we're even. Goodnight, sweetheart."

Chapter Twenty-One

I wake to the feel of fingertips trailing down my spine and look straight into startling blue eyes. Shivers follow the trail of Aaron's fingers, and I shift in bed.

And remember the events of yesterday. Guilt hits me full force in the stomach, and I part my lips to speak.

"No. Don't you look at me with guilt in your eyes," he says softly. "Cut that shit out, Dayton. What's done is done."

I sit up, knocking his arm from around me. "How aren't you mad at me, Aaron? Why aren't you yelling and screaming at me?"

"Because that would solve nothing. Am I angry at you? Yes, I am. I'm mad that you kept it from me, but not for the reasons you think. Not because you berated me for keeping her a secret in the first place. I'm mad because this, us… We're a couple, and we share this stuff. It means we don't have to deal with anything alone, but you have been." He sighs, sitting too. "And yes, Dayton, it hurts that you told Tyler but not me. I understand why you'd prefer to tell someone other than me, and I'm glad it was him, but I wish you could have been honest with me."

"I'm sorry." The words feel so inadequate, and I understand how he felt. Why he couldn't say the words in his office when I so desperately wanted him to. They seem so small and unnecessary when the thing you're apologizing for is so potentially devastating.

"I know you are, and I accept that. Now we're not going to sit here and think about what could be. We're going to get up, go to my office, and do something about it."

I swallow when he gets up. "But there's nothing you can do. You read the note."

Aaron stops before walking into the closet and looks at me. "If you believe my influences lie within the modeling and advertising world alone, you're incredibly wrong. Get up, get dressed, and make me coffee. Without all the sugar."

I can't help the upturn of my lips. His company could be destroyed at any second and he's worried about coffee. Only I could be in love with a man who has that train of thought.

I pad my way to the spare bedroom and change my underwear. When I'm back in the closet, I pull out a pair of jeans and a hooded sweatshirt. Aaron grabs them from me and chucks them on the shelf.

"No. You're not hiding. If she's keeping tabs on you, which she likely is, then you're not hiding." He cups my chin and looks at me square on. "She's playing a game, baby, and you're not going to let her win. So ignore the jeans, grab a dress, and pack that self-loathing away because we don't have space for that in our relationship, okay?"

I nod and pick a red dress from a hanger. "You know, the easy solution to all this would be to just—"

"Say it and I'm going to slap your pretty little ass until it's red and raw."

I chew on my bottom lip. "Okay. Not an option. I get it."

He smirks and spins me to do up my zipper. "Red. Good choice. I notice it matches your panties."

"Red is my color, and it's a red kind of day, I think."

He drops a kiss to the spot below my ear. "I think you're right. Now, about that coffee?"

I reach behind me and smack his leg. "I need to do my makeup. Your coffee will have to wait."

I stroll into the bathroom and grab my makeup bag from the corner of the sink. I'm brushing foundation across my cheeks when Aaron joins me.

"Coffee," is all he says.

"Is that a demand?"

"I require coffee every single morning."

I finish with the foundation and grab his arm, moving his shirt so it exposes the watch on his wrist. I tap the face lightly. "Seven thirty. There's still four and a half hours of the morning left. Your requirement can wait a little longer."

He stands behind me as I finish applying my makeup. He grabs my brush and runs it through my hair, and I meet his eyes in the mirror.

"How do you do it?"

"How do I do what?" he responds.

"Make it seem so normal. There's this huge cloud hanging over us ready to piss all over us and you're just…normal."

He smiles. "Haven't you learned anything? Great love makes the bad stuff disappear, if only for a second, and you and I? We have the greatest love I've ever felt. Don't think I'm not thinking about it, because I am. I'm merely choosing to focus on the good things, and right now, that's you. It's always you."

Aaron sets the brush on the side and grabs our toothbrushes from the holder. He runs them under the sink and squeezes some toothpaste on them. I take mine and we stand, side by side, brushing our teeth, looking like a real couple.

And it's this, the little mundane things you really do skip over, that make a difference. I never thought brushing my teeth next to someone could make such a difference, but it does.

This, right now, makes me want to fight.

And if all fucks up, if Mia Lopez is exposed and my life is thrust into the public eye, I'll fight then, too.

I'll fight like hell for the man standing next to me.

Even if he has missed a button on his shirt.

I put my brush back and turn to him, finding that missed button and fixing it. Aaron grins down at me, toothpaste around his mouth, and moves me to the side so he can spit it out. I shake my head with a smile.

He's right.

Great love makes the bad shit disappear.

I leave him in the bathroom and make my way to the coffee machine to provide Mr. Stone with his latest requirement. He's definitely getting a little requirement-happy, regardless of how many of them I like.

The coffee one? It should definitely be a two-way requirement. I need it too, ya know.

"Oh, she's learning," he quips, taking the mug from me.

I turn the sugar-heaped spoon in his direction. "Watch it, Mr. Stone, or I might decide you need some sweetening." He laughs, and I stir the sugar into my own mug. "Why am I coming to work with you?"

"Because I don't trust Naomi. If she knows you live here, when no mutual acquaintances of ours do, she's definitely keeping tabs on you. She is coldhearted and ruthless, and leaving you here alone is putting you at risk. That's something I can't comprehend. The idea of putting you in harm's way makes me sick to my stomach, Dayton. If that means I have to glue you to my side and take you everywhere with me until this is figured out, that's exactly what I'll do."

"I can't help but think it's a little over the top. Isn't that what she'll be expecting?"

"She's expecting me not to know. And regardless of what she's expecting, protecting you is my number-one priority." His eyes crash into mine. "I would kill a man to protect you, Dayton. Don't ever doubt my need to keep you safe or the lengths I would go to in order to do that."

I walk to him and wrap my arms around his waist. His words should shock me. I should coil back, reel in shock, but I'm not. I know it. I know it because I feel it too. When you love someone so intensely that it knocks your whole world off-kilter but still somehow keeps it spinning, there are no barriers to what you'll do to protect them.

"I love you," I say into his chest. "Okay? I love you."

"I know, sweetheart. I know." He envelopes me with his arms and breathes me in. "And I you. I love you so fiercely that I'm afraid it might consume me one day. So please, humor me right now."

"No need to. There's nothing funny about this."

Aaron kisses the top of my head and releases me. He downs his coffee and grabs his jacket from the bedroom. "Are you ready to go?"

I nod and drop my cell in my purse. "I'm ready."

He links his fingers through mine and takes me downstairs to the car waiting to take him to the office. I stay by his side through the journey, his arm wrapped around me securely. He waves the security guard off when we arrive at Stone HQ Seattle, and the elevator clears when we step inside.

That must be a thing. Very Devil Wears Prada.

We step out onto his floor, and Dottie, his assistant, is sitting behind her desk. She's in early. I know she doesn't start until nine, and it's just after eight.

"Dottie." Aaron waves at her over his shoulder, and she grabs some paper and a pen and follows us into his office. He sits me in the chair behind his desk. "Dottie, this is Dayton, my girlfriend. Dayton, my assistant and the woman who keeps my business in order, Dottie."

"It's lovely to meet you properly, Dayton," Dottie says, offering a tentative smile.

Oh yes. The last time I met her, I was an angry mess of a woman. *Oopsie.*

"And you, Dottie. I'm sorry last time I was less than desirable."

Aaron pokes me in the back. "Okay, enough chitchat. You two have plenty of time for that. Dottie, we have a situation, and I need you to help me."

I swallow. *Oh, god. No.*

"Anything I can do, I will." She sits up straight and clicks her pen. "What do you need me to do?"

"I need you to get someone to find out where my ex-wife is staying."

Dottie's eyes widen, and I'm sure my expression mirrors hers. "Mr. Stone—"

"She's taken it upon herself to blackmail Dayton, and as you can imagine, I'm less than happy about it. We know she holds some important details about Dayton's life that could impact both her and the business, and it's in everyone's best interests if this *story* doesn't make it past the printers into the public eye."

"You want me to send out some feelers and see who, if anyone, has this information."

"And this is why I pay you." Aaron smiles and leans forward on his desk. "How soon can you find out?"

Dottie clicks her tongue and rocks her head from side to side. "Around noon, give or take an hour or two. I happen to have a couple of reporter friends, and one works at a local tabloid. If there's anything to reveal, she'll have the scoop. And I can ask my boyfriend to see what he can find out. Is there anything else I need to know?"

"If you hear the name Mia Lopez, you're on the right track."

Dottie scribbles that on her paper and stands, nodding. "All right. I'm on it. I'll let you know as soon as I find anything out."

"Thank you. Oh, and, Dottie?"

She pauses by the open door and glances over her shoulder.

"If you get me this information, your next pay will have a considerable bonus in it."

Her lips twist to one side. "I'm not doing it for money, Mr. Stone. I'm doing it because we've all noticed how happy you are now. And, if you'll excuse my language, Naomi is a raging bitch."

She closes the door behind her, and I laugh. "I like her. She gets it."

"Dottie has worked for me for four years, and Naomi spent the majority of that time trying to convince me to fire her." Aaron perches on his desk and folds his arms across his chest.

"Why?"

"She didn't like her. Dottie was fresh out of college when we hired her. It was supposed to be for the summer so she could gain a little experience doing admin work. She took to being my assistant like a duck takes to water when my previous one got pregnant, so I kept her on permanently. Naomi was jealous of how closely we work together. And that Dottie has a crush on me."

I roll my eyes. "It's a good thing there are no trust issues here, isn't there?"

He smiles. "Very."

We stare at each other for a long moment, and he leans in slowly to take my mouth with his.

"Can I...say something?" I ask quietly.

"The amount you talk, I'd be worried if you didn't."

I backhand slap his thigh, and he laughs. "No. Have you ever considered that maybe Naomi is in love with you?"

Aaron pauses, his eyes still on mine. "Once or twice. The problem is, Day, I know her better than anyone else. She loves the money and influence I have more than the man inside."

"I think she's in love with you," I say softly, looking away. "And that's why I think she's doing this."

"Hey." He crouches in front of me and tilts my face into his. "The only person whose feelings matter is the woman I'm looking at right now. I have loved you since the moment I laid eyes on you all those years ago. I never stopped, not even for a second. You have my heart in a viselike grip, Dayton, and I hope to God you'll never let it go. Naomi hates that. She knows I never loved her, and yes, she probably is in what she has come to perceive as love. Money, influence, and social standing don't equal love or a successful relationship. Love is what's beneath the surface, beyond all of those things, and that's what you see. You see the man beneath it all. You see *me*, baby. You look at me and see the way I look at you, not dollar signs. If I have to hurt her to keep you safe, then I will."

"I know."

"Nothing is as important to me as you are. When you understand just how much you mean to me, you'll understand that I'll walk all over anyone who keeps me from protecting you."

"I know."

"I mean it, Day. I'll walk until I can't—"

I tug his face to mine and silence him with the touch of my lips to his. "I know," I murmur. "So please, shut up and kiss me now before you make me cry."

"No more crying," he orders, curling his fingers around the back of my neck. His mouth sweeps across mine in a firm way that backs up his words.

I agree. No more crying. No more doubting or worrying or crying.

I have to put my faith in the man kissing me like I'm the air he needs to breathe. I have to believe that he'll take this mess I escalated and spin it into gold, keeping us both safe in the process.

I have to believe in him, and I have to believe in us.

And I do.

I believe in us.

I believe we can conquer anything thrown our way.

We just have to do it.

⤜⤏⤛

I sigh and lie back on the sofa, lifting my legs and resting them on the back of it. I'm all for Aaron keeping me safe, but I'd like to be amused. As it is, I've run through all my lives on Candy Crush, dropped all my coins on Coin Dozer, and listened to the Spotify top chart five times. Okay, the songs I like on it. That lowers the time consumption considerably.

And now I'm bored. Really, really bored.

I sigh again, this time the breath escaping through pursed lips, and kick my legs. Aaron's in the meeting he left yesterday because of my mini meltdown that left me on the kitchen floor, and he has some damage control to do.

I think. I could be exaggerating. I have no idea how this business stuff works.

My third sigh leaves as a huff. How long does it take to negotiate a contract? Half an hour?

No, that's silly. I've been here alone for at least two hours.

He really needs to invest in a coffee machine for this office. Stat.

The door opens, and I roll my head to the side. A smirk curves Aaron's lips as he flicks his eyes over my body and takes me in.

"Comfortable?"

"Comfortable but bored," I reply, flexing my ankles. "Did you get your contract?"

"Don't ask me such stupid questions, Dayton. I was in charge of the campaign. Of course I did."

I swing my legs around and sit up straight. "Even though you ran out halfway through the meeting yesterday?"

He raises his eyebrows. "Every person in that meeting was married. They understood my need to leave."

"For your girlfriend? Married and girlfriend are different things."

"For one second, will you stop doubting your importance to me? Fuck, Day, it's driving me insane. Do you honestly think I wouldn't walk you down an aisle tomorrow if it wouldn't freak you the hell out? I love you, and love is love, regardless of a piece of paper declaring forever. My heart has promised you forever and that's the fucking end of it."

"I don't doubt my importance. I was just asking. And I'm bored. So my brain is kind of numb right now."

"You're bored? How bored?"

"I-could-claw-my-own-eyes-out bored."

He crosses his office and leans over me, one hand on the back of the sofa, the other flattened on the cushion by my side, and curves his lips. "Bored enough you can cope with me in here for an hour until my next meeting?"

"Debatable. I might get annoyed. You know what they say about couples that work and play together."

"Oh, believe me, baby. I have no work on my mind. Only play."

He covers my mouth in a kiss so forceful I push my hips up. Shit. His tongue slides along the seam of my mouth, flicking between my lips and begging for entry. I allow him, opening for him, letting my tongue sweep against his. He squeezes my waist and lowers his body on top of mine, hard and defined and so fucking perfect.

I slide my hands beneath his jacket and tug his shirt free of his trousers. The skin on his back is hot beneath my fingers as they creep under the hem of his shirt, and he groans quietly when I wrap my legs around his back.

The way my body arches into his, the tensing of my muscles that hold him to me, the deep sweep of my tongue across his—they all say how much I need him. They tell both of us how much my body needs his, how much it craves the sweet touch of his skin against mine.

He loosens his tie and loops it over his head, still knotted, and slides one hand up my dress to my ass. He squeezes lightly, and I tug desperately at his jacket. It falls to his elbows and I tear his buttons open, his shirt following shortly after. Then he slips his hands beneath my body. They flatten against the small of my back and hold me to him.

Aaron lifts me, walking me across his office, and perches me on the edge of his desk. "I told you I'd fuck you on this desk, and since everyone is gone for lunch, I'm going to fuck you hard. Hard enough that you scream my name so the whole building can hear you."

My body arches into him in response to his words. I don't need to say anything. This is the time my body says everything I can't put together.

He swipes his hand across the desk, and holy fucking shit, the papers and pens scatter just like they do in the movies. Before I can wonder when this became my life, he lays me back and eases my dress up over my hips.

Once again, my mouth is taken by his, this time hot and desperate, needy and forceful. I'm a prisoner beneath his body, my bare ass against the chill of his glass desk, while he runs his hands over my body.

They find my hips and, eventually, my aching, wet clit. He rubs me through my panties, making my back arch and my breath hitch, but it's not enough.

I want all of him. I want every inch of him inside me until I forget the crap hanging over us and give in to the sheer pleasure I know only he can give me.

"Aaron, please," I whisper into his neck, grabbing his back desperately. "I need you."

"How badly do you need me, Day? Tell me. Tell me how badly you want me to fuck you right now." He kisses down my neck to my collarbone, sucking lightly on my pulse point, making me tighten.

"Don't fuck me around Aaron. Just fuck me. You know how badly I need you."

"No, I don't," he breathes, grinding his erection against my throbbing pussy. "Tell me, Dayton."

"Tell you what?"

He slips two fingers inside me. "Tell me how desperately you need me to fill you and stretch you until you throw your head back and whisper my name. Tell me how fiercely you want me to drive my cock into you. Tell me how hard you want me to hold your hips against mine. Tell me how much you want this." He unzips his fly and positions the head of his hard, gleaming cock at my opening. "Tell me how desperately you need me inside you until you're incapable of screaming anything but my name."

"You demanding?" I flex my hips, trying to get more of him inside.

"Requiring, baby. Tell me right the fuck now or I'm zipping my pants and leaving you here wide open and begging on my desk."

The idea of that sends a lightning jolt through my body, and I dig my nails into my skin. I lift my face to his, my mouth by his ear, and I give him what he wants.

"I want you inside me, Aaron. I want you to sink into me until you forget where you end and I begin, until we forget what's real and what isn't. I want you inside me until you're fucking me so hard all you can think of is the sweet heat of my pussy clenching around you as I cry your name into your ear and bite your shoulder in pleasure. Is that enough for you, baby? Is that what you want? To know I want you to fuck me until I see motherfucking stars from the sheer force of the pure pleasure you give me?"

He drives into me in one swift thrust, stretching every muscle and making them clench. "Yes. That's what I want to know, Dayton. I want you to know you'll see nothing as you come around me."

"Then you should stop talking and fuck me right the hell now."

And he does. He pulls me into him, tilting my hips up, and pushes himself so far inside me that there isn't a part of my core untouched by him. The heat from his penetration spreads through my body, taking each of my limbs hostage by the beauty of the feeling.

He pushes deep with every thrust into me, each one harder than the last, more desperate, more frantic, more needing. I claw at his back and push my body into him, loving the rawness of it. This is pure. Unadulterated. Desperate. The very thing I need right now.

He pinches my nipple and rolls it between his fingers. I moan at the body-filling feeling. Desire hotter than I've ever felt encompasses me as he takes my other in his mouth, still pounding me.

He releases my nipple, and at his groan, the sex turns carnal. It changes to a fuck in the purest sense of the word. It's primal, and the only goal is pleasure. A scream and a clench and a release.

Our skin slaps together as he drives himself into me relentlessly, his only goal to come. I tilt my hips up and take him farther, allowing him to hit every spot inside me.

Then the skin above his cock rubs my clit, the stubble from his trimmed hair harsh and brutal against the tender nub, and I give in.

To the harsh pounding, to the desperate breaths in my ear, to the clenching of my muscles, to the digging of his fingers at my hips.

I come. Explosively. Suddenly. Incredibly. An all-encompassing shudder of my body that tenses every muscle I have. A crazy, out-of-this-world release that takes all of me hostage.

Aaron's fingers dig as deep into my skin as mine are into his as he grunts my name. I push into him, milking every drop of his orgasm.

The feeling of his skin against mine is something to savor. No matter how many times I grind my hips into his and pull every drop of salty come from him.

Aaron slides a hand into my hair and turns my head into his. "Good thing I just cleared my afternoon for you, Miss Black." He pulls out of me, a hard kiss taking my lips.

"No. You reschedule and get the hell on with it, Stone."

"No. We have other things to attend to this afternoon." He stands and buttons his fly, tucking his half-hard dick inside his boxers.

"Like what, exactly?"

He wipes some tissue along me, tenderly wiping me clean, and passes me my panties. "Sorry. I don't have clean ones," he murmurs. "And things I don't want to discuss while you're lying on my desk after I fucked you."

I sit up, courtesy of his arms around my back and lifting me, and brush my thumb along his jaw. "Let's deal with it, baby. Together. As one."

"We will be, but I'm still not discussing it while you're on my desk."

"Oh, for fuck's sake." I stand, stepping to the side of him. "There. I'm not on your desk anymore."

Aaron looks at my hand. "And you're also not wearing any underwear."

I tug my dress down my thighs and stuff my wet panties into the pocket of his pants. "And I won't be for the rest of the day, so that's a moot point. Now. Talk."

His phone rings and he holds his finger up. "Yes?"

"Mr. Stone?" Dottie's voice comes through the speakerphone. "I gathered the information you asked for this morning."

"Thank you, Dottie. Can you bring it in?"

I cough quietly and point at the floor. More precisely, the mess of papers, files, and pens covering it.

Aaron runs his tongue across his bottom lip. "On second thought, give me a minute."

"Of course." She clicks off the line, and Aaron stalks toward me, a fiery amusement reflecting in his eyes.

"You realize you'll be reorganizing all these later, yes?" He scoops the files and papers up in one swift movement and replaces the pens in the jar next to his laptop.

"Why? You're the one who put them there." I poke him in the chest with raised eyebrows.

He slaps my ass slightly. "We're not getting into this when my assistant is walking into my office in…right now." He kisses me quickly and turns to face Dottie as she eases the door open after a couple of light knocks.

"Mr. Stone?"

"Come in and shut the door behind you," Aaron orders, sitting behind his desk.

I stand to the side and wrap my arms around my stomach, the playful, sexy mood of only minutes ago dissipating into a much heavier one that feels somewhat suffocating.

Dottie takes a seat on the opposite side of his desk and places a folder in front of her. "I called around this morning and put some feelers out. What I know, so far, after promising an intern at The Seattle Insider that risking her job would be worth her while…" She pauses, catching my confused look, and one side of her lips quirk up. "After bribing her," she adds. *Oh. Ah.* "Naomi met with them on the day after you and Dayton returned from London."

"The day after I moved in." I look at Aaron. He nods once and puts his hand out without returning my gaze.

Dottie hands him the folder. "She promised them the 'scoop' on Dayton's past employment for a fee higher than it's worth. The story—as you can see in the file—is ready to go into print at the first word from her."

My fingers dig into my sides. Shit. She's really planned it all out. I step up behind Aaron and skim the paper in his hands.

A sick feeling rises in my stomach.

I don't know how she managed it, but she's uncovered everything but my bra size. My clients, my schedule, my fees… Everything. She knows absolutely everything.

"The Seattle Insider, you say?" Aaron looks up and taps his finger against his mouth thoughtfully. "What would they want with this? It's not sleazy tabloid material. Why isn't she running it with a bigger press?"

"Because they're desperate. They've been running out of stories for months, and their readership has been going with it. They're willing to pay a lot of money for something that will put them back in people's hands. A story on Seattle's version of royalty is the way to do that."

"Interesting," he replies after a long moment. Slowly, he turns to look at me, and I see a spark in his eye. One that screams of an idea, something that could only be accomplished by someone with money. The money he has.

He looks back to Dottie. "Get Sheila to deal with rearranging my afternoon schedule. I want you to send out more of those feelers and see if you can find out just how desperate the Insider is." He pulls his wallet from his pocket and slides several bills across the table. "I might be interested in broadening my portfolio of investments."

Chapter Twenty-Two

"You're going to buy The Insider?"

Aaron looks at me across the table, sucking up a string of spaghetti like a child. I wrinkle my nose at the action, and he laughs.

"Why are you looking at me like I've gone completely crazy?"

"Buying a tabloid. You could pay them off instead."

"Paying people off doesn't always work. As soon as the money is in their hands, all bets are off, especially for a company like them. Dottie said it herself—the only reason they're running the story and paying Naomi an extortionate fee is because they'll fold if they don't. If I step in, buy the company, and keep them afloat, they have no need to pay her and run the story."

"Okay, so I understand that." I put my fork on the table. "But do you really want to be associated with them?"

"They'll have a regular investment from a silent partner. My name wouldn't be connected to them in any way."

"You say it like it's so easy. Like, what? You'll just roll up to The Insider's office and tell them you're buying them? Slap a contract on the table in front of the dude who owns it?"

He smirks slowly, the curve of his lips both tantalizing and amusing. "Don't be ridiculous, sweetheart. I'll tell them I'm buying their company or they'll find themselves unable to sell another paper regardless of the supposedly breaking news stories they print."

"Really? You'd destroy their company?"

He levels his gaze on me. It's steady and firm, honesty reigning supreme in the blue of his eyes. "I told you this morning that I'd kill a man if it meant protecting you. What makes you think I won't rip a shitty little tabloid to shreds to do the same thing?"

A sheen of sweat covers my skin as I pound my feet against the treadmill. After more than two weeks of not exercising, I feel a little bit out of it. A lot out of it.

But I need this. I need to feel the burn in my legs and the thumping of my heart as I put all of my frustration and tension into this workout. I need to let go of some of it, or who knows what will happen. I sure as shit don't need to have another anxiety attack.

The gym on the floor beneath Aaron's apartment is a happy discovery. And since it's early afternoon and everyone is at work, I'm here alone. Which means I'm here to pant and scream and grunt my way through pushing out the heaviness of the last few days.

Yesterday is still niggling at the back of my mind though. I'm still feeling uncertain over Aaron's proclamation regarding The Insider. I'm also aware of the fact that it doesn't cover all our bases.

We don't know if she sold the story exclusively or not. Still, it doesn't matter. I wish that it did. The story won't run, so she can sell it again. She can sell it to any number of papers in this city alone.

Not to mention nationwide. Stone Advertising is a staple in so many industries, not just the fashion and modeling worlds. They run campaigns for fragrances and music and food. They're everywhere because they're the best.

Any number of the shiny, glossy magazines I eye every time I walk past the stand in a store would buy that story. My story.

I close my eyes and slow my pace. How did she know everything? How could she possibly know every little detail about my life? The only ones who know anything like that are…

The people I've worked with.

Monique wouldn't do that. This much I do know, and I'm completely certain of it. The informal contract we sign upon joining her dictates that work never leaves work, and personal details are never provided to anyone.

But the girls…

The escort world isn't dissimilar to the modeling world in the sense that your looks are everything. The prettiest, sexiest, most alluring girl gets the big players. They get the big pay at the end of the week and keep drawing them in. They get the regular, strong income.

That makes for jealousy. I don't know anyone who does that job because they truly enjoy it. Really, having sex with numerous men isn't fun. It's not the kind of thing that makes you bounce out of bed excitedly on a morning. That's the bottom line, and the only thing that sweetens the fact you're a fucking toy for whoever buys you is the money they pay.

It isn't irrational to believe that one of the girls I worked with for the last couple of years would have broken the story.

After all, I got the fairytale. All bullshit aside, I was the top girl. I met the guy. I won his heart. I left the business.

I did what they want, however unintentionally.

And now that could destroy everything.

I wipe my face with a towel and take the elevator up to Aaron's apartment. Our apartment. I really have to get used to saying that—which is a problem when I'm not used to sharing.

I run the shower and grab my cell from the kitchen side, ignoring the blinking message icon, and call Monique.

"Pick up, pick up, pick up," I mutter.

"I have," she responds. "This better be good."

"I hope you mean good-important and not good-good."

"Nope. I was hoping for a marriage announcement or the like."

I snort. "About as far from it as I can get, Mon. Listen, we have a problem."

"What the fuck now?"

"One of your girls sold me out."

Silence. Nothing but her heavy, controlled breathing. Until… "What the fucking hell do you mean? Sold you out?"

I reel off the whole story, ending with my realization of just moments ago. She hisses out a string of angry words, none of which are remotely understandable, and I hear a door slam behind her.

"Let me check the appointments from four and five weeks ago. There has to be something out of the ordinary. I'll get back to you in half an hour." She hangs up, and I drop my phone on the sofa.

I strip off my clothes and step into the shower. The water beats away the tension in my shoulders the way the treadmill sweated it out. The only thing this can't solve is my annoyance.

No, it's not annoyance. It's anger. One that's only set to increase when I find out who turned my shit inside out and sold it.

I don't doubt Naomi paid for the information. Which means it would have been one of the lowest-earning girls on Monique's books. One of the most jealous, desperate ones. One of the ones who needed the money the most.

Which means…

"Shit!" I rinse the conditioner from my hair and grab a towel, my wet hair dripping down my back. Then I shut off the shower.

My cell rings as I run into the front room. "Monique, it was—"

"Lori. She had a random two-hour long client who paid a lot of money for her time around the time you called to cancel Aaron's payments."

"Just before Naomi came to see me. Fuck! What's her address?"

"3A Juniper Avenue."

"Wow. Thanks. I didn't think you'd actually give it to me."

A knock sounds at the door.

"My girl or not, she doesn't fuck with you. Call me later when you know for sure. If she sold you out, she's out on her fucking ass."

"Gotcha. Bye." I hang up for the second time and look through the peephole in the door. "Tyler! Perfect timing."

"It is?"

"Yes. Grab a coffee." I shut the door behind him. "Or tea. Whatever the hell you want. I need to get ready. Then you can take me somewhere."

He raises his eyebrows, a welcome glint of amusement reflecting throughout his expression. "I can, can I?"

"You can and you will." I point at him, walking backward.

"You've been taking lessons on ordering people about from my cousin," he calls through the apartment.

I smile. It seems that way. Well, that's something that will come in handy in the next half hour.

I change quickly and blast my hair through with the hairdryer. When it's damp, I braid it to the side so it hangs over my shoulder. A flick of mascara and I'm ready to go. Ready to go and do what I'm going to refer to as "doing an Aaron."

"Let's go." I open the front door.

"But I just made tea."

"Fuck your tea. I'll make you ten cups later. Move it, Ty."

He sighs and puts the mug down, leading me out of the apartment and into the elevator. "You know what, Dayton? You're lucky you're Aaron's girlfriend. The last woman to boss me about this way found herself bent over my fucking car."

"Nice," I say dryly.

Tyler opens the door of his rental car and I get in. "Where are we going?" he asks.

"3A Juniper Avenue."

"Hang on. Oh, yes. Got it. I know exactly where I'm going."

I hit him in the arm. "I'll direct you. Now let's go."

"Where are we going, exactly?"

"Right. Now left. That's it."

"Day."

"I know who sold me out."

"Ah."

❦

The elevator in Lori's apartment block is broken, so I climb the stairs, thanking myself for putting on flats instead of my usual heels. I'm not thanking the seven flights of stairs, I admit.

I bang on the door and fidget while I wait for her to answer. I knock again, and I hear her call, "One minute!"

I take a deep breath, trying to rein in the annoyance running rife through me. Screaming at her won't do any good.

She opens the door and her eyes widen when she sees me. "Dayton. What a surprise."

"I'd imagine it is. Can I come in?"

"I don't—"

"Thanks." I squeeze past her and look around her apartment. You wouldn't look at this place and believe she was the lowest earner on Monique's books. "Nice place."

"Thanks." She closes the door softly.

"How much did you have to sell me out for to pay for it?"

Lori draws in a sharp breath. "I don't know what you're talking about."

"Don't treat me like I'm stupid, Lori." I turn to her, my hands on my hips, and pierce her with my gaze. She freezes. "I know for a fact you told Naomi everything about me."

She says nothing, but she pulls her gaze from mine and looks at the floor.

"I'll take your silence as an admission. Why would you do that, Lori? Why the fuck would you go and break the unwritten rule we all lived by? We weren't friends, but we weren't enemies either."

"You had everything." She looks at me again, her eyes harder than a moment ago. "You had fucking everything. The big clients. The biggest cut for Monique at the end of the week. You coasted through life without as much as a damn pimple on your chin."

"And that's a reason to sell my life story to my boyfriend's jealous, manipulative ex-wife, right? So she can blackmail me into paying her the money she didn't get from their divorce?" I raise my eyebrows, and her face whitens. "Oh, she didn't tell you that. I didn't think she would have."

"Fuck. I-I didn't know. I'm sorry."

"I don't want your apology, Lori. You've fucked everything— for yourself as well. Did you think you wouldn't be found out? What do you really stand to gain from this?"

"I was in debt. She offered me enough to pay it all off and then some."

I don't have it in me to feel bad. I just can't feel an ounce of sympathy or pity for her.

"I hope it was worth it, and I hope you truly thought through what you were doing. You haven't just put my identity and Stone Advertising at risk. You've put your own life and Monique's business at risk, too. It wouldn't take much to link me back to Monique."

"Naomi said that wouldn't happen."

"Naomi is a lying bitch, Lori. She can't control what happens when she sells the story, what digging journalists do. And she has, by the way, sold the story, and now I'm trying to do damage control. Aaron has one hundred other things he needs to be doing, but because you decided I was worth a few thousand dollars, he's busting his ass trying to make this right. I hope you're proud of yourself. You can expect a call from Monique later tonight."

"Wait, what?"

I open her front door. "Do you honestly think she'll keep you on her books after this? You've put every single one of us at risk of exposure, and in some cases, you've put us in genuine danger. Angry wives are ruthless, as evidenced by the woman who put us here."

She pales even further. "Fuck. I didn't think," she whispers.

"Evidently fucking not." I step through the door then pause and look over my shoulder. "And, Lori?"

"Yeah?"

"If this story breaks, if my whole life is splashed over the pages of some sleazy tabloid, you can bet your damn life I'll be slapping a lawsuit on your ass."

Her eyes widen.

"And as much as you know about my life, I probably know a lot more about yours. If I go down, I'm sure as hell taking you with me."

Chapter Twenty-Three

I push the door to Aaron's office open and look around it. He's leaning forward on the desk, one hand in his hair, a phone to his ear.

"Every one, yes. Make it clear that, if they print it, we'll be coming down on them with the force of a fucking avalanche… Yes… Thank you, Alexander. Email them over tonight and I'll take a look. Then we'll send them out… Perfect. Goodnight."

He puts the phone down and sighs heavily. He spins in the chair and slowly runs his eyes up my bare legs to the hem of his shirt skimming my thighs. After taking the rest of me in, they find my eyes. There's none of the expected heat in them.

Just love.

"Come here," he mutters, holding his arms out.

I cross the room and curl onto his lap, resting my head on his shoulder. His arms go around me securely, holding me against him, and he buries his face alongside mine.

"That didn't sound good," I whisper.

"There are several other presses who have the story. Naomi sold it to both paper and digital outlets, hoping we'd miss one. I believe she planned to have you exposed regardless of her receiving the money."

I shiver. "What are you sending to them?"

"Lawsuits," he mumbles into my neck, sweeping his lips across my skin. "They're being warned of what will be handed to them if they publish the story. Alexander Carlisle Jr. is the best lawyer in Seattle. He'll fuck them so hard they won't have a choice but to not run it."

"Alexander Carlisle?"

Why does that sound familiar?

"Do you know him?"

I sit up and bite my lip. I know I do... But where? How? I gasp. "Oh shit."

This could get awkward very quickly.

"Day?"

"I can't believe I didn't make the connection before. Um." I laugh nervously. "Do you remember that night you were outside my house? When you pinned me to the door and kissed the shit out of me?"

His lips twitch. "How can I forget?"

"Yes. Well. I had been to work that night, but I couldn't do the job."

"Why do I get the feeling I know where this is going?"

"He was hosting a function and your parents were there. I recognized your mom before I entered and apologized." I smile sheepishly. "This is slightly awkward."

Aaron stares at me for a long moment. "Amusing is what I'm thinking. More the fact Alexander had to hire someone to accompany him to his own function."

"Oh yes. Imagine that. Having to hire someone to be your date."

He grins and slides a hand up my back to cup my head and pull it forward. "Well, I'm very glad I hired you first. Otherwise, I may have had to kill him for you."

"Protecting me, right?" I murmur against his lips.

"No. That's me being a selfish bastard. Haven't you noticed? I'm ruthless when it comes to something that belongs to me."

"I'm a thing now, am I, Mr. Stone?" I stand and look down at him.

"Not *a* thing, no. You're my thing."

I fight my smile. "You really know how to romance a woman, you know that?"

"Romance, seduce. Is there a difference between the two?" He smirks. "You've never said so."

"I made dinner. It's probably cold by now though."

"You cooked in my shirt and you didn't tell me?" He stands and grabs me. He tugs me into his body. My breasts squash against the hardness of his chest, and I feel his erection press into my hip.

"You were on the phone, remember? Besides, I wasn't aware I was required to tell you."

"From now on, any time you wear my shirt, cooking or otherwise, you're required to tell me. Especially if you're naked beneath it, which seems to be your new uniform."

"Is that an ironclad requirement?"

"Set in fucking stone." He smiles at his own words, kisses me softly, and drags me into the kitchen. "What did you cook me?"

"The usual. Food. Ouch!" I clap my hand over my butt cheek. "What was that for?"

"Your sass," he grins. "That and I happen to enjoy smacking your ass."

I've gathered that. I narrow my eyes at him. "I made steak."

"You cooked me steak?"

"No, I cooked it for the security guys. Of course I cooked it for you."

"She wears my shirt and she cooks me steak. Are you a dream?"

I laugh and put the plates in the oven to heat them through. "You're a lucky bastard, Aaron Stone."

He looks at me for a long moment, his lips slowly curving to one side, and reaches out for me. He runs his thumb along my jaw and leans down, his hot breath covering my lips.

"More than you know, Dayton Black. More than you know."

"I've changed my mind." I slide in opposite Tyler in the coffee shop. "I don't think I want to model."

He raises his eyebrows. "Really? You're a natural."

I shrug a shoulder. "I don't know. I don't think it's for me. I'm not really comfortable in front of a camera, you know?"

And I'm not. The more I've thought about it, the more certain I am that I'm not model material. My age goes against me for one thing, and I'm done showing my body for money.

It might be a different context, but if this whole blackmail situation has taught me anything, it's that only one man should ever see my body again. That man is Aaron.

"Yeah, I could tell, love. It's something you would have gotten used to, but I get it." Tyler pulls out a folder. "What are you going to do with these?"

I smile. "Keep them. Maybe I'd be better on the other side of the camera."

"I doubt Aaron will rest until you're working for him."

"And I'm not making his ass coffee." I grab the one Tyler holds out to me. "I do that every morning." I pause. "Do you have to travel a lot? I mean, I really like the idea of being a photographer. It seems kind of fun."

"It is." He grins. "You don't have to travel. I do because I choose to, but I think Aaron would have you doing domestic shoots more often than not."

Good. I need to do something now. I need to feel like I'm doing more than cleaning the shower five times a day out of sheer boredom. And this… Photography…

I really enjoyed it in London, watching him shoot. Being on Tyler's side of the camera was comfortable and enjoyable. I can see myself doing that more than being the one posing.

So it means I'd have to go back to school. I'll be twenty-five tomorrow. Is that too old? No. I'm still young, and although it would take a couple of years to finish the classes, I'm guessing, it wouldn't be too late.

"Hey, would you teach me some?" I smile sweetly at Tyler. "Please."

"I have a shoot this afternoon. Want to come with?"

"Could I?" My phone buzzes in my pocket. "Hang on."

Come home. I have a surprise for you, is what the text from Aaron says.

"Looks like I'll have to join you next time. Aaron wants me home."

Tyler grins. "I know. The shoot was a bluff."

Suspicion narrows my eyes. "What are you two planning?"

"I'm not planning anything. I'm merely the one talked into keeping you out of the way for his planning."

A black car pulls up outside the coffee shop. "Is that mine?"

"Yep." Another grin stretches across his face, and he leads me outside and opens the door. "Have fun. By the way, I'm flying back to London tomorrow. I'll think about this photography thing and call you, okay?"

"Sure thing." I sit back in the chair as the car pulls away.

Tyler waves through the window, and my thoughts immediately turn to Aaron. A surprise for me? I hate surprises. They've all been bad lately.

And since it's my birthday tomorrow, I can't help but worry that it'll be something over the top.

Oh, god. I swear, if he proposes to me, I'll shove the box up his ass.

That would be so him. He would so plan for me to have coffee with his cousin—why didn't I notice something was up then? —then do something ridiculously outrageous.

That thought hangs with me the whole journey home, and by the time I reach our apartment, my hands are sweating. I push the door open slowly and stop when my eyes find him.

He's standing in front of the bar, next to an array of covered plates. His eyes are sparkling with mischief and his clothes are totally casual. I glance at his jeans. No bulges in his pockets. No box on the table.

Stupid unnecessary freak-out.

But still…my heart pangs a little. After all his talk in London, it wasn't a ridiculous thought, and maybe moving in has made me want it a little.

That or the pressure of this blackmail bullshit is getting to me.

"Sit down." Aaron pulls me over to the barstool and sits me on it. He throws my purse on the sofa behind him and tugs my shoes off.

"What are you doing?"

"Your best friend informed me that she's stealing you for the day tomorrow for your birthday, so I'm bringing my plans forward."

"Ignoring the fact you seem to talk to Liv more than I do lately, you should be at work."

"And you should be blindfolded with your mouth full of food by now, but let's not fuss over technicalities."

My eyebrows shoot up. "Blindfolded?"

He pulls a black silk tie from his pocket, a sexy smirk on his face—the one that tugs at my core—and runs it through his fingers. "Objecting?"

I shake my head. Nope. I'm not objecting.

"Good." He steps behind me and covers my eyes with it, tying it securely at the back of my head. "Can you see anything?"

"Black silk," I retort.

He gently tugs a lock of my hair, and the warmth crawling over my cheek tells me that his mouth is by my ear. It's not even warmth. No, it's a hot caress across my skin that sets all of me on fire.

"Watch your mouth," he whispers. "You're blindfolded and completely under my control."

Shivers fall down my spine in an oddly erotic way at his words. *Oh boy.*

"I could take it off," I reply weakly. We both know I won't.

Aaron's thumb runs down my neck and chest to the curve of my breasts. "No, you won't. You'll leave it on until I tell you to take it off."

"Is that right?"

He touches his lips to the corner of my mouth, pulling away when I turn my head. "Absolutely. It stays on until I'm ready to remove it. Now let me feed you."

"It's three in the afternoon."

"I don't particularly care. I know you skipped lunch, so right now, the only time I want you to open these gorgeous lips is when I'm putting food between them. Are we clear?"

"Crystal."

"Excellent. Now, here we go."

Something slightly rough nudges at the seam of my lips and I part them. I bite into it, strawberry juice flooding my mouth, and lick my lips slowly. "Mmmm."

Aaron's mouth covers mine, silencing my low hum of approval at the sweet fruit, the simple touch heating my body. It's been a matter of minutes since he covered my eyes with his tie but I can already feel everything so much more intensely.

"Next," he murmurs, bringing another to my lips.

Some juice dribbles down my chin, and he quickly flicks his tongue against my skin, licking it up. The tip of his tongue slides along my bottom lip, and I let out a quiet moan.

Is this feeding or a lesson in seduction?

"Shh. We won't get through nearly half of these foods if you make that sound every time."

"Then don't lick my lips."

"Dayton, gorgeous"—he touches something cold in a spoon to my mouth—"your lips aren't the only thing I plan on licking today."

That's it. I'm done for.

Every spark of simmering heat in my body shoots downward at his words, settling deep in my pussy. It swirls into a heavy ache that wets my panties at his promising words.

"Chocolate mousse," I mutter. "Is this a guessing game? It's easy."

"No guessing game. Just an exercise to show you how much more intense everything is when you can't see."

And he's right.

Every drop of juice, every lick of a spoon, every sweet layer on my tongue is more potent and intense than it is when I can see it. His hand at my hip is tighter and stronger than if I could see it there.

I don't feel his touch and the taste of the food in the places I'm supposed to. I taste it and I feel it in every part of my body.

"Open your mouth," he says huskily, and I know this is getting to him too. Good. He shouldn't expect to be able to take away my eyes and not get turned on himself.

But what even is this?

I feel the cold chill of glass against my bottom lip, and I close my lips over it. The rich taste of champagne fills my mouth and assaults every taste bud sitting on my tongue as I swallow it down slowly, savoring the richer-than-normal taste.

Mango presses between my lips, and I swallow it down easily, and when he presses what feels like a grape against my mouth, I can't help the twitch of it. *Dammit, don't play with me, Stone.*

"Don't you have more important things to be doing?" I murmur against the grape.

"No. The lawsuits were distributed this morning and my afternoon is clear for you. So do as you're told." He pushes the grape into my lips and I open my mouth.

I close my lips around his fingers, ignoring the grape, and press my tongue against them as he pulls them out of my mouth. He growls low. The sound reverberates through my body, hardening my nipples and adding to the ache in my core.

"Dayton."

My name leaves him as little more than a husky whisper, and I know instantly that the power has shifted. Where, five minutes ago, he held every bit of it, some has transferred to me. Some has left him and seeped into me with the mere closing of my lips around his fingers.

I smirk, reaching my hand out and finding his. Our fingers link in a moment so intimate, and I squeeze his hand. "I'm not hungry anymore," I whisper.

"You're not done." He squeezes back and pulls his fingers from mine.

Jesus, no. I don't want food. I want him. I want his body and his touch and his tongue. I want it fucking everywhere.

I sit impatiently through three more tastings of mango, strawberries, and more champagne. The anticipation is tightening every muscle in my body, practically begging for the answer to all the questions in my mind.

"Why are you doing this?" I ask quietly when he presses his forehead to mine.

"Because you deserve to relax and forget. And I know I can take you to that crazy fucking oblivion where nothing exists except you and me."

He's right. Him and me. That's what I want. The sweet, delirious, all-encompassing, shattering shudder of my body tightening around his. Of every muscle in my pussy clenching and milking his obvious erection for everything it has inside. Of that one single moment where we're both flying high, prisoners to our pleasure.

"I won't beg you. Not today."

"No begging required."

The clink of plates reaches my ears, and his hands curve around my ass. I wrap my legs around him, and he lifts me, setting me on the bar, and presses his finger to my lips.

"One more," he rasps. "Okay?"

I nod.

"Open your mouth."

I do, tilting my head back slightly. The roughness of a shell rests against my bottom lip, and I know what this is before I taste the salty yet slimy fish.

Oyster.

"Bleurgh," I mutter.

"You live in Seattle and you don't like oysters?"

"No. I'm not a fan of shellfish," I reply, feeling him push my legs open.

"You ate shrimp in the Chinese."

"No, I threw one at you and left the rest piled on the side of my plate."

He chuckles, standing between my legs. *God, don't step forward.*

He does. I push my hips into him at the brush of his erection across the apex of my thigh, and his hands slide up my legs. He slips me across the granite and into him. His erection is hard against my core, rubbing my clit, and if my eyes weren't already closed, I swear to fuck they'd be squeezed shut so tightly I'd never see again…

This feeling, his hardness against my tenderness while he has me blindfolded, is insanely world-shaking.

Aaron crashes his lips to mine. The oaky taste lingering on him tells me that he's been sipping whisky as he's been feeding me. Somehow I've been too wrapped up in the overwhelming flavors of the food to notice, but it's a welcome taste.

It's warm, touching every part of me, even as his tongue flicks between my lips and begs for entrance into my mouth.

I let him have it, sliding my hands up his arms and into his hair. I tangle my fingers in his silky locks, dreading the day he'll cut them, and arch myself into him. The rest of his body is as hard and tense as his dick against me, and I take a deep breath.

"I'm really, really not hungry any longer."

I hear the begging in my voice. The plea. The request.

"I think you need something else."

I tug on his hair hard. "You're not the only one who can require, Mr. Stone."

His lips find my neck and trail down it, peppering kisses. "Tell me, Miss Black. Do you require me to lay you back on our bed and sink my dick so far inside you that we become one?"

"Yep. That. Exactly that."

He's the only man I've ever met who can bring me to my knees. The only one who can make me shiver in real anticipation, clench in desire, thrust in desperation.

He laughs quietly, sliding his hands across my body, and cups my ass. Slowly, he lifts me, bringing me flush against him, and carries me. I can feel nothing but the rock of his cock against my clit and the pressure of his fingertips on my butt.

I've never had a sexual experience that's lasted so long. I've never felt so strongly about needing to be filled until I scream.

Aaron Stone is a force to be reckoned with.

The softness of our mattress cushions my behind as I'm lowered onto it. I still feel his touch stronger than anything. It's almost as if he's caressing my whole body with his fingertips without really moving them, desperate for every inch of me to feel his intoxicating touch.

And I do. Goose bumps erupt across my body, snaking across my skin, making my hairs stand on end, sparking little shivers. I can feel his eyes running from my head to the very tips of my toes. Feel his gaze coast over my curves, pausing on my breasts and hips.

I don't know how I know it. Perhaps it's in the subtle way his breath hitches, getting heavier when he exhales deeply. Perhaps it's in the twitch of his fingers as they dig deeper into my skin. Or perhaps it's in the lust and arousal ricocheting between his body and mine.

It's definitely in the crushing way our lips connect.

The softness of his lips completely contradicts the roughness of his kiss, but the vigor he tugs my zipper down with is completely in line with it. Within seconds, the soft material of my dress is sliding down my body and pooling on the floor at Aaron's feet.

He pulls back, his teeth grazing my bottom lip and making my clit throb so intensely that I moan. He nibbles down my neck, making me arch my body into him. I tug at the hem of his shirt, and his mouth leaves me for a split second so he can pull it over his head.

I run my fingers down his body, tracing every groove on his stomach until I reach the 'v' that dips beneath his jeans to the part of his body I'm craving right now.

His lips across my breasts, his tongue sliding beneath the cup of my bra to brush across my nipple, his hot breath cascading across my skin. The sensations evoked by this, being blindfolded, are unlike anything I've ever felt. It's so intensely erotic that my skin is humming, completely alive.

"Look at you," he murmurs, trailing his mouth down my stomach. "Who knew you could be so well-behaved in the bedroom?"

"I can change it." I drag my nails down his back, digging into his skin when I reach the bottom to make my point.

He takes my hands and spreads my arms to the side on the bed. He kneels, his nose brushing along my core, and blows lightly on me. I wriggle my hips. Shit. If my pussy wasn't aching for him already, it definitely is now. It's throbbing, aching, clenching, desperate for his touch. Any touch.

And then it comes, his fingers pulling my panties down, and his tongue slowly grazes along my hot folds. I whimper and push into him, but it doesn't faze him. He continues his leisurely pace, exploring every part of me until finally... *Oh, God, finally...* He presses the tip of his tongue against my clit and rubs hard, resulting in a firework-like explosion of pleasure that makes me tremble uncontrollably.

My heart is pounding dangerously fast, my lungs burning with the force of my rapid breathing. I feel empty as he releases my legs, and through the blood roaring in my ears, I hear the pull of his zipper. The moment the sound of his jeans hitting the floor reaches my ears, the warmth of his body over mine returns.

It's accompanied by a long, smooth thrust inside me. A tug at the back of my head and the silk tie falls away from my eyes.

I open them and stare into the striking, lustful blue of Aaron's. I lift my legs until they're wrapped around his waist and tilt my hips up until he's buried completely inside me and we're connected as one.

"I love being inside you," he says against my mouth. "The way your hot, wet cunt wraps around me and hugs me tightly drives me crazy. It makes me want to drive into you until you're begging me to slow down. It makes me want to fuck you so hard you can't do anything but scream my fucking name."

My nails dig into his back and his name falls from my lips in a desperate whisper. The man can word-fuck me and penetrate me with those words almost as deep and as sweetly as he does with his dick.

"Whispering?" He thrusts into me harder. "I'm fucking you like this and you're whispering my name?"

I moan when he pauses inside me and grabs my chin. He turns my face toward his, demanding I look at him.

"By the time I'm done with you, Dayton, whispering will be the last thing you think of. You'll be screaming my name so loudly that it'll be completely silent."

"Requirement?" I breathe, meeting him thrust for thrust.

"You bet your tight little ass it's a requirement. If you don't scream for me every time I fuck you, I'm not doing it hard enough."

He silences whatever I was going to say next with another crushing kiss, his tongue slipping straight between my lips. He dominates my mouth the way he dominates my pussy, hard and deep, strong and determined. He pounds and he sweeps and he teases until my muscles clench around him hard and I come in a second rush of swamping heat.

Aaron's own release is seconds behind mine, and his cock swells inside me as he comes in hot spurts. His hard kisses slow, turning tender and loving, and he lowers his body to mine completely.

It's hard and sweaty and *so fucking hard,* but I don't care. I don't care about the pressure the weight of him is putting on my chest as I wrap my arms around him and hold him tight to me.

He pulls his head back after a long moment of us lying here together and looks me in the eye. His lips pull up on one side, and he strokes the back of his fingers down my cheek.

"Happy early birthday, beautiful woman."

I cover his hand with mine and smile. "Thank you, baby. I think it's my favorite yet."

"Yeah?" He rolls to the side and pulls me on top of him. "Good, 'cause I'm not done with you yet."

Chapter Twenty-Four

I've missed my best friend.

Since Aaron waltzed back into my life for a second time, I've barely seen her. Now sitting opposite her, I'm realizing just how much.

It doesn't matter how intensely you love or how consuming your relationship is. A girl still needs her best friend.

Liv tackle-hugs me, squeezing me until I can't breathe. "Have you dropped off the face of the fucking Earth into honeymoon-stage bliss or what?"

"If only," I laugh, sitting opposite her in the wine bar.

She slides a glass of wine across our table and wrinkles her nose. "Yeah, Aaron told me about all that bullshit. Do I need to claw her eyes out? I just got my nails done, and these babies are lethal." She holds her hand up for me to see, and yes, she is indeed correct.

They're long, and the square shape is definitely threatening. At least they would be if they were coming at your face.

"I'm not saying you need to, but I am saying I wouldn't stop you if the opportunity arises and you feel so inclined." I smirk.

"Sweet. Now I have permission. Aaron just looked at me funny."

"Of course he did. He doesn't understand this friendship. Shit, I don't understand it, but we're good."

She knocks my shin under the table. "I would do it harder, but since it's your birthday, I'm being nice."

"Oh, gee, thanks."

"So how is it being a quarter of a century old? You're now closer to thirty than twenty. You old bitch."

I laugh loudly. "This will be you in a few weeks, so watch who you're calling an old bitch."

"I'll always be able to call you an old bitch, and I'll do it even when we're old and grey and in Seattle's finest fucking nursing home."

I don't doubt it, except the part about the nursing home. Liv is far too fiery to let someone wipe her ass, and I tell her as much.

She shrugs. "My new agent is putting me forward for a big campaign over here in a week or so. Maybe if I make it big, I'll hire someone to do it for me."

I shake my head with a small smile that's threatening to become a grin. Jesus. "Really, Liv. You don't need an ass-wiper. You need a boyfriend."

"Oh yes. Says the woman who didn't so much as look at a guy romantically until Mr. Walking Orgasm exploded into her life."

"Things change. I changed. I kind of like love now." I'd like it a lot more if it weren't filled with everything we have to deal with.

"I know. I'm messing with you, babe." Liv looks at me honestly, her eyes bright. "Love suits you. And Aaron is a good guy. He'll make you happy."

"He will. He does." I blink harshly. "It's my birthday and I'm not having you make me cry. That's no fair. So what are we doing today?"

"We're going shopping of course." She nods toward my half-full glass and lifts hers. "Down in one go, honey. We have a store or ten to visit, and it's on your man."

I smile and lift the glass. Of course it's on Aaron. There'll be open tabs and closed stores just for us.

"Come on. Chop chop! We're on a time schedule, you know."

I grab my purse and follow her out. Of course we are.

I collapse back onto the sofa in Liv's apartment and swing my feet onto her coffee table. Our bags are dumped in the middle of her kitchen, in full view, and I want to cringe a little. There are hundreds of dollars of clothes and shoes in those bags, nearly all of them mine.

Because my best friend is as much of an enabler as my boyfriend, apparently.

Liv looks between me and the bags and grins. "Right. Where's that dress you bought early?"

My lips twist. "Which one?" I ask dryly.

"Ha! That blue one. And those black heels. Where are they?"

"In the bags."

"Hilarious. I'll find them. Then you're putting them on."

I frown, straightening from my lazy, slouched position. "Why?"

"You didn't think I was taking you shopping and not dragging you out, did you? It's a Thursday. Come on, babe. We have permission from the big man, so let's go."

"Did you just call my boyfriend 'the big man'?"

"Repeating what he said." She throws the dress at me and dangles the heels from her fingers.

We're having words about that. In no place, ever, should Aaron refer to himself as 'the big man.' Joking or serious. Just, no.

I stand with a sigh and take the dress into Liv's room. Honestly, all I want to do is curl up in front of the TV, cry a little over some goofy movie, and gorge myself on popcorn and chips and candy. It doesn't escape my attention that the last two times I've gone for a night out have been forced on me.

Perils of having a party-animal best friend.

"Has that guy at work noticed you yet?" I ask when she rolls her jeans down her legs.

"Jackson? No." She pulls her top over her head and strolls to her closet. Yes, she's also completely comfortable in her own skin and isn't afraid to show her bare ass in a v-string. "And if I undo another button on my shirt, I'll be arrested for indecent exposure. Trust me—orange isn't my color."

I straighten the blue dress against my thighs and smile as she whips a black dress out. "You'll figure it out."

"Eh." She shrugs, slinking into her own outfit. "Guys are guys. Eventually he'll notice me, but I'll be locked up with some hot-as-hell guy who knows how to play my body like a fucking violin."

And she has a clear idea of what she wants from life.

Why is she still single?

I allow her to tease my hair into a head of curls but put a stop at the makeup. That I will do myself, thank you.

After an excruciatingly long hour, both of us are ready and raring to go. We grab our purses and head down the elevator to the bottom floor, but when we get there, it's not a cab waiting.

It's a fucking chauffeured car, and the door is being held open.

"What's going on?" I turn to my best friend, and the traitorous bitch has secrecy written all across that smug-ass grin on her face.

"In." She takes my hand and pulls me outside, practically shoving me into the car.

The door slams behind her, and I repeat my question. She grins wider.

This whole day has been a setup. I'd bet anything Aaron is behind it. What the hell is he up to now? What in the fricking Hell is even going on?

We drive until we arrive at the Southfall, and my heart skips several beats. I'm almost sure it'll stop beating, and I allow Liv to lead me into the hotel and to the reception area.

A guy I don't know is sitting behind the counter, and he takes one look at us and tells us to head to the elevator. I follow her blindly, and what the fuck is happening? What is this? Why am I in a hotel? This isn't a night out. This isn't a girls' night. I don't understand. What the hell?

"Don't hate me," Liv says insincerely, stopping outside the ballroom. Mischief is rife in her eyes, sparkling dangerously, and I run my tongue along my top lip.

She pushes open the door, and I freeze. Everyone. Standing. In front of me.

Monique. Aunt Leigh. Aaron's parents. Some of the girls. More. Everyone. People—everywhere. Lining the walls, leaning against the bar, sitting at a few tables.

And Aaron.

In the middle of it all is Aaron. Clad in a tailored suit that hugs him like a second skin, he turns slowly, his eyes finding mine, and smiles. It's a slow smile, one that screams, "Surprise!" and one that warms every part of me.

"Happy birthday," Liv says softly. "And surprise."

I cover my mouth with my hand when she lets go, and she steps to the side. Aaron walks across the ballroom and stops in front of me, his hand taking mine from my face.

"You did this?" I whisper, looking up at him.

He nods. "For you."

I swallow hard, and with my fingers linked with his, I look around the room, past the people. To the red-white-and-blue-striped flags dangling over the bar. To the table cloths in the same color. To the spread of food along one wall, all French, all my favorite things. To the endless wine bottles next to it, again all French. To the cake in the shape of the Eiffel Tower—something that shouldn't even be fucking possible.

"What?" I whisper. "How? Why?"

Aaron rests his hand against my cheek and turns my face to his. "Because you are the single most important person in my life, and you deserve nothing less than the absolute best. You didn't mention anything about your birthday and I wanted to give you a day you won't forget. And the French theme…" He smiles. "It was a no-brainer, sweetheart."

I wrap my arms around his neck, not giving a crap about everyone watching us, and his arms circle my waist in the same tender way.

"Thank you," I whisper. "Thank you for being the most infuriating, demanding, requiring, relentless man I've ever met in my life."

He smiles against my skin. "I'm reminding you, Day. It's a double-edged sword. The French theme is to remind you that, no matter what, no matter what is thrown our way, no matter what we have to fight through, our love will always bring us back to each other."

I squeeze my eyes shut. I know this. I know that, despite all the bullshit life can throw at us, all the lies and the manipulation and the pressure, I know we'll always find a way back to each other.

When you have the kind of love that flows through your veins as easily as your blood does, there's no escaping it.

I release him and smile. "Always. No reminding needed. I require you to love me always, Mr. Stone. Okay?"

He lowers his lips to mine and kisses me sweetly. "I can deal with that requirement, Miss Black. In fact, I believe it's a given. Now you have guests to attend to, and I'm being incredibly rude by keeping you all to myself."

"You are." I smack his chest lightly. "I'll have a glass of wine while I greet my aunt."

He raises an eyebrow, his lips quirking with the movement. "Demanding, are we?"

"You betcha."

He winks and kisses me once more before heading toward the bar. I turn to my aunt, who is standing by my side, and another wave of emotion fills me at the raw sight in her eyes.

Before I can move, Aunt Leigh envelopes me in her arms and holds me close to her. She holds me tighter than she ever has before, and I return her embrace.

"Thank you," she whispers. "Thank you for following your heart."

"Thank you for telling me to," I reply, kissing her cheek.

Our time is cut short when Monique intrudes, snatching me from my aunt and hugging me just as tight. "I've missed your snappy, no-bullshit ways. Don't tell me you've gone fucking soft on me?"

I laugh and shrug her off me. "Don't be so stupid, Mon. If you ever needed your ass chewed out, you just have to call me."

She winks. "You got a good one, Dayton. Don't fuck this up."

"When have you ever known me to fuck anything up?" I raise my eyebrows and take the glass Aaron slides in front of my face. "He's well and truly stuck with me now."

"Rather him than me," she retorts with a laugh, shooting me a second wink.

I smile as Aaron whisks me away, introducing me to some of the people who work for him. My head spins with all the new names, and before I know it, I'm on my third glass of wine and Dottie is giggling alongside me at the bar.

"And then I told him, 'Haz, you do realize all of those models have more silicone in their body than fucking Silicone Valley?' and he told me Silicone Valley isn't really made of silicone, and I looked like a complete and utter moron in front of everyone he works with."

I snort into my hand. "And he still wants to marry you?"

Dottie holds up her hand. "Oh yes. For some goddamn reason, the man is crazy in love with me, and when he has abs tighter than a nun's vagina, who am I to argue with him?"

"Who has nun's-vagina abs?" Liv slinks in beside me, a full glass in her hand.

"Her fiancée," I explain. "Put your tongue back in its mouth, thank you. No ab licking tonight."

She sighs. "Damn. Here I thought I had a chance at getting some."

"Well," Dottie drawls, "you could always go for Daniel. He's hot and single and a rising prospect in the company. And then there's Paul. He's one of Aaron's senior staff despite barely touching thirty. And *then* there's Garrett. He's the head of advertising in Seattle, hot as fucking hell, and from what I hear, he knows his way around a bedroom and pair of handcuffs."

I blink at her. "How do you even know that?"

Dottie looks at me blankly. "I'm Aaron's assistant. It's my job to know."

"Even their sex preferences?"

"I'm an eavesdropper. So sue me."

"Wait. Which one is Garrett?" Liv taps her shoulder, and Dottie points at a guy by my cake with a bright red tie.

Liv coughs, smoothing her dress, and stands up straight. "Excuse me, ladies. I suddenly want some cake."

My lips quirk to one side as I watch her cross the room, swinging her hips. I shake my head. She's hot, sexy, and irresistible. Poor Garrett. He stands no chance against her.

Dottie has the same expression on her face when my phone pings in my purse. I dig inside it, grab my phone, and unlock it before opening the message.

You were warned.

A link follows the text, and everything stops. The music and the chatter silence and my heart stops and my lungs freeze and there's nothing. Nothing but the link staring back at me, bright blue against the white background of my phone.

"Dayton? What's wrong?"

I ignore Dottie and click on the link. *Fuck no. Please no. No. No no no no no.*

The link opens to Naomi's official website, and the first thing I see is my name and Aaron's and a photo of me.

And then there's the exact story she sent to The Insider and probably every press Aaron sent a precautionary lawsuit to.

But we never considered this.

We never thought of her own site, with its thousands of followers. We never dreamed she may put it up here.

I feel the color drain from my face, and I can barely imagine my expression as I turn to Dottie. I know I must look horrified. Petrified. Completely and utterly defeated.

She knows that Aaron knows.

That's the only explanation.

And now my identity is out.

Who I am is public.

My whole life is strewn across her personal website for the world to see.

And I have no idea what I'm supposed to do now.

Chapter Twenty-Five

Dottie takes my phone from my hand and her eyes flick over the screen. "Fuck!" She yells the word. A real, full-bodied yell, and it draws the attention of everyone around us.

Still I stare at her. I'm frozen, unable to move due to the unexplainable feeling spreading through me. Nothing I can say can make this better. I'm helpless.

"Aaron!" Dottie yells again, her voice louder than that of the music. She wraps an arm around my waist, guides me from the stool, and deposits me straight into his waiting arms.

"What's wrong? What is it?" His voice is panicked, his hand rubbing my back.

Dottie shows him the phone wordlessly, and he growls. He actually fucking growls. A primal, angry, possessive growl that vibrates throughout my body.

"Fuck!"

"Son? What is it?" Brandon appears, resting a hand on his shoulder.

I bury my face in Aaron's chest, fisting his shirt in my hands. This can and will ruin everything.

I can't believe she's done it.

I can't believe she's exposed me.

No, I can. I just can't believe it's happening right now.

My phone buzzes again, and I catch a glance at the screen before Aaron can turn it away.

Happy birthday.

"We're leaving. Right fucking now. Dottie, call for two cars then follow us down. I need you to help me. Dad, can you come? Mom?" Aaron's voice is strong, and I wonder if I'm the only person who can hear the underlying anger.

"Monique," I whisper.

"Get Monique," he orders Dottie. "She needs to be here."

Aaron sweeps me from the room with the confidence of a man who is in control of the situation. In reality, he couldn't be further from it. In reality, he has absolutely no control over it.

We travel down the elevator. Dottie has her cell attached to her ear the whole time, and I vaguely hear the words, "Mr. Carlisle... Now... Yes..." as Aaron holds me even closer.

"Dottie, you take the limo with my parents and everyone else. I need to speak with Dayton alone."

"Of course. We'll meet you back at your apartment."

Aaron deposits me in a car and climbs in next to me. I feel numb. Totally numb. I didn't need to read the whole post to know what she wrote. To know that she's exposed everything I was.

"I'm sorry," I whisper, looking at my feet. Guilt and remorse—they flood me. Consume me.

Aaron pulls me into him and tilts my face back. "Look at me, Dayton."

I shake my head. I can't. Not this time. I can't look in his eyes and know that everything we have is on the line. Everything he and his father have worked for is now hanging in limbo because of me.

How many reporters have picked that up? How many stories will I see tomorrow? How many news alerts will pop up on my cell?

"Dayton." His voice is hard. No-nonsense. "Look at me. Now."

My eyes disobey me. They rake up his body until they find a sea of bright blue.

"We will figure this out. Do you understand me? It's unexpected and sudden, but we will fix this."

Tears born of a real fear fill my eyes. "My past could destroy you. How can you even look at me?"

"I can look at you because I don't see the woman of your past. I see the woman I fell in love with, the woman I love right now. Please, baby, don't look at me like I should hate you. I can't and I don't and I won't. I love you for who you are today, right in this moment, and I will fight for that woman until the day I die."

"How?" I whisper. Vulnerability. It's not something I'm used to.

"How? Because you're the very air I breathe, Dayton. You're the one thing that keeps my heart beating."

"But you could lose everything."

"I won't." He looks so certain, and I don't understand it. "I don't pay the best lawyer on the West Coast a shit-ton of money for nothing. I don't have the best people I know around me to sit idly by while the woman I love is torn to shreds publicly. Regardless of what happens, of who gets this supposed story, I will be standing by your side through it all. Understand that, Dayton. There isn't a second I won't be supporting you. Even if I have to lift you onto my shoulders and carry your weight as well as mine, I'll fucking do it. Do you understand that?"

I nod. "Yes. I understand."

"Good. Now, please, trust me. Trust me and everyone I have around me. I don't give a fuck if I have to slap lawsuits left, right, and fucking center. No one who even sniffs this will get away with it. She made a big mistake in telling you just after she posted it. A very, very big mistake."

"How do you know? How do you know it isn't already being spread across the country?"

"Because Stone Advertising has a web hosting company integrated within it, and her website is hosted by us. It's being shut down as we speak."

I stop as the car does. I look at him. The clench of his jaw, the harshness of his eyes, the tightness of his grip on mine.

"How?"

"Dottie." He smirks slowly. "She called for a car, then my lawyer, then Miguel, the man who runs the web hosting company. That site will be down within the hour."

"You're so confident. How? I'm petrified, Aaron. I've never been so scared in my fucking life, and you're acting like she's spilled your grandma's favorite muffin recipe."

He clasps my face in his hands, his palms rough against my cheeks, his fingers brushing hair from my eyes, and leans in with a deep breath. "Because our love can conquer anything it comes across. It's strong enough to fight for a lifetime together. That's why I'm so confident. I know that, no matter what, I'll still be able to look in your eyes at the end of the day, and that's all that truly matters." He slides me across the car and lifts me out, setting me in front of him. "Now let's go and do some damage control."

"And sic a lawsuit on Naomi's ass?"

Aaron's smirk grows. "Now we're talking, sweetheart. Now we're talking."

With his arm firmly wrapped around my body, he guides me into the elevator and upstairs. When we step into the apartment, it's alive with ringing phones and voices issuing commands. There's a heavy layer of tension hovering above everyone, threatening to suffocate us with its intensity.

"Now, you," Aaron says quietly, "are going to go and sit on the sofa with my mother and you're going to let me handle this."

"This is my mess," I argue.

"And it's my solution," he responds without missing a beat. "I have the manpower to solve this. Please sit back and let me deal with this. Let me protect you."

"I'm not the one who needs protecting. It's you."

"Naomi vastly underestimated the power and influence this company has. My father will be in my office contacting everyone necessary and explaining the situation diplomatically. There are twenty people in this apartment right now fighting to make this right because I said so. I know you feel like this is your fault."

"It is."

"Not," he adds. "It isn't your fault, and as much as I adore your desire to protect me and this company, it's unnecessary. I need to protect you, Dayton. I need to protect you like I need air to breathe, so for the love of God, please go and sit with my mother and let me do this. I won't ask you again."

I take a deep breath and look into his eyes. I see the truth of his words reflected in them, but I have to argue. I want to do something. There has to be fucking something I can do to right this.

"You wouldn't be here if it weren't for me," I whisper.

"And you wouldn't be here if it weren't for me. Last chance." He kisses me hard and turns me in the direction of the front room.

Carly, his mom, is sitting on the sofa, watching me. The compassion in her eyes undoes me, and I let the fear spill over. I let the pressure and the tension and the apprehension of the last few weeks release in the form of my tears, and I collapse onto the sofa next to her. She wraps her arms around me and rocks me gently, whispering in my ear. Just the way a mother should.

I cry silently into her shoulder, savoring every moment that her arms are around me, and let it all out.

I'm helpless.

I caused this and there's nothing I can do to right it.

I'm powerless, out of control, only able to sit by and watch as everyone else cleans up my mess. Because that's how I see it. If I'd just told Aaron right away, if I'd just been honest and not so fucking stubbornly independent, this could be fixed. It would be fixed.

My cell pings again, and Dottie swipes the screen to open the message.

"Aaron!"

"What does it say?" I look at her. She bites her lip. "Dottie. Tell me now!"

"She said that if you don't pay within the hour, she'll have it distributed to a large number of websites and presses ready to run a breaking news story first thing tomorrow. They're waiting for her story."

"Will she fuck." There's no wavering in his voice. Despite his lack of jacket and tie, Aaron looks as serious as ever. "Dottie, get me her on the phone ten minutes ago." He turns. "Alexander, get something drawn up that prevents her from contacting either Dayton or me for the next fucking lifetime. This ends right now."

"Aaron, you can't pay her!" I wrench myself from his mom's grip. "Don't be so fucking stupid!"

He brings his eyes to mine. "I told you before that there isn't a price I wouldn't pay for you, Dayton. And now I'm telling you to sit the hell down and let me deal with this."

I breathe in deeply. No. He can't do this. He can't pay her off. "You can't. Your divorce terms."

"Stated she can't contact me. Not the other way around."

"She's on the line," Dottie interrupts, holding the phone out.

Everything in me wants to reach forward and grab that phone. I want to tear it from his hands and scream into the receiver. I want to yell and cry and scream until I'm hoarse, until she understands what she's caused.

Carly reaches for my hands, but I pull them away, shaking my head. Everyone in this room, this packed room, is on high alert. There are phones and tablets and laptops everywhere. There is no silence, not for the constant ringing and keyboard-tapping and talking. Even Monique is standing in the corner, her cell to her ear, speaking frantically into her phone. It's a crazy kind of organized carnage.

I follow Aaron into his office and slip inside quietly.

"No, Naomi. No. You're un-fucking-believable… No, I found out through necessity. She kept it from me because she was willing to destroy herself to protect me… No, you wouldn't understand that, would you? You have no concept of love… Regardless, your demands have been met. Visit your bank in the morning and you will find the requested amount deposited into your account, plus interest for the last four weeks. You'll also be receiving a call from your lawyer in New York explaining about the lawsuit being brought against you should you contact either of us again… Slander. Defamation of character. Invasion of privacy. Blackmail."

Silence.

"Fantastic. Then we're on the same page. One more word to Dayton or me and you'll find yourself in the middle of a legal battle you'll never win. And don't doubt me for a second. I told you before you don't fuck with the woman I'm in love with. Goodnight."

The phone hits his desk with a clatter. I bite the inside of my lip and stare at his back. At the way he leans forward, grasping the edge of his desk, and takes a deep breath. At the way he stands, turning to me, his eyes finding mine with a fierceness I've never seen before.

"You shouldn't have done that," I whisper. "Paid her. She doesn't deserve it."

"But you do. You deserve every fucking cent I have and more. Money is expendable, gorgeous. There'll always be more of it. I can always make more. I can never have another you. She can have everything, but she can't have you."

I lean against the mirror and hug myself. God, to be loved this much. To be loved in a way you don't feel you deserve, in a way so utterly that you are the center of their world. That you're the fucking axis their world hovers on, the gravity making it spin.

To be loved so much that you really are the most valuable thing they have.

Aaron touches his lips to mine gently yet firmly. A promise. A certainty. A forever.

I wrap my arms around his waist because I need him to hold me. I need to feel the warmth and security that comes from his arms, and I'm not afraid to admit that, after years of being so strong, I feel weak.

Like my world is being ripped from under me and torn into pieces. Like my fear could overwhelm me until I can no longer breathe. Like the very man I'm holding on to could be tugged away from my grip.

"Strength comes from giving yourself to another. It comes from deep in your heart, the very thing you share with that other person. It comes from knowing that fear isn't an option where a future is so certain." He cups my cheek and touches his forehead to mine. "It comes from every time we look into each other's eyes and see every ounce of love we feel reflected back."

I close my eyes and turn my face into his palm. "But it's not over, is it?"

"No, sweetheart. Not yet. So you need to let me go again and let me finish this. Okay?"

I nod. "Okay. I'm going to bed. I need to be alone."

Wordlessly, he takes me into our room. He pulls off his shirt and hands it to me. "Never alone, Dayton. Never."

My dress falls from my body and I wrap myself in the soft, warm cotton of his white shirt, buttoning it before I bury myself beneath the covers. I feel almost childlike, needing to escape the horror situation born from me.

Aaron crouches before me, cupping my head, and takes my mouth in another promising kiss I feel beating away at the fear in my veins.

"When this shit is all said and done, I'm going to take you away to somewhere no one can find us and we're going to make up for every second we've lost to another person," he whispers in the dark. "I'm going to be the most selfish bastard in the world and keep you all to myself for as long as I can."

"I'm totally okay with that," I whisper.

"It was happening anyway." He kisses me again, and a hint of amusement tugs at the corners of my mouth. Even now, in the midst of a hellish disaster, my man can make me smile.

True love, people.

Right fucking here is true love.

When everything seems dark, like it's all going to shit, but the love you have still lights up your body and sends your heart racing, you know you have a love worth holding on to. Even if it destroys you.

The door clicks shut as he leaves the room, and I pull the covers up farther. I tug them over my head until I'm fully encased beneath the warmth of our sheets and close my eyes, hoping that, tomorrow, everything will be a little bit brighter.

I wake to darkness and a welcome silence. The earlier hum of noise from endless conversations is no more. I stretch my arm to the side, feeling for Aaron, but instead, my hand lands on empty sheets.

I sit up, brushing hair from my face, and listen for any indication of him being around. There isn't any, so I swing my legs over the edge of the bed and make my way out of the room.

The city lights flood the front room, and I glance at the clock. Four a.m. Where could he possibly be at this time?

Something creaks in the direction of his office, and I walk down the hall to it. His door is cracked open slightly, and a gentle light from the television is flickering through the tiny gap. I wrap my fingers around the edge of the door and ease it open, my eyes landing on his exhausted, shirtless figure.

He's slumping over his desk, his fingers buried in his hair. His laptop is open in front of him, papers are scattered everywhere, some lying idly on the floor, and a desk light is illuminating the mess.

"You should be in bed, asleep," he mutters without moving.

I hold in my snort and cross the room. I lay my hand on his shoulder. "Have *you* been to sleep yet?"

He shakes his head in response, and I close my eyes. His fingers close over mine on his shoulder and he pulls my hand to his mouth, brushing his lips across my knuckles.

I look at him as he tilts his face up to me. His eyes are slightly glazed, dark shadows forming beneath them, and I press my hand to his cheek.

He looks exhausted, like there isn't another ounce of energy left in him.

"Come to bed," I whisper.

"No. I need to finish this." Aaron turns back to his laptop.

I reach forward and slam the top down. Slowly, he faces me again, his lips quirked to one side.

"Come to bed," I repeat, firmer this time.

"Dayton, I have to finish this. I have to make sure we've covered all our bases and nothing has slipped between my fingers." He knocks my hand from the laptop and opens it.

Once again, I slam it. This time, I climb onto the desk and sit on top of it, my eyebrows raised. I rest my feet on his chair in the small gap between his legs, and he runs his hands up my calves.

"Dayton," he sighs.

"You're coming to bed, Aaron, and I don't care if I have to sit here for another hour. You're not opening the damn laptop again tonight."

He opens his mouth, but I lean forward and press two fingers against his lips. Instead of speaking, he kisses them.

"I know you don't want to. I know you want to sit here until you collapse on the keyboard, but you're not going to. I love that you're trying so hard to fix this, baby, I do, but you need to sleep now. You're no good to me or you if you're stumbling around like something out of The Walking Dead."

He smiles. "The Walking Dead?"

I shrug a shoulder. "So I watch some TV. Please come to bed now. You can come back to this in the morning. If you checked everything now, you'd probably miss something because you're so tired. Look at it with fresh eyes. I'll help you."

Our gazes lock for a long moment, and just when I think I'm going to really have to argue my point, he drops his shoulders.

"Fine. I'll come to bed, but know that I'm going to hold you so tight you might suffocate a little."

I bend forward and touch my lips to his. "I don't expect anything less."

"And when I'm not so tired, this is happening again. You on this desk in my shirt, that is. I am incredibly tempted to fuck you right now."

I hop up and tug on his hand. "Not happening, Aaron. Come on."

He waits while I shut off the light and TV and dutifully follows me into our room. I tug his sweatpants from his hips and he steps out of them, grabbing me before I can turn. Deftly, his fingers work the buttons on the front of his shirt and he takes it from my body.

We climb into bed together, and no sooner have I pulled the sheets up than he's cocooning me in his arms. I snuggle into him and turn my face so my lips rest against the part of his chest where his heart is beating. He squeezes me tight when I press a kiss there, feeling it speed up beneath my lingering touch.

"I love you, woman," he whispers into my hair. "So very, very much."

"I know," I whisper back, tangling our legs further. "I love you a lot, too."

"Good."

I close my eyes and listen as his breathing deepens and evens out. He's asleep within a minute, but his hold on me never loosens or wavers. His arms are locked around me in an ironclad grip, and I slip one of my hands over his side and up his back.

Somehow, and I wish I knew how it was possible, she hasn't won.

Naomi might have what she set out for originally—the money—but I have to wonder if that was her real motive. If, like Carly said, she always hated me, the Paris Girl, then it wouldn't be crazy to think that blackmailing me would have some other outcome.

Like walking away from Aaron.

I truly believe that she loves him. Maybe it's in her own twisted, vicious way, but I think she does. That could be me hoping that there's a real reason behind this whole thing. That could be me seeing good in someone who doesn't particularly deserve it, but I'll never know.

Their relationship isn't my business. I don't know anything of it bar the basic facts Aarons told me, and I don't want to know. Not because I don't want to hear about him with another woman, but because it doesn't matter.

We're past the point of it having any impact on us. We're past the point of her being a thorn in our sides. At least I hope so. The threat of a five-million-dollar lawsuit if she contacts us again should be enough to keep her away.

She may love him, but she loves the money more. She won't give that up for something as trivial as trying and failing to come between us.

We've shown her how strong we are. We've shown everyone, including ourselves, how hard we're willing to work for, fight for, and hold on to this relationship. We've made it crystal clear that our love has the strength of a thousand diamonds.

Yes, you can scratch it. You can even chip it if you're really lucky. But you'll never break it.

And craning my head back to look at the peaceful, restful face of the man who possesses every part of me, I know how true that statement is.

After everything, we're still as strong as we were the first time around.

This time, we're just not willing to let go. We learned our lesson.

Chapter Twenty-Six

I swing my legs from the bar, watching the seconds tick by on the clock. The large hand approaches the twelve, crawling at a snail's pace, and I sigh when it finally reaches it.

It's ten in the morning and Aaron still isn't up.

That alone tells me how much yesterday tired him. He's incapable of sleeping past six. Crazy man.

I rock my head from side to side. If I had any idea exactly what he was doing last night, I'd go into his office and finish it. As it is, I have no idea, so all I can is sit here like a freaking orange waiting to be juiced.

I can't read because my concentration won't last beyond a page. I've done my Candy Crush and Coin Dozer thing, and if I see one more whining status post on Facebook, I'll do one of my own.

The sound of a phone ringing in his office cuts through the silence, and I pause. *Oh hell.*

I jump down and run into the room, barely blinking at the name on screen before answering. "Hello?"

"Hello? Dayton? Is that you?" Dottie's voice is a welcome sound down the receiver.

"Yep, it's me."

"Great. Is Aaron available to talk?"

"Sorry, Dottie. He's not. Is there anything I can help with?"

"Actually, I just have some good news. Miguel managed to get Naomi's website down before too many people caught wind of the post, and the ones who did get the details have all been caught up with. Between you and me, he called in his intern, who has a knack for hacking."

I blow out a long, relieved breath and drop into Aaron's chair. "That's amazing, Dottie. Did you have to send any more lawsuits?"

"None. They were threatened with it last night if they ran with the information, by Aaron, and I woke to an email instructing me to call every one and explain that the story was a lie fabricated by his ex-wife. The lawsuits were apparently for defamation of character."

"So when this gets around, the real story will be how Naomi was so jealous of Aaron finding love with me again that she tried to sabotage our relationship?"

I can't help it. I smile. Of course she wouldn't get away with it that easily.

"The idea is that the story doesn't get around at all, but hey, if it does…"

I can picture it clearly, the twinkle in her eye. The amused one that says she's as happy about this as I am. Well, that's impossible, but I know she'll be grinning.

"If it does, it does. After all, you can't tell the media what to post, can you?"

Dottie laughs. "Absolutely not. I'm going to get back to work. Can you pass a message on to the boss for me?"

"Of course."

"Tell him I've rescheduled his appointments for this afternoon and cleared next week, as he requested in his email. And that everything else he asked for will be delivered by courier at noon."

Everything else?

"Uh, sure thing. And, Dottie? Thanks. I mean it."

"Just doing my job, Dayton, but it certainly helps when the person you're helping isn't a bitch." She laughs again. "I'll speak to you soon. Bye."

"Bye," I echo, setting the phone back in the holder.

Done.

It's done.

I'm safe. Aaron's safe. The business is safe.

And I didn't do a thing to protect any of us. And boy, is that a hard pill to swallow. Handing all that control over to someone else is the hardest thing I've ever done.

I press the heels of my hands into my eyes and make my way back to the kitchen.

"Fucking hell, you scared the life out of me!"

Aaron turns slowly, a grin across his face, and holds out a mug. "Coffee?"

I shoot him my best not-impressed look and take it from him. "I thought you were sleeping."

"I was. Then I did this thing people call waking up." He raises his eyebrows, sipping from a second mug, then screws his face up. "This is yours. Not that one."

A giggle escapes me as he swaps our mugs. "I didn't wake you, did I?"

"No, Bambi, you didn't wake me. Although…were you just on the phone in my office?"

I nod, smiling sheepishly. "It rang, so I thought I'd answer it. It was Dottie."

"Anything good?"

I relay to him the conversation we just had. The tension visibly leaves him as I speak, each point relaxing him a little more. The frown lines in his forehead smooth out and the purse in his lips becomes a gentle smile. The frustration in his eyes becomes an easy happiness that glimmers brightly.

"Yes, it would be a shame if Naomi was branded as a liar, wouldn't it?"

"How do you expect to get around that, Aaron?"

"It's that or she's labeled as a blackmailer. And if that were to be public, the police would eventually pick up on it and she'd have much bigger problems than her reputation."

I scratch my cheek, watching him talk so casually. Like he really doesn't care.

And it's plain to see in his eyes. He really doesn't. As long as I'm okay and he's okay and we're okay together, he couldn't give a flying monkey about her.

"But you already have the lawsuit ready."

His eyes twinkle. "From me. You're not mentioned anywhere. If the situation arose, you would naturally work with the police and aid them in their case."

I look at him for a long moment before sitting back. "You really have thought of everything, haven't you, Mr. Stone?"

"I warned you, Miss Black. I'm a ruthless man to deal with, especially when people fuck with me. More so when they fuck with you. Naomi did both, and now if she has any sense, she'll leave us alone for good."

"You're a wonder. Also, remind me never to fuck with you. Not that it matters because I'm not allowed to pay for anything, so your lawsuit would be a waste of time. You'd be paying for it yourself."

He smirks, leaning forward infinitesimally. "Don't fuck *with* me, Dayton. Just fuck me normally and I promise not to get my lawyer involved."

"Oh, so generous of you."

"Isn't it?" He stands and glances at my mug. "Have you finished with your coffee?"

"No. I still have half left."

"That's a shame. I hate to waste it." He pulls it away from me and empties it down the sink. "Oh well."

"What the hell was that for? I was drinking that!"

"Correct. You were." He rounds the bar and tugs me from the stool, his eyes darkening. "Now we're going to make good on that fucking part I just mentioned."

"We are?"

"Yes. You're wearing my shirt again, and I believe it was some six hours ago I was promising to fuck you on my desk, so I suggest you get your ass into my office and hop up onto that desk pronto."

"You're getting more demanding by the day, Mr. Stone." I add some extra wiggle to my hips as I walk, and I'm rewarded by a low growl of pleasure behind me. And punished with a sharp smack on my ass.

"I never said anything about a demand. I'm requiring you get on my damn desk. Now move."

⁂

"Thank you." Aaron takes a large envelope from someone and closes the door behind him.

I watch from my slouched position on the sofa as he pulls a letter opener from the kitchen drawer and slices the letter open.

Because who doesn't keep one of those in their kitchen?

I resist the urge to roll my eyes as he pulls out a large piece of paper and…

"What the hell is that?"

"This?" He holds up the piece of paper. "Oh, it's the final lease for a house I just bought."

"You bought a house?" I sit up straight. "What? Where? Why?"

He laughs throatily and hands me the paper. He leans on the back of the sofa, and I catch his eyes for a second before I look at it.

My mouth goes dry. Am I reading this right?

"You bought a house in *Paris?*"

His grin widens. "Correct."

"Why would you do that? I mean. What? I'm so confused."

Another laugh. "It's not that confusing, sweetheart. I found a house I liked, I bought it, end of discussion."

"But everything always goes wrong in Paris."

"Perhaps before, yes. But not this time. When we leave Paris next weekend, we'll be very much together."

"Next weekend? Oh!" I slap the paper against the cushion in front of me. "That's why Dottie cleared your schedule for next week!"

He leans in, sweeping his lips over mine. "I told you that when all that shit was done with I was stealing you away for a little while. The only person aside from us who is aware of the Paris house is Alexander, and that's the way it's going to stay. Everyone else will assume we're heading to the Bahamas for a week at an exclusive resort."

"You picked Paris over the Bahamas? Are you crazy?"

"Perhaps, but after everything, I think we need to remember where it all began. Don't you agree?"

I sigh, unable to argue that point. He's right. We need to go back to the place it started, this time with no secrets, no skeletons, no force. We need to go because we want to, because it's part of who we are. That's all there really is to it.

"I can't believe you bought a house."

"We can stay in a hotel if you prefer."

I wrinkle my nose. "Not that I don't like Parisian hotels, but if there's a house, I'll take the house. Besides, isn't the first rule of buying a house with your significant other that you have to make love on every surface in every room?"

His eyes darken. "Is it?"

"I believe so." I get up and spin around him, my hands clasped behind my back as I walk backward. "It's practically a requirement."

"Far be it from me to deny you a requirement, Dayton. I suggest you go and pack a suitcase while I call and get the plane ready. It looks like we're flying out early."

"How early?"

"Tonight early. I want to make sure I leave myself enough time to enjoy you everywhere possible, per house-purchasing requirements."

The depth in his voice, the husky undertone, leaves me no doubt that he intends to do just that.

I open the closet door, my eyes skimming over my half.

Perhaps I should pack just underwear instead.

"Here."

Red floods my vision, and I step back into Aaron's hard body. When my eyes focus again, I look at the red corset he got me in London.

"Pack this," he orders. "There's a bay window seat in the master bedroom that looks onto the Eiffel Tower."

"What relevance does that have to the red corset?"

He lowers his mouth to my ear, whispering, "It'll add to the view when I bend you over the seat and fuck you."

I clench my thighs together. Jesus, he was only inside me an hour ago and I'm already aching for him. Damn him and his word-fucking.

"Keep talking like that and you'll be rearranging the plane again."

"You're insatiable, woman."

"Coming from the man who just informed me he's going to bend me over a window seat and fuck me right after doing something very similar."

"I appreciate the view of your ass while I fuck you. Are you complaining?"

The ache intensifies a little as I remember my most recent orgasm. "Nope. No complaints."

"Then be quiet and pack." He throws a suitcase onto the bed. "Don't pack too many clothes. You won't be needing them."

I smirk, unzipping the top of the suitcase. I drop the corset in, much to his delight, and put my hands on my hips. I watch him maneuver his way around the closet easily, so certain of what he's taking and what he isn't.

My eyebrows go up when he drops a pile of clothes on the bed. I count them—six pairs of pants. Oh no. If I'm on clothing rations, then he is too.

I cough, motioning to the pile, and he smirks himself, grabbing two pairs and depositing them back on his shelf in the closet.

No.

I grab another two pairs and skip past him, laughing, shoving them on top of some shorts before he grabs me and spins me round. His fingers dig into my sides, and I laugh louder, squirming and wriggling.

"Two pairs for a week? What do you think I am, woman? A tramp?"

"No," I breathe, holding my side through the tight pain there. Damn him. "But you said"—I take a deep breath—"not too many clothes. Applies for you, too."

He laughs, pulling me against him. "You can take as many clothes as you want, but they won't be worn for long." He trails his hand down my back and inside the waistband of my shorts to cup my ass.

"Making a point, Mr. Stone?" I gasp when he grazes his teeth down my neck.

Oh crap.

"Point for what?"

"How long my clothes will be worn for?"

He squeezes my behind and brings his wrist up, glancing at his watch. "We have time."

"Again?"

"Mhmm."

"Oh no." I wrestle myself from him. "No, no, no!"

I laugh, running through the apartment. And as I slam the office door shut behind me, I realize my mistake.

You never run from someone willing to stalk you until he can catch you.

"Dayton." He hums my name through the door. "Do I need to break the door down?"

"That's a habit for you."

"Open the fucking door. The longer you keep me waiting out here, the harder I'll have to fuck you."

Oh, silly, silly man. When will he realize that that's not a bad thing at all?

I giggle and tap out a random beat on the door. Truth is, I have no intention of letting Aaron Stone fuck me right now.

I plan to sit him on that fancy-ass leather chair and fuck *him*.

Slowly, I turn the lock and grab the handle. The door opens before I can pull it down, and Aaron steps forward, his eyes locking with mine, hunger and lust glaring from them.

The temptation to let him do what he wants with me is so overwhelming that I almost do exactly that.

"Gonna catch me?"

"Do I have to chase you?"

I tilt my head to one side. "Depends if you're gonna catch me or not."

He steps forward and tugs me to him before I can think about running. "Looks like I already did." He trails his nose down my neck, his lips peppering kisses as he goes, and pauses at my collarbone. "And we're back in the office."

"So we are." I fist the front of his shirt and walk backward, pulling him with me.

"What are you playing at, Dayton?" he murmurs.

I grin, spinning us and pushing him back into the chair. "Why, Mr. Stone. If you want a hard and fast fuck, it's only fair that I get to do the fucking. You already had your turn today."

He pulls me onto his lap and his erection rubs against me. He's hard and ready, and I could spring him from his pants, tug my shorts and panties down, and lower myself onto him without any foreplay.

"You're one sexy woman when you start demanding things." He pushes his hips up into me.

I smile and kiss him hard, running my tongue along the seam of his lips. "Remove your clothes, Mr. Stone." I slip my hand between us and cup his cock over his pants, teasing the side of his length with my thumb. "We don't have long."

Chapter Twenty-Seven

There's something insanely crazy about walking into a house in Paris, my favorite city in the world, and knowing it belongs to us. Well, technically, Aaron, but if I say that out loud, he might kill me.

I think I'm finally used to the yours-mine-ours thing. Most of it, at least. This house I can see as ours. He might have bought it, but he knew exactly what I'd want. He picked the perfect Parisian property. Complete with the bay windows he mentioned before and a balcony off the second bedroom, not to mention the gorgeous rose garden in the backyard, it's perfect. I can see the Eiffel Tower from almost any room in the house.

Believe me. I've looked from every one.

I don't want to think about how long he searched for this or how much he paid for it. I don't want to think of anything except the fact that it belongs to us, and in the four days since we arrived here, we've gradually made it our home.

It took me two hours to tear down the old curtains and drag him out for new ones. Of course, that meant returning with new rugs, throw pillows, and some adorable bedding, but everyone knows that house shopping is extensive.

And now I'm picturing crazy things.

I'm picturing mini breaks here, not just two of us, but three of us, maybe four. I'm picturing walls adorned with pictures, both professional and natural. I'm picturing a high chair in the corner and mucky fingerprints on the glass doors leading from the kitchen to the backyard. Maybe little crayon scribbles in hidden places, a Lego brick here, a toy car there.

I'm seeing the kind of future I never let myself imagine.

It was never in the cards. Even when Aaron came back into my life, I couldn't believe it was a possibility. Then when I did, that was torn away brutally by a secret I never knew existed.

Then it was fixed again. His relentless pursuit, his refusal to give up—they made me believe that maybe… Maybe we could make this work. Maybe we really do have a shot at it.

And Naomi took that. She made me question everything—until Aaron answered every single one of them.

This is the first time since I walked into that booth in the Southfall Hotel that our relationship hasn't been based on money or clouded by lies. It's free, and true, and honest. The way a relationship should be.

I can feel it. Our smiles are wider, our eyes brighter, our touches lighter. It's almost as if everything that was buried before is now simmering away on the surface, mixing with our ever-present lust and attraction. It's a heady mix, one that gives me a nearly constant delirious high.

There will be more lows. Of course there will. It doesn't matter that we may have had more than our fair share of them in such a short space of time. All that matters is that I know, and Aaron knows, that we'll come out on the other side.

I will be more confident of that if we leave Paris in one piece. Our track record isn't exactly great.

Our track record can be changed.

I step out of my robe and into the large corner tub, shutting off the taps as I do. The hot water ripples when I lower myself into it, and I've barely lain back when I hear the door open.

"Move forward," Aaron orders.

"This is my bath."

"It's our bath," he replies, and when I look at him, he's totally naked.

I huff and move forward, giving him enough space to slip in behind me. He does, and he lets his legs fall open to the sides. I slide back and lie against him, linking my fingers through his as he wraps his arms around me.

A happy sigh falls from my lips. This is a part of Paris I remember and adore. Both of us lying together in a bathtub full of bubbles, not speaking, just holding each other. These are the moments I cherished, and I smile at the thought that I don't have to think back every time I want to remember this feeling. I simply have to drag him into the bathroom and run a bath.

"What are you thinking?"

I turn my head to the side, gazing out of the window. "I'm thinking I love Paris."

"I love Paris, too." He kisses my shoulder. "It gave me you."

"It's very generous that way," I tease. "Although the return gift leaves something to be desired."

He prods me in the side. "I think I found desires you weren't aware of over the last few days."

Ah, this much is true. Who knew having sex in front of a large bay window in the middle of the day was so fun?

"I was very much aware of them. They'd just never been satisfied before now."

"They'll continue to be satisfied, too."

"I should hope so."

He laughs quietly, burying his face into my neck. "Sit up. Let me wash your hair."

I do as he says, and he grabs the showerhead from the little holder I put it in for easy reach. When the water is the right temperature, I lean my head back and let him wet my hair.

"Tyler's coming back to Seattle in a few weeks."

"He is?"

"Hmm. He said he'll call you to arrange your photography lessons when he's found a place to live."

I lick my lips. "I forgot to tell you about that. With everything–"

"I'm not mad, sweetheart. Would you believe I'm happier at the thought of you being behind the camera instead of in front of it?" He pauses in his massaging motion, and I crane my neck round to look at him.

"Would you believe I'm not surprised in the slightest?"

We share a smile, and he turns my head again. "He said you were thinking of going back to school."

"Yeah. I was considering it."

"He didn't tell you, huh?"

"Tell me what?"

Aaron rinses the shampoo from my hair with the showerhead before he replies. "Tyler is trained to teach photography. He used to do shoots for us on the side, outside of classes, but he loved the photography side so much he gave up teaching."

"Tyler is a professor?"

Well, shit me.

"There are a lot of things about Tyler you don't know, Dayton. He'll teach you so you don't need to go back to college."

I consider this. "Like an apprentice?"

"Yes, exactly like that. It's the best training you could get, and from the best photographer I know. He'll continue his freelance work for us while you work together."

"So technically I'll be working for you."

"No. Tyler isn't employed by us." Aaron trails his fingers down my back. "He's self-employed. We commission him to do shoots for us, so you'll be working for yourself."

I shrug. I can deal with that, and I actually prefer it. Imagine working for the guy you live with. Aside from the fact that I've never really worked for anyone in my life, no matter what people say, you don't leave stuff at the door or at work. It'll carry over. Having an argument at home then having to go to work with him would drive me insane.

Aaron lifts me from the bath, and I smile. It doesn't matter if I can do it myself. He's going to do it anyway, and this is a battle I'm choosing not to fight. No point wasting my energy on something I won't win.

I curl myself into the thick, fluffy towels we bought yesterday and shuffle into the bedroom. Hanging over the door is a knee-length red dress with a flirty skirt. I glance at Aaron and narrow my eyes at the shit-eating grin on his face.

"Humor me," is all he says before opening the closet and pulling out a white shirt and black pants.

I blink a few times, watching him as he dries his powerful body. "What are you playing at, Aaron Stone?"

He looks up from his position, one knee on the bed, the towel wrapped around the thigh, and smiles. "Remember those plans I canceled last time we were here?"

"How could I forget?" I reply dryly.

He smirks. "I remade them, and it's what we're doing tonight."

I glance from my dress to his clothes and back to his blue eyes. His lips curve even more before he turns around to dress.

I stand here, hugging my towel around my body with my hair dripping wet, and stare at his muscular back. If he thinks I missed that mischievous glint in his eyes, he's mistaken.

What is he playing at indeed?

The Eiffel Tower at night is a sight to behold. The way it lights up, reflects onto the flowing water of the River Seine, and illuminates the dark night sky is something close to magical.

Aaron takes my hand and slowly pulls me toward the tower. I raise an eyebrow, but he says nothing, letting his feet do the talking as we get closer and closer.

"Are we going up?"

He smiles, and we enter the elevator that will take us to the top. I'm surrounded by the strong feeling of déjà vu. We did this once, the first time, and it was the night he told me he loved me.

Aaron squeezes my hand as we go up, and I gaze out at the city around me. At Notre Dame, the Champs-Élysées, the Louvre—all lit up in their own unique ways. The lights spread out in a romantic way no other city in the world can recreate, and I step into Aaron's side. His arm goes around me, his lips brushing my temple, his touch warming through me.

"Dinner," he whispers, leading me into the exclusive Le Jules Verne restaurant. The empty, exclusive Le Jules Verne restaurant.

Empty.

"You booked the whole place?" I look at him in awe.

"For you? Yes." He leads me to a table in the corner, one that provides an uninterrupted view of the Louvre. One he knows I'll love, and I do.

He pulls my chair out and I lower myself onto the seat, taking in the table. Candles. Wine. A beautifully printed and embossed menu.

Aaron pours two glasses while I sit here, overwhelmed. This is what he planned before? It's no wonder he was pissed when he had to cancel. But still…

Every day, he amazes me a little more. This time, I admit, it's the fact that he's strolled in here and booked out the whole damn restaurant like he's buying a stack of newspapers.

"Is this a special occasion I've missed?" I question, accepting the glass of wine.

"No." He smiles. "It's a just-because." He lifts his menu, ending that line of questioning, and I can't shake it.

Something is going on.

A server appears from nowhere and asks for our order. Aaron reels it off for both of us, which is good since I've only glanced at the menu and certainly not at the food list. He gets it perfect—of course he does—and looks out of the window.

I stare at him. I stare at him until my eyes hurt, wordlessly, until our food is brought out.

Even as I eat, I watch him, and after a while, he returns that gaze. Our eyes lock across the table but no words are exchanged, and I can see it. In his eyes. That glimmer that knows something I don't. That betrays his 'just-because' excuse.

I'm not getting it out of him no matter how hard I try. I know he won't give anything away until he's good and ready, so I'm stuck sitting here in my awkward limbo until he does. Stuck here, wondering, waiting, what-iffing.

Our plates are cleared away and replaced with our main course. Again, it's eaten in silence, our eyes flitting from our plates to each other's. The only difference is that there's a zinging of tension, one tight enough to cut, and I swallow hard. My fork clatters as I put it against my plate and look at him firmly.

"Do you want dessert?" he asks innocently, his steady voice betraying the tightness between us.

"No. I want to know what this is."

"This? It's dinner in the Eiffel Tower, sweetheart."

"No. What is it? Why are you doing it?"

Aaron waves his hand and the server reappears and removes our plates a second time. I chew the inside of my lip, keeping our gazes connected, and wait for him to speak.

"Can't I take you to dinner and just have it be dinner?" he questions, resting his forearms on the table and leaning forward.

"Of course you can, baby. Just not in the place you told me you loved me for the first time."

"You remember that."

"I never forgot. I didn't forget anything. I just chose not to remember it the way you did. Now I know something is up, so don't sit in front of me and tell me it isn't."

His lips quirk, teasing into an amused grin. "Don't freak."

"I don't freak."

His eyebrows twitch, the amusement in his eyes evident, and he reaches into his pocket. My heart stops at the small box he places on the table, and I can't breathe as he slides it across to me.

"What. Is. That?"

"Open it."

I know what it is. I think. You don't book the most exclusive restaurant in Paris to give someone a pair of fucking earrings.

What is happening?

I take the box with a shaky hand and open it. A glittering ring stares back at me, a simple design, classy and elegant, and I look up at him. To the ring. To him. To the ring. To him.

"It's not what you think," he says slowly, his lips curved even through his words. "So you can breathe, Dayton."

I laugh awkwardly. "Um, if it's not what it looks like, then what is it?"

He reaches across the table and takes my hand in his, kissing my fingers. "It's a promise ring. Not an engagement ring. I'm promising you that one day, when you're ready, I'll ask you. This is me promising you that I'll be yours without you having to voice the same commitment, despite its truth."

A lump forms in the bottom of my throat, and I blink harshly as I swallow it down. A promise ring? Like…

"Oh hell no, Aaron Stone." I take my hand back and shut the top of the box. "If you're going to promise me you'll be mine for the rest of my life, you're gonna do it properly or not at all."

I shoot the box across the table and fold my arms across my chest. A promise ring indeed. What the hell is—

What the hell is he doing sliding off his chair and bending in front of me? On one knee?

"I was hoping you'd say that," he murmurs, "so I came prepared."

Oh shit. Oh shit oh shit oh shit.

He pulls a second box from his jacket and leaves it closed as he stares up at me from his position on the floor. My mouth opens and closes again. It does this a few times as this crazy moment hovers between us.

"Seven years ago, you exploded into my life in this crazy burst of color that made me blind to everything else. When you left, you took it with you, leaving me in an ugly world of black and white. Then, four months ago, you did it again.

"When you walked into that booth in a crazy twist of fate, Dayton, I realized that nothing would ever be the same again. I realized that, this time, I had to keep you and not let you take that color I was, and am, so incredibly in love with.

"I know it didn't work that way. We've both made mistakes, but that doesn't matter. What matters is that we're here, right now, and we have the rest of our lives to be together. What matters is that I'm never letting you go again. I'm never even giving you the chance to leave.

"And since you refuse to accept one promise without the other, I'm asking you to promise me the same thing. That you'll be there every morning and every night. That your voice will be the first and last thing I hear every day, that your touch will be the one to calm me when I'm angry, that your lips will be the ones I get to kiss whenever the urge takes me."

He pauses, and forever could pass in this moment and I wouldn't know. All I know is that I can't look away from this man in front of me as he bears his soul to me and asks me for the one thing I never imagined I'd be able to give.

He slowly opens the box, revealing the most beautiful princess-cut ring I've ever seen in my life. The diamond glitters up at me, beckoning me, promising me the future.

"So whenever you're ready, Dayton Lauren Black, will you marry me?"

Epilogue

Four Months Later

"No, no, no!" I drop my forehead to the table. "Why is this so hard for them to get right? Champagne and ivory are not the same color. The seat sashes are supposed to be champagne, not fucking ivory!"

Liv pats my shoulder. "There, there, Bridezilla. You have three months still to chew their asses out until they get it right."

"Liv, with the amount Aaron is paying them to get it right, I shouldn't have to be chewing asses." I sigh and straighten again. "This is crazy. Why can't we just elope in some tropical country and get married without all this fancy crap?"

My best friend laughs and shuts the laptop down. "Okay, babe. Let's get you a drink. You and I both know you wouldn't want to have this any other way."

"I know. I just… It's three months away and already I'm being bogged down by shit. Why can't these people just get things right?"

Two glasses of wine appear on the table between us. "Listen to me, Dayton. You will get this fixed. Has Aaron chosen his best man yet?"

"Yes. He had him picked three months ago. He just got his ass in gear and asked him."

Finally. He can't even use the whole face-to-face excuse because Tyler moved to Seattle a month after Aaron popped the question. No, he's just been lazy about it.

"Who is it? Anyone hot and rich from his company?"

I snort at the way she perks up and reopen the laptop, bringing up my email. "His cousin. Although, Tyler is hot and rich. And kind of from the company. I mean, he's a photographer. He's the guy training me. I don't know how you two haven't met yet. Hmm."

I glance up at her when she doesn't reply and take in her face. Wide eyes. Parted lips. Flushed cheeks.

"Uh, Liv?"

"Um." She takes a deep breath. "Did you say Tyler? A photographer?"

"Yeah. Why?"

"I know him already."

I tilt my head to one side. "Well, I suppose that will make everything easier. The whole maid-of-honor-best-man thing. You guys have to get along."

"Oh, we do. I can't say we've talked much, but we get along just fine."

It clicks. I stare at her, my jaw dropping, and she flattens her mouth into a thin line. Slowly, I close the laptop, unable to process anything except this very unexpected information.

My best friend has slept with my fiancé's cousin.

Oh holy crap.

THE END.

Liv and Tyler's story, currently untitled, will release later this year.

Acknowledgements

Thank you to my incredible partner, Darryl, for accepting and living with my special brand of crazy. And for putting up with all my sighing and constant hammering at my keyboard. And for being told to shut up numerous times because I was too lost in Aaron and Dayton. Love you, Mr.

My babies, for sometimes coming second to the people inside my head. I hope that one day you'll understand that this is all for you.

My agent, Dan Mandel, for loving the idea of this series from the moment I sent it. Thank you for believing in my ability to write erotica, and for encouraging me to publish it. And my foreign rights agent, Stephanie, for all you do. It makes my head spin like whoa.

My critique partners, Heidi Joy Tretheway and Katie Ernst, and my early readers, Kendall Ryan, Zoe Pope, and Holly Baker. You all begged me for more Aaron—and Dayton—and your enthusiasm and ahem, desperation, kept me writing when it got hard. I love you all tons.

Sofie Hartley—I expect that leg hump in July for your surprise early copy of this. I can't wait to go in, fuck shit up, then strut out with you.

To the bloggers who have helped spread the word from day one—I'm not even going to name you all this time because I know I'll miss someone. But if you've read and reviewed *Late Call*, or even just read it and loved it, thank you. This wouldn't be possible without your epic buzz-creating skills and excitement.

My editor, Michelle Kampmeier, and my proofreader, Emma Mack. Thank you, ladies, for cleaning up my words. They're now shiny and sparkly.

And for you guys, my readers. Thank you for loving Aaron and Dayton and fiercely as I do. I hope this book is everything you were hoping for.

<3

About the Author

By day, *New York Times* and *USA Today* bestselling author Emma Hart dons a cape and calls herself Super Mum to two beautiful little monsters. By night, she drops the cape, pours a glass of whatever she fancies—usually wine—and writes books.

Emma is working on Top Secret projects she will share with her followers and fans at every available opportunity. Naturally, all Top Secret projects involve a dashingly hot guy who likes to forget to wear a shirt, a sprinkling (or several) of hold-onto-your-panties hot scenes, and a whole lotta love.

She likes to be busy - unless busy involves doing the dishes, but that seems to be when all the ideas come to life. She has since invested in a dishwasher, meaning the ideas come at the same time as her son's dirty nappies. She is in the market for a bum-changer due to this.

Emma's works include new adult series THE GAME and MEMORIES series. The CALL series is her first adult erotic romance series, but it's been so fun to write, she doubts it will be the last.

Find Emma online at:
Blog: http://www.emmahart.org
Facebook: www.facebook.com/EmmaHartBooks
Twitter: @EmmaHartAuthor
Goodreads:
http://www.goodreads.com/author/show/6451162.Emma_Hart

Printed in Great Britain
by Amazon.co.uk, Ltd.,
Marston Gate.